At the Court of Charlemagne

ROBERT ADAM

ISBN 978-0-46326-755-4 (ebook)

ISBN 978-1-79808-805-0 (paperback)

CONTENTS

Chapter One

Bars of light flickered over the walls of the lift as I rode alone to the top floor of the Berlaymont building and Kramer's office. My home city, Hamburg, was Protestant, but every time I came here I felt a little sorry for the nuns of the Dames des Berlaymont who'd been evicted from the site. One hundred years ago, when they'd built their convent and school, they had no idea the EEC's headquarters would one day land there like an oversized spaceship on its lower storey of stilts. Back then too, if you had tried to describe either a spaceship or the EEC to them, the sisters would have been equally baffled.

After nearly three years working here, at times I still felt out of place myself - I didn't fit neatly into any of the main groups of people in the four thousand-strong organisation: the younger university-educated technocrats who often treated it as just another employer, the middle-aged civil servants with stalled national careers hoping to relaunch themselves in Brussels, and the elder statesmen put out to grass in semi-retirement.

Outside, the clear morning air promised a perfect day, bright and crisp after the dreary winter - a damp squib at the end of that year of drama for Europe, nineteen sixty-eight. Inside, the office of the French *chef de mission* was typical of those enjoying the top layer of the cake - views over the Parc du Cinquantenaire, a sleek desk in blond wood and soft leather sofas around the low meeting table. All spoke to modernity, a fresh start, a putting behind of the past and of the old ways of doing things.

1

The previous afternoon I had been asked to come up this morning for what I was assured would merely be a friendly conversation. My job in the Internal Affairs department took me to many levels within the EEC, but meeting the most senior French bureaucrat for the very first time, on such a vague invitation, warranted playing safe and wearing my best dark suit.

I sank deep into one of the sofas, whilst on the opposite side of the table Kramer leaned forward, slowly stirring his coffee with a solid silver spoon, as he got himself ready to pronounce my fate.

'Herr Lenkeit, I'm sure you know who I am, but before we start, tell me something of yourself.' He relaxed back into the calfskin, sprawling slightly to take up more of his sofa than I did on my side.

I quickly marshalled my thoughts, opportunities such as this interview didn't come along often.

'Well sir, I joined here from the uniformed Hamburg *Landespolizei* in nineteen sixty-six, on the suggestion of a former colleague. I always wanted to serve in the police and never really saw myself doing anything different, but I also never thought I'd get the chance to have a career abroad.'

Kramer nodded slowly.

'The job here suits me very well - similar to the *Kripo* detective work I was hoping to eventually do in Hamburg - but with the chance to improve my French.' A little sycophancy never hurt at the Berlaymont.

'But you were never actually a detective? That's different to the impression your department director gave.'

I silently cursed my boss for over-selling. Our job was really a combination of expenses auditor, the occasional muscle for our parent department, Personnel, and only the odd true investigation into bribery by suppliers or into petty theft within our various office buildings.

I tried to reinforce my credentials. 'We have to cover many areas here with a small team. Part of what we do does require investigative skills, and even in the uniformed police we were taught and had exposure to those.'

He pondered for a moment. 'And the political aspect? This isn't the normal neighbourhood policing you used to do, breaking up bar fights, arresting drunks and the like.'

I risked a smile. 'You might think that, but it depends which department is organising their after-work party.'

He returned the ball back over the net with a wry expression. 'I suppose the Social Affairs Directorate like to fully live up to their name?'

Despite the shaky start, Kramer was already sounding twice as human as that cold fish, my own national *chef de mission*, von Barten.

'We tread very carefully, politically. We honestly do try to be blind to people's nationality - after all, isn't that the whole point of the EEC?'

'So, you're a true believer?'

'Surely one ought to be, if you work here?'

'As an experienced Brussels hand to someone starting out, my advice is always firstly to ask what people think they are being true to.'

He looked at me searchingly and seemed to come to some sort of decision.

'Very well - but enough of the politics, or rather, moving on to something that's very political - a delicate problem has arisen, sensitive in the extreme, so sensitive, in fact, that in a couple of minutes we're going to walk down the corridor to see your compatriot von Barten and chat with him about it too.'

Little surprised me after my three years. Forget party drunks - many times it turned out that people had been suggesting their rivals as subjects for Personnel investigations. Marooned on board the EEC spaceship in the middle of Brussels, where people soon found out they had little real prospect of returning to their national careers, positions at the Berlaymont were jealously protected. Salaries free of your home country's income taxes were worth defending too.

If we were about to discuss an Internal Affairs job, with only myself and the two senior officials from the leading nations present, then I could only guess at an investigation intended to provide a fig leaf to someone very senior indeed. Wrongdoing high enough up in the organisation such that procedures had to be seen to be followed to allow a valid exoneration, but conducted by someone like myself, so low down the pyramid, such that there was no real chance of any misdemeanours being uncovered and the political apple cart being upset.

Kramer expanded on his theme. 'Because this is so delicate, we do need a committed volunteer, not a hired hand.'

The strident private warnings of our platoon's hard-bitten sergeant during my fifteen months of army conscription, never to volunteer for anything, rang out loud and clear in my head. However, working on behalf of the top people was something to be grabbed with both hands. If, by their standards, the outcome was successful, I would bank it for the future – sponsorship was the currency of Brussels, the oil in the machine of career advancement.

'I want you to have the chance to say "no" - you can tell that to me much more easily than you can to von Barten.'

'I'm listening, please, carry on.'

Kramer continued, 'So, how to keep the story simple? I need you, we need you, to track down and recover what you can of some long-forgotten, perhaps long-lost papers. Something from wartime. How does that sound so far?'

'Who exactly lost these papers?' I asked.

He sipped his coffee and gave a faint grin. 'You'll find that out in due course, if you agree to take on the assignment.'

'Sorry, but I don't really get to decide that. Our department director hands out investigations to the individuals in his team.'

'This time you do get to choose though, I already asked to meet you specifically this morning.' That was somewhat disconcerting. A direct request for one of his staff by name meant my boss would probably take it literally and only put me onto the case, giving him cover if the job went badly. Of course, that wouldn't stop him taking credit for the department if things went well.

'So, what more are you able to tell me now?'

'You need to visit some genuine "old comrades", charm and persuade them to give up what they know, force them when necessary. You're too young to have overlapped with their past and they won't see you as any kind of threat, psychological or otherwise. But I trust you can be open-minded towards them for the sake of the task in hand.'

I didn't really have a choice, not if I wanted to have any kind of a career at the EEC after this.

'So, young Lenkeit, what's it to be - yes or no?'

'Very well then, of course I will.'

He pressed the intercom call button for his secretary to warn von Barten.

'Let's go.' he said, standing up.

I had been in von Barten's office once before, and I had met von Barten himself at various official functions for German employees at the EEC, where his homilies were admired as masterpieces of suavity. His room was of similar size to Kramer's, but without the sofas, and decorated with his own personal touches - watercolours of pine forests and seascapes from the Baltic coastline of Germany. Von Barten was a somewhat aloof character, not given to humour with those outside his inner circle. Nearly twenty years successfully stalking his rivals in the jungle of EEC and European politics had given him the assurance of being untouchable. This he disguised only to a limited degree - even to outsiders - but we recognised that he'd earned it.

Von Barten was already sitting at his conference table, we joined him and waited for him to begin. He tapped the ash from his cigarette into an ebony ashtray, laid it carefully on the tray edge and clasped his hands.

'Well, my dear Lenkeit, Kramer and I have a task for you that will give you a great opportunity to shine whilst doing something even more worthwhile than your current role normally allows.' Pomposity came naturally to him, along with that touch of arrogance.

'Indeed sir, Monsieur Kramer has already alluded to as much.' When needed, I too could be as oily as the best of them.

Von Barten warmed to his theme. 'Kramer has briefed me already, but before he explains the situation to you, let me paint a picture using my own words, a shocking picture from nineteen forty-four, although we already have a plentiful supply of those. Imagine it is November, you are an official in Vichy France, and the war is clearly lost.'

For the briefest of moments, his eyes glazed, and he seemed to be far away from the Berlaymont. 'Your country has been deceived into an alliance with its invader, you personally have been sucked into the very heart of their war effort. Believe me, I should know, I was required to do the same for Germany, whilst working secretly against the regime, of course.'

Von Barten's story was well known to all of us, he wore it as a badge of pride. He had worked in one of Speer's special industry groups, orchestrating the production of steel and coal across France, Germany and Belgium for the war effort. At the same time, he had been a member of the Kreisau-Zirkel, a resistance network of the great and the good in Germany, who had debated plans for a post-war political settlement whilst certain of their members plotted the active overthrow of the Nazi regime with varying degrees of enthusiasm, if not any actual success.

'So, you know your time is up and you have nowhere

to go. Actually, that's not quite true, your government has decamped en masse to Sigmaringen, in south-western Germany, to run a government-in-exile, the mirror-image of de Gaulle's alternate government in London. As you sit awaiting the end, what do you do? Some take to drink, drugs, affairs, seeking oblivion from the storm clouds about to burst over their heads - and not without reason, the French Resistance killed twenty thousand collaborators in reprisals during 'forty-four and 'forty-five.'

Kramer nodded solemnly in agreement. Von Barten continued, 'What can you salvage from this disaster? You start to think about Europe after defeat - how can the achievements in European cooperation which the war threw up be built on?'

'What would those be?' I interjected, not liking von Barten's tone, regardless of his personal historical credentials.

'Acting with a single purpose when it came to industrial coordination for the common war effort: coal, steel, weapons, aero engines. Despite the aerial bombing we increased production threefold in all the main categories between nineteen forty-two and 'forty-four. Going further, if you momentarily suspend disbelief, some former generals even point to the Waffen-SS as a prototype for a multi-national European army.'

Kramer picked up the baton before I had a chance to respond. 'Let me tell it a different way. Over the previous four years, the occupied countries of North West Europe had begun, under different levels of compulsion, to start to work together in the face of a supposed common enemy. But even at a distance from overseas, the legitimate Dutch and Belgian governments in exile were already looking ahead to a new era of pan-European cooperation when they agreed to create the Benelux customs and currency union in nineteen forty-four.'

He leant forward and lowered his voice.

'At different points in time, but at Sigmaringen for

sure, the Vichy French started to commit their ideas on post-war cooperation to paper. Those discussions were, and remain, irrelevant to today, apart from one aspect - they start to look too similar for comfort to the Project.'

Von Barten interjected. 'Now their secret papers have resurfaced, and we suspect not accidentally either. In the wrong hands they could taint us by association and it's difficult enough pushing the Project along as it is.'

Kramer's face hardened, 'Two weeks ago, a former minister in the Vichy government turned up at the SDECE, our secret service. He said he knew of a highly detailed Nazi blueprint for what we now call the EEC and he believed some of his old comrades were about to release it. We at the EEC only learned of this approach on Saturday, three days ago. No-one at the SDECE had thought to alert me as the senior French representative here, for which they got given a roasting in Paris yesterday.'

My ears pricked up at the possibility of working with the secret services. I was suddenly desperate to get started on this – it sounded ten times more interesting than my day job.

It was my turn to speak. 'Now, I assume, someone is blackmailing us, threatening to release this blueprint? But to whom? To the Soviets? East Germany will have a field day, they already accuse West Germany of being some kind of Third Reich successor state, obscene as it seems to us. Their full name for the Wall is the "Anti-Fascist Protection Wall" to make sure the whole world knows it too.'

Von Barten picked up his cigarette and drew on it slowly while Kramer replied. 'Calm down Lenkeit, don't get carried away. There's nothing as definite as blackmail - yet. We've merely been told about the blueprint, but there is the unspoken suggestion of trouble ahead. We need you to meet this ex-minister, dig deeper, and ultimately find and retrieve these papers - if they really still do exist.'

I had already committed to the task back in Kramer's office, but it was now becoming clear just how far it lay beyond my experience of the minor infractions I'd dealt with in the past three years. Furthermore, I wouldn't just be operating under the watchful eyes of the two senior bureaucrats in the EEC, the affair was maybe even a threat to the entire organisation. The three of us looked at each other in silence for what seemed like a minute.

'Who am I reporting to on this assignment?

'To us directly, of course, and only to us. You can have whatever resources: time, money you need - but no assistance from your rest of your department at this point in time.' My earlier guess had been correct. 'For now, this is a solo effort, very strictly need-to-know, *"streng geheim"*, as you Germans would say. It goes without saying that no breath of this will ever get to the outside world.' As Kramer spoke, Von Barten fixed me with narrowed eyes, the tip of his cigarette glowing bright.

'Tomorrow,' continued Kramer, 'you and I will meet with this Monsieur Freybourg, who in Sigmaringen ended up as an overqualified fixer for Marcel Déat, the Vichy Minister of Labour. Earlier, back in France in his glory days, Freybourg had rejoiced in the title of "Plenipotentiary for Anti-Tank Ammunition Production".'

Kramer smirked at the ridiculous-sounding name, glancing at von Barten. 'In the meantime, finish up or get rid of any ongoing jobs. Given that the most convincing lie is the truth, simply tell your colleagues that you're working on a theft of sensitive documents - that's what we told your boss.'

'I have one last question - why me? I'm not the only investigator in the department.'

'That's obvious to us, but for your sake, let's see,' von Barten began to count on the fingers of his free hand.

'Firstly, you are German - and my French colleagues want Germany to be involved to demonstrate multi-national collaboration on such a delicate issue. Secondly, you speak passable French for a non-university graduate - you'll need to go there, interview the civil servants of the *ancien régime* and dig around in the dirt.'

'Thirdly, you,' now he pointed directly at my chest, 'have nothing to lose in the game of career politics. You've been here too short a time to have built up a list of sponsors to protect from investigation, but on the other hand this is your chance to make a mark with some powerful potential supporters. I therefore expect you to upset the right people to get to the wrong answer, if you understand what I mean. Think of this as your lucky break.'

All the above points were factually true, but not only for me. Maybe the aim really was simply to find the most junior member of the department and put them onto its most important task.

They stood up together, the interview at an end. We shook hands, but when I turned to leave, the two of them sat down to confer again.

Back across the street at the Charlemagne building I quietly pushed open the door of the office I shared with Bernd. We were both ex-Hamburg police - he was a little older than me and had joined the EEC two or three years before I did. He was the one who had given me the nod when a junior position alongside his had opened up in Brussels at Internal Affairs. Unlike on the top floor at the Berlaymont, we had grey painted metal desks, an organisation chart pinned to the wall covered with a spider's web of alterations in red and green marker, and a view across the courtyard to the opposite wing of the office block.

Bernd was one of the few people I was close to in Brussels, so this conversation was going to be tricky. At least I could switch back into German.

'What did your new best friend Kramer want?' he asked, rising to his feet. I perched on my desk, looking up.

'He's volunteered me to find some missing documents that seem to have vanished into some Frenchman's back pocket, but it's a cold case.'

'How cold is cold? They've only just realised they're missing now? Sounds like a wild goose chase just to cover someone's backside by claiming they tried to investigate and failed.'

'I didn't have a choice - it seems to have all been arranged well before today. I've been detached from our department to work for him and von Barten directly, as a favour.'

'Both of them directly, eh?' he said appraisingly. 'Why are the two of them involved in this?' I could sense the jealousy bubbling up just below the surface and tried hard to deflate it.

'I think it's because, when completed, the papers were originally meant to be given to our people - so Kramer now wants to make sure von Barten is happy with how the investigation is run.'

I slid off the desk and sat down on my swivel chair with its fraying fabric.

'Neither of them gave the impression though, that there was a high chance of recovering this material. I assume that our boss will only be too happy for Internal Affairs not to be associated with this one.'

Bernd silently weighed this up for a while.

For all its supposed spirit of goodwill to humankind, I'd found that the EEC had even stronger cliques than the police in Hamburg. There, the original officers of the newly-purged post-Nazi force had been recruited by the British occupation authorities when they ran the city in the late forties. Back then, those who later were to become the old lags of my cadet days had often been part-time black marketeers themselves, both before and after they joined the police. They helped their own when it came to promotions and were suspicious of those who'd arrived after the force had returned to local German control.

That was part of the reason I suspected Bernd had left - he was impatient to move on faster than he ever could in Hamburg. Knowing him better now, as I did, I wouldn't have been surprised if his original idea in recruiting me was to extend his own patronage network and have a tame colleague to support his ascent at the EEC. He'd told me on several occasions of his ideas for what came next for him and perhaps, us. From Internal Affairs we could move up within Personnel, transfer to Financial Audit, or, if the EEC ever required new, niche functions, such as counter-espionage to protect our trade negotiators, try to establish ourselves there too.

Bernd mostly managed to keep his ambition in check, though, and not to let it spill into life outside work. At heart, he really was a decent sort, ready to crack a joke in the bar after office hours. Given his ambition, he was also a useful sounding board for the internal politics, for which he had an excellent nose.

It was Bernd who knew who was up for a promotion, who had offended whom, who was on their way out. He had a healthy respect for von Barten's skills - how the dry civil servant had glided, seemingly effortlessly, up the ladder to become the senior-ranked German official, with the informal position of spokesman for all the German nationals at the EEC.

Kramer, as it turned out once Bernd had bought my story and opened up, was more of a mystery figure. He was younger than von Barten by at least ten years and an object of continuing interest to Bernd.

'What did you make of Kramer then?' asked Bernd, always keen to increase his store of knowledge. Like the policeman he still was at heart, his philosophy seemed to be that if someone hadn't already committed a crime it was only a matter of time before they became a suspect. Almost subconsciously, he collected and mentally filed away facts on everyone of consequence whom he came across.

'Hard to read, spoke to me privately first, then he let von Barten lead their double act when they told their story of woe.'

'A double act eh? That is interesting. The year before you came, in nineteen sixty-five, the EEC ground to a halt for six months until the French and the Germans kissed and made up after a big fight over its future direction. There was a rumour, only a rumour, mind, that at one meeting Kramer and von Barten had to be pulled apart before they came to blows.'

'No sign of that today.'

'Well watch out for him, watch out for both of them. There's something about Kramer that unsettles me. Can't really say, it's just that he doesn't seem to belong here somehow, even though he goes way back, almost as far as von Barten.'

Bernd was pacing up and down now within the narrow confines of our office, from door to window and back again.

'Did you know that Kramer helped run the Saarland Protectorate for the French until they lost the referendum there in 'fifty-seven and had to hand it back to us? - that's when he joined the EEC. His career since then has followed the normal path up through the senior grades, but there always seems to be some different agenda to his choices.'

'No-one in high position here has had a normal career, whatever that means - but I take your point.'

The point being that no-one in Brussels was ever truly your friend. Unless perhaps you'd known them from before, or if they were family - nepotism being as natural as breathing here - but sometimes, not even then.

Chapter Two

The following morning, I walked over to the Hôtel Métropole from our office in the Charlemagne to give me time to think about the questions I needed to ask Freybourg. I was curious to see what Kramer would be like in action, never having worked directly with someone so senior.

Kramer had told me to meet him at the hotel's Café Métropole. It was a place I'd always found fascinating, a fin-de-siècle cornucopia of gilt, marble and mirrors, where you could imagine the cream of nineteenth century society, aristocrats and artists, industrialists and rubber barons from the Congo mixing together for afternoon coffee and cakes. Easier than imagining the nineteenth century from the cityscape of Hamburg after what the British and Americans had done to it.

Kramer was already seated in an alcove behind a palm tree with a diminutive man dressed in an old suit with shiny elbows which was now too large for him. He had the demeanour of someone used to crouching in corners, of having spent half a lifetime learning to avoid attention.

'Lenkeit, allow me to present Monsieur Freybourg.'

Freybourg got to his feet and gave a half-bow. He shook hands limply, gazing at me uncertainly, the same reaction I would occasionally have received when I was on duty in my police uniform back home.

'Enchanted to make your acquaintance Monsieur,' I said. My spoken and written schoolboy French had improved dramatically over the past three years with

14

almost daily use, but it was going to get a real test from an assignment potentially spent entirely in France reading old documents.

We sat down, and Kramer opened the meeting, deliberately enunciating his words, as if speaking to someone hard-of-hearing or weak-minded. 'Monsieur Lenkeit here has been asked to help us find the papers you worked on when you were in Sigmaringen.'

Freybourg raised an eyebrow.

'Perhaps you can start by telling Monsieur Lenkeit in your own words what you did there and what just happened a couple of weeks ago?'

Freybourg clasped his hands in front of him, eyes closed. When he opened them to speak, his voice was stronger than I expected. 'Before I begin, you must understand that many years have passed since the war. Ideas which seemed right at the time have been utterly disproved, their dark side exposed for what it is. I am not the person I was in nineteen forty-five.'

'Very well,' I said.

He continued, 'Now that I've come to understand your Project, it is of great importance to me that it's not hindered in any way. Indeed, without realising it before, it appears to be what I've been striving for all my life, even during my earlier career, when I didn't know that there would be such a thing as the EEC in the future, or the path that the Project would take.'

He was sounding more like a true believer now than Kramer himself. Freybourg drew himself together again, as if to haul his story up from the deep well of the past.

'I was a junior minister in the Vichy government. Just after the fall of Paris, in September nineteen forty-four, we were evacuated to Sigmaringen in Germany. There the French State carried on, right to the end of the war, a French enclave on the Danube with flags, ambassadors and ceremonial guards. Some of us fatalistically waited the end, some of us plotted escape to a new life outside

Europe after the war, and some of us, with time heavy on our hands in our new unemployment, reflected.'

The din of the cafe faded away as his words flowed more strongly.

'I was one of the latter, and with a few, a very few, former colleagues - both French and German economic administration officials - we discussed what we would have done differently. We also tried to imagine how our two about-to-be defeated nations could work together in the future to again build a strong European homeland for our peoples.'

I shifted a little uncomfortably in my seat. Growing up in Germany I had come across the full spectrum of reactions to the war and its motivations: those who claimed they'd been tricked by Goebbels' propaganda, those who claimed they had a moral obligation to follow orders, those who claimed things hadn't really been so bad under the Nazis - that atrocities had either been exaggerated or were no worse than what the Allies did, especially the Soviets. But I'd rarely been in the company of someone who was so open about their former support, support that had gone on right up to the very end.

'We took ideas on European-wide economic organisation which had been discussed in Berlin in the earlier war years. We took our practical experience of coordinating steel and armaments production for the anti-Bolshevik war effort across France, Belgium and the Ruhr area of Germany. We fleshed those ideas out, combined them with our experience, and came up with plans for how we could cooperate again, but even more effectively next time. And we worked out those plans for each of the post-war political scenarios we were able to envisage.'

My eyes widened as Freybourg warmed to his theme. 'Remember that in nineteen forty-four it wasn't clear whether France would be under Allied military government, as Germany finished up, or whether de Gaulle would be allowed to simply declare himself leader without a mandate from the French people.'

I laid my notebook on the marble-topped table between us. 'We wanted to make sure we played a role in Europe after the war ended, whoever was in charge, or perhaps, whoever thought they were in charge. We had been defeated militarily, it didn't mean we were defeated though.'

He re-folded his hands with a self-satisfied expression on his face. This was pure Fourth Reich conspiracy material, but I wasn't buying, not yet anyway. I glanced at Kramer for confirmation that Freybourg was for real, but no help came from that quarter.

I tapped my pencil on the table and started taking notes, waiting to see if Freybourg would fill the silence.

'We considered how we could create step-by-step an ever-closer cooperation in all areas of economic life, and how that would lead to a natural political understanding.'

He sighed regretfully. 'The old way, during the war, where Germany dictated production quotas, set prices and exchange rates would have to go. If the German leadership had only sought to harness and truly encourage the willing allegiance of other civilised and semi-civilised nations, we wouldn't have lost half our European territory to the Communist bloc.'

Kramer still wasn't helping, it was up to me to rein Freybourg in from his paean of praise to himself, otherwise we'd never get onto the details of the case.

'Why were you in Sigmaringen in the first place?'

'Eh … because we would have been shot if we'd stayed.'

'So why Sigmaringen and not Argentina? Whose idea was it to go towards the problem?'

Kramer finally broke in. 'Because the Germans made them - they wanted to maintain the fiction to their own people that France was still an ally and that their setbacks in the West were only temporary. It also gave them the excuse to force escaped Vichy Milice paramilitaries into the Charlemagne Division of the Waffen-SS. These were the regime supporters who had fled France, sometimes with their families, and who really did have nowhere else to go.'

'So you were all in Sigmaringen under duress? And who were these people who still wanted an eventual political union with Germany?'

Freybourg pursed his lips. 'It was an eclectic mix of people who worked on the plans, as I've already said, some of the German and French industrial co-ordinators, political scientists, philosophers.'

'And how were these plans going to help them, specifically there and then in nineteen forty-five?'

Kramer stared at me momentarily. 'I think the idea was to get ready to negotiate for new jobs in the Allied military governments - even Himmler and Goering assumed they would be needed by the Americans to rebuild Germany for a near-term conflict with Stalin. Naive, but there you are.'

I kept pressing Freybourg. 'Monsieur Kramer has asked me to help track down the papers. I need names of people to investigate, those who might still have them and might be threatening now to release them. Who was in your planning group and who took copies?'

Freybourg relaxed. 'At least six copies were made, distributed between both French and Germans - not to me - but to people we thought had the best chance of political rehabilitation after the fighting in the West was done. Those who were young enough, without obvious ties to the fascist regimes, and thus able to work their way into the post-war institutions and promote our ideas.'

'And who were these people?'

Freybourg's ivory skin flushed pink. 'My memory isn't what it was, there was someone from the propaganda ministry, although that perhaps too grand a word for what it had become by that time, a certain Dupont. Then Latour, he was in the trade department. Also, Suffren from the diplomatic service. There were also a couple of

Germans, involved in trade negotiations, whose names I have now forgotten.'

'Do you know of these people, Monsieur Kramer?'

'Suffren was shot after the war's end as a collaborator. His copy must be presumed to be lost or destroyed a long time ago. Dupont and Latour were rehabilitated but have since retired from public service.'

I shook my head slightly and turned back to Freybourg. 'If you've known about these documents since nineteen forty-five, why bring them to our attention now?'

'Because two weeks ago I received a letter sternly warning me not to speak about Sigmaringen, should I read anything in the press in the coming months about what had taken place there. It said that I had done enough damage to France already, but if I kept silent I would be spared. All of us live with this knowledge, that one day someone will decide it is time for the past to catch up with us.'

'But you were rehabilitated too?'

'Yes, but memories are long. Think of what the Israelis did to Adolf Eichmann eight years ago - the past decade has seen more and more examples of adherents of the former regimes, previously cleared, now being reinvestigated and sometimes tried again in court. As the war fades into history, the immediate necessity of the early post-war years to forgive and forget has also diminished. There's a new generation which wants to make sure justice, in their eyes, is done before we're permanently out of reach.'

He gave a rueful smile, 'Which for some of us will be sooner than for others.'

He passed over a sheet folded three ways. The paper was of low quality, the typewritten letters smudged. The text was as Freybourg had described it, sparse in its use of words and terse in tone.

'What do you think the letter means?' I asked.

Kramer replied for him. 'Someone knows what

happened at Sigmaringen, someone plans to announce it - that's all we can say for sure, but we also know that whatever the intent, it's not good news.'

He lowered his voice, until I had to strain to hear his words.

'Maybe there'll be a hatchet job on a politician who has successfully sanitised or even buried their past until now, maybe a smear against the concept of the EEC itself and those politicians who speak in favour of deepening the Project.'

He glanced at Freybourg and continued softly.

'There are any number of reasons, personal, grand-strategic, or both at the same time. We just don't know, but in France we don't like these shadows of the past any more than you do in Germany. We have a shared interest in pre-empting whatever is coming our way.'

'Can you find Dupont or Latour? We should at least interview them. Why can't your SDECE pull them in?'

'Because we're not in East Germany. This needs finesse, not an assassin from the Service Action - we chose you because you're not French, so you're less of a threat to them.'

I wasn't so sure about their respect for the law. Borders certainly weren't any obstacle to the SDECE - given that they had even bombed a ship in Hamburg harbour in the late fifties which had been running guns to the Algerian nationalists.

'What if they think I'm some kind of German Nazi-hunter then?'

'These are the only threads we have to follow. At the very least, if we can find out where the copies are now, we can start to follow the trail back to the author or authors of the letter.'

'And if the copies went nowhere?'

'The fewer we leave out there,' Kramer waved his hand towards the other customers, 'the greater the control we have of the story. We might be able to doctor the text, make it seem less incriminating to us, sow doubt as to the authenticity of anything that does surface later.'

'Six copies are a lot, though, given how far and how widely they may have been dispersed over the last twenty-five years. Some will have been lost or destroyed for sure, but if you want all six tracked down, that isn't a small job and probably not for one person, at least, not if you need results quickly. Plus, we don't really know how long we have until the threat in the letter is followed through.'

'At the minimum we need to secure one copy – firstly, so that we know what we're dealing with concerning the content, and secondly, as I already said, so we can manufacture a new version if we need to.'

'If these people had intended to infiltrate and influence the post-war order in Europe, how do you know they didn't do so? And since their day, even if they're already long gone themselves, how do you know they didn't collect followers and successors for the positions they ended up with after the war? You know how patronage works at the EEC, Monsieur Kramer.'

'We can't solve every possible problem, we need to fix the ones at hand first - which for now is killing dead any idea that there were Vichy or Nazi plans to subvert the western institutions.'

Kramer clicked his fingers at a passing waiter to bring another drink.

'Anyhow, and so to practicalities. You need to find a way to speak with these people without scaring them into silence.'

'They don't draw a salary from anyone, they haven't committed a crime, there's no official reason to pressurise them into an interview. Beyond taking the time to befriend them over weeks or months, it has to be in the form of a request - research, maybe someone collecting memories of Vichy France for a newspaper article,' I suggested.

'Too aggressive, newspapermen are always looking for a scoop. Tell them you're from Hamburg and they'll think that Bild is on to them.'

Freybourg suddenly spoke up. 'Why not academic research? On a boring topic, for a thesis to be published in some years' time.'

'There you go Lenkeit,' said Kramer, 'your chance to pretend you went to university and are now hoping for a doctorate.' That was a somewhat low, especially as most of the higher- and middling-level Germans at the EEC seemed to be titled 'Herr Doktor'.

I still didn't like it - if there was some kind of existential threat to France's position at the EEC, I didn't understand why their police or security services couldn't take a more direct route to the source.

Freybourg was taken with his idea though.

'I can provide letters of introduction to both Latour and Dupont. If you need me to be present to make an introduction in person I can do so too, but only if you can't get an interview yourself.'

I bristled. 'So you know where this pair are living now?'

Kramer replied for him. 'Give our authorities some credit, they got moving once I set off my rocket under them. Dupont now lives in northern France, in a resort town on the coast, Latour lives only a few kilometres from Strasbourg.

'What were they like back then, and how do you think they will react to questions now?'

Freybourg licked his narrow lips. 'They both felt bitter at the end of the dream, were determined that Europe shouldn't be dominated by either the Americans or the Soviets, but that it should steer its own course. I imagine both will have mellowed somewhat, but I haven't seen them for twenty years, so I can't really say.'

Kramer seemed to have had enough of my questions and brought the meeting to an abrupt close.

'Lenkeit, go and find us a taxi back to the Berlaymont. I need a few final words with Monsieur Freybourg.'

I emerged into the spring sunshine, looking back I could see the two Frenchmen deep in conversation. I had to hold the taxi for almost ten minutes until Kramer finally came out.

As the driver pulled out onto the Boulevard Jacqmain, Kramer turned to me across the back seat. 'What do you think?'

'Not a lot to go on. Surely if there is a Vichy, or a Nazi document you should be getting your political response ready in case it does comes out.'

'Why do you think von Barten is already involved? You've already forgotten you were told yesterday we wanted a German to work on this. You're part of the political solution.'

'Speaking of Germany, what can we, or what should we do about the German copies?' I riposted.

'Freybourg doesn't know who on the German side was entrusted with the plans, he says they didn't seem to take them as seriously as the Vichy side did, which isn't surprising. And we, or rather I, have no easy means of tracking them down even if we had to.' Kramer added.

'Von Barten would be our route to help get that done. In any case, something sourced from Germany alone can be more easily dismissed as a crackpot Nazi idea. But if it was proved that Franco-German collusion was going on at the end of the war you can see why that looks more serious for the EEC.'

'So, if we take the French copies out of circulation, that's enough you think?' I asked.

'It will have to be.' He ran his fingers through his thinning hair. 'In some ways, it was all so much easier during the war and then the Liberation afterwards.'

'May I ask, what did you do during the war?'

'Me? I was lucky. By chance I was a junior in our embassy in London in nineteen forty when de Gaulle fled there to declare the continuation of the war by France - I was simply in the right place at the right time. I returned to

France in 'forty-four untainted by collaboration and thankfully still on de Gaulle's good side. He could be extremely sensitive to imagined slights, even we French thought so.'

He drummed his fingers on the handle of the passenger door. 'Listen, I spoke with Freybourg some more back there. We'll take care of making these appointments between us. If you have any leave due, take a couple of days this week, or just skip work on Friday - once this investigation kicks off properly I need you to be available at any time round the clock. If anyone asks where you are in the next few days, tell them to speak with me.'

I needed to think some more about the student idea, not having been to university myself. I knew how students were expected to behave, but I wasn't sure I could create and sustain a story which required some level of academic knowledge on twentieth century European politics – fortunately, I knew someone who did.

Chapter Three

I decided to follow Kramer's suggestion and go home to Hamburg for a long weekend, but before I did, I went to see another Brussels buddy, Jan Stapel. He was only ten years older than me, but was already an associate professor at the Free University of Brussels. We had met one night eighteen months ago when Bernd and I had been out drinking on the Rue du Midi, and Bernd bumped into a friend who was there with Jan. Since then, we'd got together every couple of months, apart from late last year when he was finishing the paper that had ultimately secured him his tenure.

Jan fancied himself a man of the people and enjoyed mixing with those outside of his social class. I guessed it was all part of his efforts to maintain his left-wing revolutionary credentials with impressionable students. Outside his academic duties, when not writing pamphlets, he could sometimes be found at bars in working class districts or, more often, at protests outside the American embassy for whatever was the cause du jour - be it the Vietnam War or nuclear disarmament.

But I had asked to see him on business, so we were now sitting in his office which overlooked a grassy quadrangle. Books lined the walls and spilled onto every surface, from the windowsill to the curved tops of the heavy iron radiators.

'Nice trinket you have up there,' I said, pointing at a tiny painting of Lenin in a wooden frame on the wall behind his desk, well away from the clutter. It was executed in the style of a Russian Orthodox icon.

'Bought it off an old member of the Parti Communiste de Belgique, claimed he had been given it on a visit to the Soviet Union in the nineteen twenties.'

'Looks like they painted Lenin as a saint.'

'Yes, that's why I liked it, the inherent tension it represents … "the creatures looked from pig to man, and from man to pig, but it was impossible to say which was which" … you know your Orwell?'

'We did some in our English class at school, I'm not completely ignorant.'

'So, what brings you to the world of modern European history - and a word of warning, by "modern" we don't mean much that happened after nineteen hundred.'

I had thought about this - despite the warnings of Kramer and von Barten for total secrecy, anything other than an approximation of the truth would sound more suspicious than something I could invent out of thin air.

'I've been asked to look into some lost documents relating to the years before the EEC, telling the story of the start of European cooperation. I have to go to France and interview some persons of interest, and I need a cover story, perhaps as a student researching a thesis.'

Jan looked at me quizzically. 'Really? How could that be of interest to people in the EEC today? These documents must be pretty important to want to look that far back.'

Despite the bumbling academic act, he hadn't got his tenure for nothing. I was sure he saw straight through my thin smokescreen.

'Anyway, what makes you think you can pass as a student?' The man of the people facade slipped somewhat, but I forgave him that one for the sake of our friendship.

'What else would you suggest? I need to go digging around in the affairs of some old comrades, if you get my meaning, I don't want to frighten the horses.'

'Oh really? Well you have landed yourself a delicate job

then.' He looked at me even more shrewdly now.

'I need to know more of what went on before the birth of the European Coal and Steel Community. Maybe I've been making assumptions all these years about how the EEC itself came about.'

He tipped his chair back on its hind legs, ignoring the creaks of complaint from the wood.

'As I said, modern history stopped in nineteen hundred, but it's no surprise that after that disaster of diplomacy which ended up as the Great War, the first pan-European movements began to emerge. The clearest thread to follow is the story of Jean Monnet - during the First World War he passionately argued with anyone who he could get hold of, from the French Prime Minister downwards, for the creation of organisations to coordinate the Allied war effort. He was only twenty-six at the time.'

Jan stared at the ceiling for a moment, as if he saw himself there, button-holing Clemenceau on the steps of the Hôtel Matignon.

'And after the war?'

'Monnet tried to get the Allies to build trade cooperation into the peace treaties, but without success. He did manage to get himself appointed as the Deputy Secretary-General of the League of Nations for a while, but then dropped out of public life in the early nineteen twenties. He became an investment banker in America and China for the rest of the period between the wars. During the Second World War he worked for the British and then later for de Gaulle, coordinating the purchase of war supplies from the Americans.'

'Still a long way from starting the EEC though?'

'It all fed his developing internationalist philosophy. The received wisdom is that it would later be a small step from pushing for trade links to advocating for some kind of political union.'

Jan crossed his feet on the desk, pushing a pile of unmarked essays off onto the floor.

'After the Second World War, as you know, it wasn't clear if Germany would be allowed to exist again as an independent entity. Lots of people, from Morgenthau to de Gaulle, wanted to carve it up into agrarian statelets. De Gaulle wanted France to become the industrial centre of Europe, so Jean Monnet obliged him with a plan to detach the Saarland coalfields from Germany and turn the region effectively into a new colony of France.'

This I already knew instinctively. It now made sense to me why, as children, we'd celebrated the return of the Saarland in nineteen fifty-seven by beating up a kid in the schoolyard whose mother happened to be French.

'The Americans eventually pushed back though, when they realised that Germany needed its coalfields and steel plants if it was going to have any chance to rebuild its economy and not turn to Communism. The Germans themselves were none too happy at what had been done to them by the French, under the noses of the other Allies.'

He started jabbing the air with his forefinger.

'So the Allies created the International Authority for the Ruhr in mid nineteen forty-nine, partly to stop France getting the same ideas about the steel plants there too. By putting the Ruhr under joint Allied control, it was also a payback to the French for them allowing the creation of West Germany out of the three Western allies' occupation zones. In late 'forty-nine the new West Germany was allowed to send its first national delegates to the IAR. They acknowledged international control of the Ruhr, trading this for an eventual end to the ongoing dismantling and removal of production plant by the French and the Soviets as war reparations.'

He paused to check my expression. I was stony-faced, my earlier warmth towards Kramer cooling with every minute that Jan carried on speaking.

'The pendulum was now swinging further against the French - by the start of the fifties they had failed to permanently annex the Saar or the Ruhr and had failed to prevent the creation of a German political entity in the West, an entity with the potential in the future to outcompete France and dominate Europe once again. Monnet's next plan was now to put all French and German coal and steel assets under one supranational body. He promoted his idea through Robert Schuman, the French Foreign Minister.'

'What was Monnet's official position at that time?'

'As he had always been, since the end of his League of Nations days - an administrator, an appointee, an adviser to politicians - but never actually elected to office himself.'

'An éminence grise.'

'Exactly - and in nineteen fifty-two, when the European Coal and Steel Community was established, he eased into office as its first President.'

'So all this had nothing to do with the Third Reich?'

'The Nazis had no original ideas of their own. Everything, and I mean everything, was recycled from other countries, or from earlier times - even if it was wrapped up in their own language of cod-science.'

He got up and went over to a political map of Europe hanging behind the door.

'Look.' He circled a swathe of Central and Eastern Europe with a sweep of his hand.

'Back in nineteen nineteen at Versailles, at the very time Woodrow Wilson was smashing up that early model of supranationalism, the Austro-Hungarian empire, into component parts which were more-or-less ethnically homogenous, ideas of an even larger European federation were already germinating.'

'Because ideas have a life of their own, don't they? They get picked up and recycled by all sorts of people, as you say. Different people can find themselves wanting the same thing for different reasons.'

'That's just what I said. The Nazis brought nothing new, they were only ever able to subvert concepts that had already been invented or proposed. By "subvert", look at how Europe's economy was organised by the Nazis during the war and ask yourself if the EEC today really bears any resemblance.'

'You're going to enlighten me?'

'In the early years the Germans found themselves in the delicate position of persuading the authorities in the occupied territories to build weapons for them, whilst needing to steal from them at the same time to fund their war. That theft was in the form of promises - promises on the value of the Reichsmark which they fixed at an artificially high exchange rate to the currencies of the occupied countries.'

'And later on?'

'Slavery. Volunteer and increasingly forced labourers taken from Eastern Europe, Holland, France and Italy to work in German arms plants, replacing their own workers being sent to the front. But forced labour was also supplied to other non-German European corporations too, in order to drive up their arms production, and profits, of course. All whilst funding the SS at the same time when they charged those corporations for the use of their slaves.'

'Sounds like a descent into insanity.'

I was thinking about Freybourg's comment on how at Sigmaringen they had realised a new system was needed.

'How did Germany persuade French and Belgian corporations to work for its war effort?'

'Yes,' said Stapel grinning, 'I noticed that displacement, talking about "Germany" and not "we".'

'That was a little low.' Naturally we'd never talked much about the war before at all. He was now being as smug with me as he was when holding forth in the bar on the evils of America and those he denounced as class traitors.

'Do you want to know or not?'

'Go on then, how did they do it, at the point of a gun?'

He smiled, 'By appealing to their base capitalist

instincts, of course, seasoned with a lot of fear. It was either make profits from fulfilling the orders given to them by Speer's ministry for tank components, coal, steel and the rest or have their businesses appropriated - either by other industrialist collaborators inside their own country or by the Party itself.'

He paused again for effect. 'The Nazi Party's own industrial combine, the Reichswerke Hermann Göring, went throughout Axis and occupied Europe gobbling up businesses through management control agreements and forced transfer of shares. The regime were the biggest kleptomaniacs in Europe, of things and people, since the Romans.'

'More like organised criminals than political pioneers, I suppose.'

He snapped his fingers, pointing at me. 'And don't forget it - also, during your "research", at all times remember to ask who benefited personally out of these deals.'

I thought for a while. There was plenty of organised crime for sure in Hamburg, and the wartime and post-war black market had helped its roots grow deeper, even if the men running the rackets had changed over that time. One thing was sure, though - none of them had ever willingly given up either leadership of their gangs, or their accumulated wealth.

'So, what happens next for the EEC?'

'It's currently in a period of stasis. Four years ago, there was an almighty bust up between France and Germany over the role of the European Parliament and over national voting on EEC policy - it had been brewing for some time, to be fair though. When de Gaulle came back into power in 'fifty-eight he started to apply the brakes on the spread of the pure religion of supranationalism as taught in the College of Europe.'

He turned his head to do a mock spit on the floor.

'What?'

'Whether the EEC should be a "*Europe des patries*" - independent states working together, led by de Gaulle's France, of course - or whether it should continue to be run fundamentally on a "supranational" basis where the decisions of the organs of the EEC take precedence over national assemblies and, incidentally, where those organs accrue more and more policy-making powers over time.

'So what happened four years ago?'

'To understand, you have to go back a couple of years before that. In nineteen sixty-three de Gaulle and Adenauer signed a Franco-German friendship treaty – but it didn't end up as de Gaulle intended.'

'What was the problem? How could a friendship treaty be the cause of disagreement?'

Jan shook his head slowly, amused at my naivety. 'On the surface, it looked very collaborative – joint meetings of the Foreign, Defence and Education ministers from both countries to agree common policies – the first steps towards what might be interpreted, by those who wished to, as a political union. But Monnet's followers in Brussels saw through it – successful cooperation by independent states in those three sensitive areas would erode the rationale for a single supranational body to eventually take over those same portfolios, obstructing the path to a single federal European state.'

'And now you're going to tell me how they twisted the treaty?'

'You got there before me – yes, a combination of fear of de Gaulle dominating the proposed partnership, but also, of course, the influence of the supranational lobbyists here and in Germany. The result was that the German parliament altered the agreed text, reaffirming Germany's intent to work with France, but through the existing EEC institutions.'

'So de Gaulle was mightily displeased, but what happened four years ago then?'

'Nineteen sixty-six had been set as the date for the

introduction of majority voting at the Council, meaning the EEC institutions as a whole could start to independently direct policy, overriding the objections of any individual member state. When Hallstein published the details of how he wanted it to work, de Gaulle had a fit and withdrew all the French national representatives from Brussels.'

'So not the French employees of the EEC then?' I was thinking of Kramer.

'The compromise, in the end, was that majority voting would still take place, pleasing the supranationalists, but that individual countries could have a veto on matters of so-called "national interest", which has chilled the climate for the out-and-out federalists.'

'Is federation really a likely outcome?'

'Look at the tortuous path it has taken, since nineteen sixty-two, to get to the agreement to be signed later this year on the long-term sources of funding for the Common Agricultural Policy. Whatever date the EEC proposes to implement a certain policy by, even in the areas they control, it always takes longer than they think. Because of the voting compromise, the eurocrats can kiss goodbye to any further serious integration, as they call the transfer of powers, for another ten years at least.'

'Why ten years?'

'It's my guess – but as more nations start to join the Six inside the EEC, the need for strong central direction will grow, and the supranationalist wing will inevitably end up as the winners, especially given the supranational bias built into the very heart of the founding treaties.'

'Is the division still between France and the rest?'

'You work there, you know better than me. You tell me who is on top right now.'

'I have no idea, you forget how low down in the organisation I am. We work on catching expenses cheats and people stealing wallets from the office cloakroom. From what I can see, at the top they all look out for each other, regardless of nationality. But back to my original problem - how do I pass myself off as a student to these old boys?'

'You told me you were a policeman before you were in the EEC, so you'll have met the full range of personalities in your work. Some interviewees don't need any excuse to talk - you just turn up with your notebook and they'll tell you everything you need and more. But if someone is suspicious, it doesn't matter how good your cover story is, they won't open up.'

'At least give me something to read, so that I have something to say to these people, to pass myself off to them. Or something to use as a stage prop - what does a political history student carry around with them?'

'What, apart from weed? Just find a study or a briefing paper from your archives to take along.'

'Can we take a look in your archives? What do you have here?'

'You're not getting your grubby fingers on any of our good stuff. Just take a look see what you can find at your library on the Rue Van Maerlant. Or, here, take this.'

He dug around in a pile of papers on top of a filing cabinet and handed me a loose-leaf folder, bound with string ties.

'Here you go – "An Account of the Development of the International Authority for the Ruhr" - sounds dry, but it's a set of notes giving a precis of other research. It'll give you a quick insight into the subject.'

'And it looks handwritten, as if I made it myself. Thanks, that'll do. Where did you get it from?'

'I was going to write a paper, but only got as far as doing some background reading and making notes.'

I reddened with embarrassment.

'How can I pay you back?'

'Well, now that you've got me interested in the EEC again, let me know who's up and who's down in the power struggle. Any gossip will do - it's a good excuse for a drink in the evening.'

As I walked out to my Volkswagen and started the engine for the eight-hour drive to Hamburg, I realised that Jan and I had never really properly talked about the EEC before. To my surprise, he knew far more detail and had a much greater interest in its historical background than he'd ever previously advertised. Also, no-one normal cared about office gossip at the EEC - its inner workings were designed to be grey, boring and impenetrable to the outside world.

But if nothing else, the conversation had underlined, that on this job, I'd been set down plumb in the middle of a Franco-German minefield, where I suspected both sides wouldn't overly care if I misstepped.

Chapter Four

I'd arrived in Steilshoop, the suburb of Hamburg where I'd grown up with my mother, late on Thursday night. She was still living in the home of my childhood – an apartment in a four-storey concrete block of flats built in the fifties to house bombed-out families. It was small - comfortable enough for two people with a decent-sized living room but a tiny kitchen. My father had been killed in the war. She never talked about him and I had finally stopped asking questions as a teenager.

My mother had arrived in Hamburg as a refugee from the eastern territories of Germany at the end of the war, and I had arrived into a new world at the end of nineteen forty-five.

She told me that she had been a German Red Cross nurse during the war, and in Hamburg she carried on nursing – working at the Catholics' Wilhelmsburger hospital in the south of the city, over an hour away from where we lived.

While she had worked her shifts, I had grown up mainly in other people's flats and houses - thanks to the kindness of neighbours who looked after me as a child and watched out for me as I grew into adolescence.

I had another reason to be grateful for their kindness - one of those replacement father-figures was a retired policeman, who had encouraged me to join the force after my army conscription, opening my eyes to a career that would otherwise have passed me by.

Overall, I had a happy upbringing, despite our

36

disadvantages. I knew she was proud that I had joined the EEC - she saw it as a cut above the Hamburg police, as I did myself when the call came that day from Bernd, back at the end of 'sixty-five.

On the Friday, the day after I arrived, she was working a long shift again. I'd spent the day doing odd-jobs in the flat, finishing the painting of the hallway that she'd started. On the Saturday, we'd gone shopping for food, cooked and watched TV together until I went out for the evening.

Before leaving Brussels, I'd called a friend to arrange to go out with tonight, another of my ex-colleagues in the Hamburg police. Jorg had made senior sergeant in the three years I'd been away and had also married his girlfriend, the tiny, bird-like Bettina. He'd more been a contemporary of Bernd's than mine, but we'd clicked, perhaps because he'd lost his father in the war too, an artillery observer who'd died somewhere near Kiev, just before Christmas nineteen forty-three.

He'd looked out for me during those difficult early months for every probationer cadet, guiding me on which officers to listen to and which others to respectfully ignore. And memorably, he, Bettina and Bernd, specially back from Brussels, had come to my leaving drinks in spring 'sixty-six in St. Pauli. That was the night which had ended around three in the morning with a group of us linking arms and rolling down Grosse Freiheit, singing 'These Boots Are Made for Walkin'' in atrocious American accents.

This time, we'd arranged to meet up at a bar near his flat in Altona, just outside St. Pauli. We all arrived together, and I was surprised to see that he'd brought Bettina along. I'd always had a soft spot for her - she'd been friendly on the occasions we'd met in the past, but I didn't think my leaving drinks had been such a blast that my return warranted her coming out for a beer again tonight. Maybe now they were married she just liked to keep a closer eye on Jorg, to see what he got up to of an evening, or maybe it was simply that she didn't fancy staying behind in an empty flat.

Bettina and I sat down at a booth while Jorg went to fetch the first round of drinks.

'So, how's life married to the force?' I'd thought carefully about this opening - any questions about her having tamed Jorg or having finally pinned him down to marriage would only make her defensive, and I knew from the past that her stature belied her fierceness.

'Same as before, lots of waiting around when he's on night duty - tell me about Brussels instead, when do you finish work each day?'

So, a comparison with the Hamburg police then. 'It's quite different from the police, which I realise now - it's an office job, really - not sure Jorg would like it.'

'I wouldn't like what?' his meaty hand clasped around three foaming litre glasses.

'Investigating the little people in Brussels to give the impression that the big guys are clean.'

'How's that different to dealing with the Hamburg gangs?'

'What are they up to these days, anyway?'

'Mostly being slowly pushed out by the Turks, and not liking it, but not organised enough to stop it either.'

'Anyone we know of getting hurt along the way?'

'Not here. Tell you some other time.'

Bettina looked at him askance. 'Tell me Oskar, what's life like in Brussels, as exciting as Hamburg?' she said, looking around the bar. A man in a dark donkey jacket was eyeing us from a booth against the far wall, as he leaned over his beer.

'The EEC is a world within a world. It's an international community living in a former imperial capital, whose own local Dutch dialect, until recently, was being squeezed out of public use - giving the Belgians a taste of their own colonialism.'

'Listen to you, you've turned into a politician since going there. Not for me,' he shook his head and glanced over at Bettina, frowning as he caught sight of the watcher.

I couldn't help but wonder if she had come out tonight, just to force this very question on him. She'd seen Bernd leave and then me, and my guess was she wanted Jorg to think about it too.

I thought some more, I didn't want to be the cause of a domestic dispute. 'It's not policing. It sounds like it but it's not and moving away to Brussels is a big gamble compared to what you've got here. Anyway, you're already sergeant now, you're on your way.'

I smiled encouragingly at Bettina and continued, 'I wasn't cut out for the police in the same way you are.' And there I had to stop, because the other reason I'd left was the low level, cloying corruption that hung around the force like a bad smell. It couldn't be avoided in a port city with rocketing levels of prosperity - so my choice had been to get out before I gave in. I didn't have a senior sergeant's ability to shrug it off, to bend and not to break.

We reminisced some more, Jorg related again the famous story of how Bernd had answered a call on the station's switchboard number from the Senior Police Director - equivalent to a Brigadier in the Army - demanding why an honour guard hadn't been provided for a visiting official from the Federal Ministry of the Interior. When the Director had asked, 'Do you know who I am?' Bernd had replied with the same question, and when was told 'No', had hung up.

In turn, I told Bettina the story of how Jorg had protected me from being stabbed by someone we'd been arresting through the quick use of a temporary street sign as a shield. '"Stop" was the right word at the right time,' I grinned. Bettina smiled back approvingly. Flushed with goodwill, she asked, 'So Oskar, any girlfriend in Brussels?

One of the Italian secretaries catch your eye?' I was glad for Jorg's sake he hadn't asked that question.

'Excuse me, I need a moment,' he got up and I watched as he walked down the bar towards the alcove where donkey jacket man was still sitting.

'There was a girl last year,' I said, turning back to Bettina. 'One of my friends set me up, but she turned out to be an obsessive - wanted to know what I was doing every evening, tears at every imagined slight, called me at work most days.'

'What did you do in the end?'

But I didn't get to tell her how Jan had finally rescued me, in embarrassment, by taking his student out himself a couple of times before dumping her with a warning about her grades.

'Let's go,' said Jorg, walking past our booth and on to the doorway. He waited a moment there while we hurriedly gathered our things and caught up.

'What's going on?' demanded Bettina.

'Someone back there I don't want you to meet.'

We walked out in silence, neon lights of every hue reflecting off the wet pavement. Jorg led us across the street and a few metres down an alleyway on the far side, then turned back towards its mouth, saying to me, 'Wait here with Bettina.'

Her eyes were wide and bright in the darkness. 'He's been nervous for the past few weeks, I know something's wrong,' she whispered.

Standing alert by the corner of the alley, Jorg reached into his jacket and I raised an eyebrow as he pulled out his gun, reversing it to use as a club. If he was carrying off-duty, then something certainly wasn't right.

In my narrow angle of vision, I watched as donkey jacket man came out of our bar, made his way through the groups of late night revellers and approached the entrance to the alley. Jorg half turned to me and said, 'He pulled a knife on us first, remember you saw that.' I nodded, even though he couldn't see me, Bettina was very still behind me.

The man came around the corner but stopped when he saw the two of us. 'The boss says no more games, Bulle.' For answer, Jorg brought the butt of his gun down hard on the top of the man's head, who slid slowly to the ground.

'Come on, give me a hand.'

We each took a grip under a shoulder and dragged him into the street, to some befuddled looks from the people there. 'Take Bettina to the Davidwache station and tell them to bring a wagon. I'll see you back there.'

It was supposedly Germany's most famous police station - even the Beatles had been guests there - a classic red brick edifice built in the last years of the Kaiser that seemed to have made it through the bombing. No one that I knew was on duty, and I had a job to get their attention, having to rack my brains for the names of lieutenants whose faces I remembered to prove my credentials. After a long wait on a hard bench with Bettina, Jorg finally appeared from behind the counter. It wasn't the Saturday night any of us had planned, but Jorg seemed much happier, and when she saw his face, so did Bettina.

'Thanks for that.'

'It was nothing, I saw his knife,' - in his jacket pocket for sure, but still, a switchblade was a switchblade.

Naturally I wanted to ask what was going on, but I judged it was probably something Bettina needed to hear from him in private.

'Let me know if there's anything I can do to help. I might have left the police, but you never really leave, if you know what I mean.'

'Sure Oskar, you always were a good sort. I knew you'd stick with me.'

'It was nothing - tell me about tonight some other

time.'

'Next time you're in town. Listen, we have to get back now, sorry to leave you like this, but never a dull moment in Hamburg, right?'

And that was that, whatever its problems and the seedy side it presented to the world, the city was alive in a way Brussels never would be.

After the excitement of Saturday night, there was a little tension between my mother and I the following morning. As the years had gone by, she had become more and more religious - the church had provided a type of family network which she didn't have in the West. We'd started going to church more regularly when I was already in my teens, and although she never forced me to go every Sunday, I could sense her dissatisfaction when I skipped to play football or go ice skating with kids from school.

I didn't really have anything against the church or religion, but today I just didn't want to have to answer questions from people in the congregation on how life in Brussels was going or endure the sly hints and nudges from parents to strike up conversation with the unmarried girls of my age who'd stayed in Hamburg.

But when she spoke, her embarrassment wasn't about me not going to church.

'I've invited someone from church back to lunch here, before you leave for Brussels.' Her voice was shy.

I was taken aback, I'd never known her before to have anything approaching a boyfriend.

'Of course Mother, who is it?'

'Someone new to the church who I've got to know in the past couple of years. I'd like you to meet him today, if you'd like to come along ...'

'Not today, thank-you. But I'm looking forward to getting to know him at lunch.'

I stirred the meatballs in white sauce on the stove and laid the table whilst she was out. I even got out the special Meissen porcelain cups for coffee before we sat down to eat.

Stefan was a bluff man, of similar age to my mother, but his silvering hair and reserved manner made him appear older. He was a divorcee, with a son of around my own age living in West Berlin.

'Nice to meet you, Herr Benke,' I said, wanting this to go well for her.

'So, you're the young man she talks about the whole time?' My mother blushed.

'Indeed, although she has more interesting stories about herself and the hospital I'm sure.' The pink in her cheeks faded.

'Perhaps. What brings you back from Belgium this weekend?'

'I had some leave due, so took the chance to come home.'

'And what do you do there again exactly? Didn't you have a steady job with the police here?'

My mother went out to the kitchen to start bringing the food through.

'It's like a police job - but an internal one. We watch over the employees at the EEC.' I didn't add that that included negotiating with the Police Locale when certain senior members of the staff refused to pay their parking tickets.

'May I ask, what do you do, Herr Benke?'

'I work at the airport, maintaining the radar equipment. Like I did during the war in Holland.'

We sat round the table to eat. Between mouthfuls I asked him more. Although we never spoke of the war in our family, as the fifties had turned into the sixties people had started to open up about the past. When I was a boy there were still Wehrmacht prisoners of war in the Soviet Union - the last ones hadn't come home until nineteen fifty-five.

He explained what he'd done in Holland. 'For the last three years of the war I was stationed on the Dutch coast on our radar picket line. Every night we waited for the stream of bombers to come over and then to feed our reports back to Deelen, where there was a gigantic underground command centre.'

'Did you have much to do with the local population? You must have got to know some of the people well, over the three years you spent there?' I was curious as to whether the European nature of the war effort everyone had told me about since Tuesday had actually filtered down to the lower levels.

'Yes, we were billeted with local people for a time, and we got to recognise faces in the village after a while. We weren't any threat to them, we weren't there as an occupying force to repress them. Everyone knew we were simply stationed in the dunes because Holland was on the flight path of the bombers. Certainly, some were unhappy that we were helping to shoot down Allied planes. On the other hand, there was one family in the village with a son in the Dutch regiment of the SS. According to his family, once they'd opened up to us, he'd seen the posters in the town and volunteered for what he thought was an anti-Bolshevik crusade to save Europe.'

'Did you see any evidence of that in the wider population? People treating the war effort as a common cause?'

'Not really - just the token Dutch force fighting for us on the Eastern Front. I remember a large Philips factory in Eindhoven though, they made radios for our fighters, and some of our radar equipment was made there too, I believe.'

I watched my mother from the corner of my eye as Stefan recounted his stories. She sat quietly, not contributing to the conversation or trying to steer it. After a while, she got up to busy herself in the kitchen.

'To be honest, I had an easy war - until near the end, of course. We had enough food rations, even in nineteen forty-five when the Dutch went without. Most people in

Germany did well too, at least until the very end. I remember newsreels from the middle of the war showing the arrival of the first trains from the Ukraine laden with grain and even eggs - which made me wonder how they got them back through partisan territory without breaking.'

My mother brought in an apple strudel for dessert.

'Ah Maria, you're too good to me,' Stefan said with a contented air.

Jan would have been disgusted by such quiet domesticity, but I could imagine getting to like Stefan. He was unpretentious and clearly fond of my mother. I wondered how far she was planning to take the relationship and what it would mean to our wider family.

'Have you heard recently from Aunt Hilde?' I asked. My mother's sister had stayed behind in the East after the war and was now on the wrong side of the Wall.

'I got a letter, last month, your cousins are growing up fast.'

'Have you ever been there Maria?'

'No, it's very difficult, as you know. I send money when I can.'

I wasn't quite so sure - family visas were hard to arrange, but they were available. Sure, there were restrictions on when and where you could go, and when you were there you had to pay what was effectively a sales tax when you exchanged western hard currency at the official East German rate. But it wasn't impossible, and the sisters hadn't seen each other in nearly twenty-five years. That was another area of the past that we skirted round carefully, without words.

'We're only fifty kilometres from the border, I could drive you there one day,' he said, somewhat hopefully.

My mother went very still. 'Maybe one day,' she said quietly.

I didn't want to leave her on a down note, but I had to start the journey back to Brussels.

'Mother, that time has come again.' It was what I used

to say at the end of each leave from the army. 'Herr Benke, a real pleasure to meet you, and I hope to see you both again soon.'

I picked up my bags in the hallway and we stood for a moment embracing. She gave me a kiss on the cheek and watched as I walked down to my car. Every time I left Hamburg I vowed to fight my way up through the EEC ranks, so I could afford something better than a scruffy Volkswagen and make her prouder of me. Maybe it was an unconscious desire to lift the sadness shrouding the relationship with her family, to try to compensate for whatever damage they'd done to her.

Chapter Five

I arrived in Saint-Valery-sur-Somme, where Dupont was now living, late in the afternoon. I'd got his details from Kramer's secretary at the Berlaymont when she'd again summoned me to the top floor this morning after my return on Sunday from Hamburg. I then set off for France immediately, my overnight bag still in the Volkswagen after my trip home.

Before dinner, I scouted out Dupont's house on the seafront promenade. I walked past once, then turned down a side street to take a look from behind. It was three storeys tall, solidly built with windows freshly painted and iron railings still sound, despite the salty air. Whatever his past in the war, Dupont didn't seem to have unduly suffered during the peace. The whole town had a discreetly genteel air, built on quiet money invested cautiously.

The town was now in darkness and a chill wind was blowing off the Channel. The bar at my hotel was almost empty but seemed as good a place as any to spend the evening. I got into conversation with the bartender as I sat at the counter on a high stool while he polished wine glasses.

My French was almost unaccented, which was no surprise given the mixture of people from all regions of France and wider Europe who worked at the EEC. I wasn't in a hurry to reveal my nationality, though - earlier I'd driven past a bar by a crossroads just outside the town called 'L'Embuscade' with a bronze Free French *Croix de Lorraine* mounted at the side of the doorway - I guessed it to be the site of a Resistance attack on my countrymen rather than a celebration of the cocktail.

'This town has some beautiful houses on the front - before the war you must have had plenty of holiday visitors from Paris?'

'Better than that, we had a real writers' colony here in the nineteenth century - Victor Hugo and Jules Verne both had villas on the promenade.'

'Anyone famous still live here?'

'It's more a place people come to now when they want to get away from society. Why are you here?'

'I'm seeing a retired politician tomorrow, Francois Dupont, for some academic research.'

'I know of him - he comes here on occasion, somewhat of a bon viveur, at least he was in his younger days.'

'How old is he now then?'

'I don't know, maybe seventy, or thereabouts.' He waggled a glass at me inquiringly.

'Calvados, please. What does Monsieur Dupont like to drink?'

'Wine, whiskey, his tastes are catholic from what I remember.' More drinkers arrived, and he took their orders.

'Was he well-known in the past?'

'He was some kind of politician or civil servant I believe. There's one story about him that I do know.'

I leaned forward in my chair in anticipation.

'Churchill was on holiday in the late forties on the Riviera. Dupont and he are staying at the same hotel and somehow a debate on which is the best marque of champagne ends with Dupont under the table drunk on Pol Roger with Churchill not much more sober.'

I leant back, not much of a story then. But, to my ears, a surprising feat of rehabilitation for a Vichy official all the same.

The bar started to fill up further. A girl came in from the outside and propped herself up on the counter, at the opposite end to me.

The bartender nodded towards her and spoke softly under the growing hubbub. 'If you want company tonight, you could ask her, maybe for a price.'

I glanced over. She was wearing a burgundy satin dress, a little too high over the knee than was suited for thick pale thighs. I'd seen enough of the trade whilst on the beat in Hamburg to put me off for life. It was the brazen artificiality that was the worst - the superficial pretence at romance. I supposed it was necessary for some customers.

I discreetly shook my head. 'In a town of this size?'

'We still get visitors.'

'Who is she?'

He waited until she slipped off the stool to buy cigarettes from a vending machine on the opposite wall, working her way through the crowd of drinkers.

'No better than her mother, who also did the same thing, part-time, for the Boches in the war. The rumour is that Claudine was the result. However, her mother wasn't badly treated afterwards, like some of the horizontal collaborators in other places - no head shaving or parading through the streets here. All that it proved, though, was that some families don't deserve second chances.'

I swallowed the rest of my drink.

'Until tomorrow then.'

He nodded at me. I scanned the girl on the way past to my room. What a way to end up, stuck in the same trap as your mother.

The next morning dawned clear and bright with a fresh breeze off the land out to sea. It felt like an auspicious start, now that my part of the job was finally starting for real.

Kramer's message said the meeting had been fixed for ten, so after breakfast I sat a while on a bench looking out across the estuary towards Le Crotoy on the opposite bank, killing time whilst the gulls screamed and wheeled overhead.

Dupont sounded like he'd been an old soak for years - instead of academic papers I wondered if I would have more success getting him to talk in his retirement with a bottle of brandy as a gift.

I pondered again as to what was really going on. It seemed like the EEC was making a considerable effort to chase down a rumour. The letter to Freybourg might simply have been the work of a crank wanting attention. Now here I was, far from Brussels, sitting on a lonely bench, with my future career in the balance if I didn't do whatever was expected of me. That was the real puzzle I had to solve - what did Kramer and von Barten want out of all this? And which one would it benefit me the most to try to please?

With German exactness I pulled the doorbell twenty seconds after ten. Dupont opened the door himself, his silk cravat and plaid jacket somewhat raffish for a retired politician or civil servant - I still wasn't quite sure which. I made to show him the letter of introduction from Freybourg, but he waved it away.

'Well then, my German friend, you've come a long way to speak with an old man. Do come in, do come in.'

What I assumed was a chihuahua, or at least a small lightly-built dog with long silky hair, came from round behind him for a friendly snuffle.

Both the little dog and I followed him upstairs to a study overlooking the neatly clipped front garden and the ever-changing sea beyond. The desk in the bay window was clear of clutter, the swivel chair tucked tightly underneath. Dupont sat back in a soft leather armchair at the side of the fireplace, the dog cushioned on his lap. I took a settee with linen antimacassars covering its arms at the back of the room, facing the window.

'So, what connection do you have with Freybourg?' He smiled with a knowing expression.

'I was searching for a title for my doctorate

dissertation, and my professor suggested this.' I pulled Jan's folder of notes on the International Authority for the Ruhr from my case and laid it on a side table next to the settee.

'He also suggested that I researched the earlier background to the IAR and said he knew of someone who had been involved in the discussions at Sigmaringen - Monsieur Freybourg. I interviewed Freybourg the other day and he in turn kindly offered to introduce me to some other people from his time there.'

Dupont gently stroked the dog's ears.

'Who else agreed to speak with you?'

'Latour, a trade official.'

'Ah yes, I remember him. Nasty little man, obsessed by that fact that he hadn't managed to skim off much, if anything, from the money changing hands at Vichy back then. He was determined not to miss out the next time.'

'How do you mean, the "next time"?'

'When the next political upheaval shook capital back into motion. And we didn't have too long to wait, nineteen forty-eight, after the Communist coup scare the previous year. That's when the American funds arrived with the Marshall Plan and our economy started growing again.'

'So did Latour benefit at that time?'

'Well no, he was still keeping a low profile in the years after the war, so low that people eventually forgot about him. His network of contacts dissolved away and when he came back into circulation politically he didn't have any influence to offer.'

'But you didn't get forgotten about?'

'It called for careful judgement, timing my return to public life. Too soon and I might have been caught up in the *Epuration*, like poor Brasillach, only thirty-five, shot whilst we were in Sigmaringen. Can you imagine the savagery? - how can a nation which calls itself civilised execute its authors and turn writing into a crime?'

'Maybe you expected too much when it came to

people's willingness to forgive. Isn't that what drove you into exile in Germany in 'forty-four?'

'It was a wild time, too many passions in the air. I thought I'd be better off lying low outside France until the end of the war. But it was no picnic - no sir! Too many refugees crammed into too small a town and, worse, food was short too.'

'I thought you had a high position in the Information Ministry, from what Freybourg told me?'

'It didn't make the food go any further though, not unless you were Pétain or Laval living in luxury on the upper floors of the castle with your sixteen ration cards. That's why I helped write Freybourg's manual, to get extra rations from our German sponsor.'

'You called it a "manual" then?'

'Well, it was more of a collection of other documents and papers. We wanted to show our sponsor quick progress, so we bulked it up with existing work and some linking text. Don't forget that deception was our speciality at the Information Ministry.'

'What was the gist of this manual?'

'Oh, it was good stuff, especially the bits we created ourselves, of course. Freybourg knew exactly what he wanted to show his sponsor. I polished up the part on how we should sell the ideas, Latour supplied the economic rationale.'

'And Suffren?'

'Don't remember him being involved, or even remember much about him. What did he do?'

'I was told he was a diplomat.'

'Maybe he contributed some material to Freybourg after I was finished.'

'So Freybourg was the editor, so to speak?'

'You could say so, but he was always under direction himself.'

I left that line of questioning for now. Now came the moment of truth. 'You were going to tell me, what was the plan in outline?'

Dupont tapped his feet and pushed the dog off his lap.

'Oh, I don't know,' he threw up his hands. 'It was written in a rush twenty-five years ago, and I only wrote part of it, remember?'

He relented a little and threw me a bone. 'It was something along the lines of the League of Nations but for Europe, where the big countries would set the direction and together make rules which the other nations would have to follow. Five votes for France and Germany, one vote for Denmark - that kind of thing.'

He didn't seem to realise this was exactly the principle behind the allocation of votes to each of the Six in the Council of Europe.

'And what rules would this "League of Nations" have set?'

'There would have been a customs union, I presume, like the Benelux arrangement that the Dutch and the Belgians signed up to after the war. Perhaps a defence union, although from memory I think we discussed it in principle but didn't write it up.'

'Did you keep a copy?'

'My dear boy, no. I wrote it to eat, not as my political testament or suchlike. No, no, I simply agreed to take a copy home, so as to get authorisation from our sponsor to leave Sigmaringen. Once I was over the border and alone, a match, whoof!'

The question had to be asked, I couldn't put it off any longer, no matter what he said next.

'Who was your sponsor?'

'I forget exactly, another trade official, in the Allgemeine-SS, with some connection to Himmler. A real nutcase, just like his boss.'

'And his name?'

Dupont looked out of the corner of his eye and asked slyly. 'Now why is that important?'

'I want to understand how far up the chain this plan

went.'

'To Himmler, I just told you! Our chap was a Müller or a Bäcker, or some other such boring name.'

The chihuahua wandered over and jumped up onto the settee beside me. I decided to change tack, to try to tease out what he really knew of the contents.

'What if Germany had won the war? What kind of arrangement for Europe would have they have actually allowed, as opposed to the one you dreamt up with your boring German colleague.'

Dupont settled himself deeper in his armchair and steepled his hands.

'The first thing you said could never have happened. Germany was effectively bankrupt before the war even started because they had rearmed faster than the natural capacity of their economy allowed for. They only kept going for a time because of massive transfers of assets from the occupied countries - labour, armaments, gold reserves - not in France's case though, because we sent our gold to America just in time. Latour could tell you more about that.'

This next question was going to be the most delicate of the day.

'So France didn't realise all this, when …'

'We capitulated? Have no fear, I won't take offence young man. I too was once young - and things looked very different back then. One day you'll remember nineteen sixty-nine and find it as strange a place as I do today when I think about nineteen forty.'

I put Jan's file back in my case. The chihuahua nuzzled my hand as I reached over, I picked it up onto my lap.

'We agreed to an armistice because we hadn't learned any lessons from nineteen thirty-five onwards. Once again, we thought we could reason with Hitler. We traded a partial loss of sovereignty in exchange for avoiding another destructive war on our territory and another lost generation of young men. I myself lost many dear companions in the last year of the Great War.'

His lower lip trembled, and I held my breath, worried he was about to shed a tear, but he recovered with a shake of the head.

'Some of us doubtless even imagined we were doing a noble, self-sacrificial thing and could direct the Austrian away from the path of a general European conflict, if we joined him as an ally and allowed him his triumph in the West.'

'Was your work at Sigmaringen a kind of absolution, a chance to show Germany how France would have run Europe? Instead of what actually happened.'

'You might interpret it as that - but that wasn't my intention, I said already, I had to eat.'

I was getting nowhere. In fact, if I took him at his word and the document had been destroyed, my trip here was over. But I didn't have to leave until the early afternoon for Latour's town and my interview with him there the following day. And in France it never hurt to keep digging in the dirt - after all, you might find a truffle.

'Allow me to offer you lunch, it's the least I can do.'

'An excellent suggestion, I propose the Hôtel du Somme. They serve a heavenly *crabe tourteau*. But let's walk a little first.'

We went back downstairs. Dupont selected a polished cane walking stick from a stand and clipped a lead on the little dog.

As we walked down the promenade to the start of the saltings, then back up towards the town, he reflected. 'At my stage of life, there's no point in holding back from enjoying food.'

'Do you live by yourself?'

'Yes, quite alone, apart from Léon here,' he tugged at the lead. 'But I have friends in the town, and a woman comes to cook and clean during the week.' He pointed with his stick. 'And the view of the sea and sky changes every day.'

At my hotel we both nodded to the bartender as we went through to the restaurant tables angled in the seafront conservatory.

Dupont attacked his crab with gusto. As the bottle of Riesling between us got lower, he got into his stride and opened up further about his life at the heart of the Vichy regime. He told me of the artists and writers his Ministry had co-opted into supporting the National Revolution. He told stories of blurred lines and cooperation between the Allies and Axis - prisoner exchanges and secret clearing bank meetings in Switzerland.

As the second bottle got lower still, I sensed he was losing his inhibitions and that we were at that narrow place between the point where hidden truths might be uncovered by a loosened tongue and the point where the alcohol started to garble everything being said.

'Back to your manual and what it contained, did you consider, or write up, any kind of plans to infiltrate the Allied organisations set up to run Europe immediately after the war?'

He gazed at me with rheumy eyes.

'We didn't have to plot - where else were they going to find administrators from? De Gaulle's government didn't drop in by parachute from England in nineteen forty-four. For sure the minister holding the portfolio might be a Gaullist, but they needed us *collabos* to actually to their work. Even in Germany itself they couldn't put eight million Party members in camps, not when most of the school teachers and virtually all the judges had carried the card. Think of your own Chancellor today.'

This I had gradually worked out for myself over the years. The Allies had found the Nazi Party membership records, which had been saved from destruction right at the end of the war by the owner of the incinerator they'd been sent to. The Americans, especially, had then extensively questioned POWs and civil servants on how closely they had supported the regime, trying to assess the role they had played and make an objective judgement of guilt. In the end, though, the system collapsed under the weight of four million forms, and denazification checks had been stopped as a practical necessity in nineteen fifty by Adenauer. Most Nazi Party members ended up as Category Four or Five anyway – classified as either 'fellow travelers' or 'exonerated', receiving a slap on the wrist at most.

'So the people who planned a new European order with you in Sigmaringen could be working in the EEC right now?'

'People like myself work everywhere now, if they haven't already retired, so why would that be a surprise? What did you say you did there anyway?'

'I'm a student, at the Free University of Brussels.'

'Of course, my pardon.'

He pushed back his chair and nodded at the waiter to bring him a Benedictine. 'You want one?'

'No thank-you, too sweet for me. So tell me, what kind of people did keep their position in society when the democracies were restored? How did you manage it and Latour didn't, apart from getting the timing of your return right?'

He smiled self-satisfiedly.

'I told you already, Latour was a bitter man, even back before nineteen forty-five. When I was in the Information Ministry and persuading actors, intellectuals and the like to support us I wasn't pretending to be their friend. I took an actual interest in their careers, was understanding of their foibles, treated them as individuals, didn't classify them by labels.'

I poured the last of the Riesling into my glass.

'When they came to me to get their sons exempted from *Service Travail Obligatoire* in Germany, or to complain about censorship, I expressed genuine sympathy, even if I couldn't do much to help them. Whether they had agreed to collaborate with us or not, I was still sympathetic, and they didn't forget it afterwards when I returned to France.'

He pointed at me with his glass.

'You too need friends in life and not just hard-heartedly for the sake of your career. You need to listen to everyone, discern who people really are underneath. Judge them when you have to, but remember that you are almost certainly no better at heart. If you had been in France in nineteen forty would you have chosen any differently?'

I nodded along.

'We were the lawful French government - yes everyone calls it "Vichy France" now, but that was de Gaulle's inspired invention to spare France's blushes at the Liberation. After the capitulation in nineteen forty we simply carried on with the system which had always been in place. Only a very few people, like de Gaulle in London, could have had the willpower to imagine into existence something new, more real to them and to others than the place they left behind.'

When Kramer said he'd been in the right place at the right time at the embassy in London, might he also have been implying, even unknowingly, that if Chance had dealt him other cards, he too could have ended up in Sigmaringen?

'How did you end up here, on the coast, away from Paris?'

'I finished my career in state television, with the RTF. The people I had known from the early days were getting fewer and fewer, and I wanted a change, to return to the coast and the countryside where I had grown up. We despised the *paysans* in pre-war Paris, but come the end of the war and the years immediately after they were the ones laughing with their easy access to meat and butter.

Dupont was obsessed by food in a way I recognised from the same generation from back home. He eventually brought our conversation round to that too. 'When were you born then?'

'Nineteen forty-five.'

'How did your parents feed you?'

'It was only my mother - I don't really know, I've never thought to ask.'

'How old was your mother when you were born?'

'Twenty.'

'H'mm - do you ever think about what she had to do to provide for you in your first three years? No German currency until 'forty-eight, so food was only available if you had something to barter.'

I wasn't quite sure what he was driving at, and I wasn't sure I wanted to.

'It can't have been easy whatever she did - don't forget that. When we're young we despise our parents, we assume bringing up children comes without cost. But I assure you, the regrets will come later if you don't make your peace now.'

Maybe I didn't always fully appreciate what my mother had done for me, bringing me up alone, but I wasn't a monster.

'When do you plan to see Latour?'

'I have to get to Rosheim tonight - it's just outside Strasbourg. I'll interview him tomorrow afternoon.'

'You're welcome to stay the night at my house and go tomorrow.'

I guessed he didn't get many visitors, maybe he was lonelier than he admitted and would welcome the company. I declined as graciously as I could.

'That's kind, but it's a eight-hour drive and I need to start soon. But I'd like your permission to come back, if I have any further questions.'

The wrinkles in the corners of his eyes deepened as he smiled. 'By all means, I'm sure there's more you'll need to know, in time.'

I was also sure - that I wasn't ever coming back to Saint-Valery, but I didn't say so.

Chapter Six

Latour left a message at my hotel in Rosheim the night I arrived, asking me to meet him the following day for lunch at a restaurant in what passed for the centre of the town.

Rosheim was dreary by comparison to Saint-Valery - all heavy half-timbered houses and grey streets, looking more like Germany than France. It was a nowhere place with no personality, at the edge of a cluster of other equally boring towns half an hour from Strasbourg.

At least Latour lived on the coast with the sea- and skyscapes he loved. But here, even the sanest person would go crazy if they had to spend their retirement with a view of the flat, damp floodplain of the Rhine.

As I looked around the restaurant searching for Latour, I realised it was a lot smarter and the prices were probably a lot higher than the pavement bistro I'd been led by his message to expect. I guessed, given that there wasn't anything else to do in the town, the proprietors had a near-monopoly on entertainment and could charge accordingly.

As the maître d'hôtel oiled his way towards me, I wondered if Kramer and Freybourg had inadvertently given Latour the impression that I somehow had access to the expense account of an investigator at a big bureaucracy.

I wasn't happy - I was pretending to be a student, and if Latour wasn't going to pay the bill, then my settling it wouldn't help my credibility. Eating with Dupont yesterday had been different - I'd already established my story by lunchtime.

Latour was already seated and, by the half-empty bottle in front of him, he was obviously on his second or third aperitif. His suit was clean and well pressed, but, like Freybourg's the other day, wasn't cut in a modern style. He stood to greet me, clicking his heels and welcoming me in German. I pursed my lips as we shook hands.

'Thank-you for meeting me Monsieur Latour - do you prefer if we carry on in French or German?'

'German. I don't have the opportunities these days to speak the correct, standard, German like I used to get - will you indulge an old man?'

I thought this was somewhat stretching credulity - unlike Dupont, Latour was well into late middle-age, but no older. It was also both somewhat sycophantic towards me and insulting towards the Alsatians, whose names on the street signs and shops underlined the fact that we were in the middle of the highest density of native Germanic language speakers in France.

This conversation needed to be handled robustly, otherwise his germanophilia would steer him towards telling me what I wanted to hear, rather than what I needed to know.

We sat down, and I opened the menu. Alongside pork served with the Alsatian sauerkraut that I had expected to see, they also offered fish and game. Instead, I chose the potato noodles that my supposed student budget might stretch to.

'As you know from Monsieur Freybourg, I'm researching the structures of economic cooperation between the former regimes during the war and how they influenced the post-war bodies. I understand you were in the Trade Ministry during that time, correct?'

Latour took the bait with relish. 'Yes, I'd just started working for Paribas before the war. The bank owned interests in chemical and steel concerns in different parts of Europe, so I got to know trade officials in Germany. In 'forty-one I was recruited by Bichelonne to help him run the office allocating raw materials to the French corporations supporting the war effort.'

He took a sip of wine and looked at me over the rim.

'When he was made Minister for Industry, he took me with him, and I ended up running the negotiations on the removal of custom tariffs on raw materials traded with Germany for the war effort. Coal from the mines in the Pas-de-Calais region, steel from Luxembourg, that kind of thing.'

He was enjoying telling his story, so I encouraged him to keep going. 'It all sounds quite organised, even clinical, or business-like I suppose?'

'When Germany occupied northern France in nineteen fourteen, during the Great War, they simply took the coal and anything else they wanted, including labourers. This time we decided it was better to cooperate with Germany - and it worked to a degree, for instance Bichelonne managed to persuade Speer to exempt French war industries from the forced labour draft. You know they got on quite well at a personal level, Speer and Bichelonne? They were both of a kind, young technocrats who thought they had the real answers to the problems of society, who secretly despised their political masters.'

He jabbed at me with his bread knife.

'Of course it wasn't perfect, but they were the first tentative steps towards a better, more enduring means of coordinating industrial effort across Europe. The European Coal and Steel Community that was started in nineteen fifty-two, when you were barely in school I imagine, was advertised as a means of locking France and Germany together to prevent war. Ironically, it was truly that - not least because it simply re-established the same wartime networks from when we'd fought together on the same side.'

'But that was seven years after the war ended. Surely the ECSC was a completely fresh start with a different set of people to those who ran the wartime networks?' As I said it, I realised I'd forgotten about von Barten.

'Some were involved - and why wouldn't they have been? If the Americans have been able to use former SS rocket engineers to accelerate their space programme, why couldn't specialists in other areas also have been rehabilitated?'

Dupont had said something similar yesterday, but I had no means of testing how widespread it was, apart from trawling personnel files back in Brussels. It was time to direct him towards Sigmaringen, in the hope he'd get even more carried away and simply volunteer his copy of the manual, if he still had it.

'Wernher Von Braun took the Americans his drawings and his plans, what did trade officials have to offer - the work you did at Sigmaringen with Monsieur Freybourg?'

'So you were paying attention to Freybourg. Sometimes the best ideas come when under pressure. Right at the very end, in exile, we held a series of conferences, about which I'm sure Freybourg has already told you in detail. We brought together experts who had actually made cross-border industrial cooperation work in practice, not just in theory, like Monnet.'

This didn't seem to be the rushed, cobbled together effort that Dupont claimed he helped create to earn extra bread rations.

'We gave thought to the propagation of the project, we drew on all of our propaganda expertise to devise ways to promote the ideas after the war, to camouflage them so that the victors would believe them to be their own.'

I looked around the room to see if anyone was paying attention. This was hot stuff, much more interesting, or even you might call it, exciting, than Dupont's tale by far.

'And now you want to know what happened next - who ended up influencing the EEC from the inside? I'm surprised Freybourg hasn't told you already, given he has such good connections there.'

I desperately wanted to know, but it was the document I was after first and foremost, for now.

'The EEC is later than my area for research - my thesis is on the International Authority for the Ruhr, which existed only up until the founding of the ECSC.' I pulled out Jan's folder again and laid it on the white tablecloth between us.

'I'm interested in Sigmaringen, so I can understand the immediate background to the IAR. I have a few more questions, if I may.'

Latour poured himself more wine and leaned forward, willing me on.

'You've told me that you came together in Sigmaringen to discuss the future, but why did you do that, apart from wanting to have something to offer the Americans?'

It was Latour's turn to purse his lips, a sour look came over his face as he remembered.

'At heart, I think it was because we wanted to justify to ourselves that the struggles and sacrifices over the previous four and a half years hadn't been in vain. The initial humiliation of surrender to Germany and then switching sides to join them in their fight against our former allies.'

'Which sacrifices hurt the most for France?'

'Too many to list them all, let alone rank them. The nearly million workers we eventually sent to the Reich for the war effort, if you include the prisoners of war the Germans took in nineteen forty. And not just France's sacrifices, but Europe's - the deaths of ordinary people in French, German and Italian cities in terror attacks from the air. The blood shed by the allied armies in the east, in the war against Communism, a war we lost thanks to international finance conspiring with Stalin to subvert the West's own best interests.'

He ran out of steam just as the food arrived at the table. I held fire until the waiter had returned to the kitchen.

'You were in international finance once.'

He cocked his head to one side. 'You know the people I mean.'

'Oh, that.'

I buttered another piece of bread, looking down at my plate.

'So you simply wanted to salvage something from the whole mess?' It was what von Barten had said that first day back in Brussels.

'We weren't going to roll over without a fight, we weren't going to let the Allies deconstruct our nascent European Order.'

In Brussels, and from Dupont, I'd been led to believe Sigmaringen was a madhouse for the delusional. Latour was describing a motivation that seemed a lot more rational and a lot more sinister.

'So you can't have been pleased when de Gaulle himself tried to deconstruct Germany by surgically removing the Saarland and attempting to do the same with the Ruhr?' I patted Jan's folder.

'Of course not, that was simply remaining imprisoned in a medieval past where the winner takes all, but loses it again the next time around - just like this very region,' he said, pointing around the room with his fork this time.

'France on its own, no matter how many assets we might have been allowed to strip from Germany during our post-war occupation, could never achieve as much as we would be able to do together. The war proved how effective Europeans could be when we worked together for common goals.'

I wasn't sure about how effective Germany and its European allies had been, given that we'd lost the war. Maybe he meant some different goal.

'You've told me why you did it, but who was the driving personality behind the work in Sigmaringen? Did the leadership come from the French side or the German?'

He flicked his eyes to the side. 'Ah - it came from both camps. We all wanted to win the peace after the war.'

'What role did Freybourg play? Was he the lead author?'

'Author of what?'

'Whatever it was that you wrote down as a result of your discussions.'

'Why would we have written anything down? You're the one who's made that assumption during the course of this conversation. What would have been the point of making a written record on the eve of capture by the Allies? We were trying to avoid the guillotine, not give them an excuse to use it.'

If this was true, then the wheels had completely come off Freybourg's story.

'So how were you going to take your ideas forward? Wouldn't a briefing paper from a neutral body that could be fed to the Allied military governments have helped?'

That's how think tanks were used at the EEC, so it was a fair question.

'Nothing we discussed or agreed on could have been acted upon in the immediate post-war period. We thought the best use of our time was to thrash out details, imprint the plan on people's minds, and then each go our own way after the war, committed to the cause of European unity.'

'Nothing? There really were no memos, studies or the like?' I tapped the folder again.

Latour looked at out of the corner of his eye. 'Of course, anything that did survive could be very valuable because of its rarity.'

'And did it?'

'I agreed to meet you today, despite not knowing you, or having any real interest in your work, because I am not a rich man. Unlike some of my former colleagues who were able to reinvent themselves, I was too exposed politically from my involvement with the French State - thankfully not enough to lose my head. All the same, I was left unemployable at the same level I was previously used to and with no private wealth which survived the war.'

I felt no pity - and it was nonsense anyway. Even the head of the Vichy police from nineteen forty-two, René Bousquet, had managed to convince enough people that his collaboration was ambiguous. He'd ended up as a consultant to Banque de l'Indochine and sponsoring Francois Mitterand's presidential election challenge to de Gaulle in 'sixty-five. Latour just wasn't very good at persuading people to like him.

Maybe too, it was because in Freybourg and Dupont, I'd met people, who, if they hadn't apologised for their actions, at least recognised their folly and had shown no misplaced loyalty or inclination to revisit those times.

'What are you trying to say Monsieur Latour?'

'I can help you, but I need money.'

'What are you selling?'

'You want historical papers? You want to write a doctorate which will get you noticed by every history faculty in Europe?' I tensed.

'I want some money upfront as a goodwill gesture - fifteen thousand francs. Then I'll show you what I have, and then we negotiate further and find out it's worth to you.'

I did a quick calculation, fifteen thousand was roughly half my annual salary at the EEC.

'Are you crazy? What do you think doctorate students earn these days?'

'I didn't think they were salaried, but I'm sure if you explain it to your faculty, whoever they are, funds will be forthcoming.'

I gave him a stare. I might have been born yesterday in Latour's eyes - but that didn't mean that Latour had recent practice at this sort of negotiation. Presumably, you only got to sell your trove of pilfered Nazi documents once. In the police we used to make small payments to low-level informers, and I saw Latour as just another type of snitch.

'What evidence are you going to give me to help sell that idea?'

Latour thought for a moment or two. 'I can give you a sample of some material - we'll need to go back to my house though, after we've eaten.'

The rest of lunch was a dismal affair. In Latour's mind, our business was almost done, and he made no effort to keep the conversation going. He'd ordered from the top end of the menu, and when we were finished, asked me to pay, as I had feared.

I grumbled and made a show of being in difficulties, but he simply sat there with a sardonic look as I slowly extracted the notes from my wallet.

Afterwards, I followed him back to his house on the edge of town. We must have looked a strange sight, an odd couple with grim expressions and nothing to say to one another. Latour's house was more of a cottage - a narrow-fronted two storey building, sandwiched between taller neighbours on either side.

We stepped inside - there was no hallway and the front parlour took up the whole width of the house. Through the open doorway to the kitchen at the rear I caught a glimpse of a tiny courtyard backed by a high wall. Modest the house might be, but not easy to approach by stealth.

Latour left me in the front parlour while he climbed the staircase crossing up over the kitchen door. I looked around, the furniture was antique, but solid - I suspected it had belonged to the house long before Latour had moved in. The cottage was almost devoid of personal touches - I took a quick look into the kitchen and noted the single dirty plate and cup in the sink. His bookshelves were mainly filled with titles on philosophy and politics - unlike Dupont, it seemed that Latour had found a career, seen it come prematurely to an end, and never moved on.

I had pulled out a couple of books, looking at the flyleaf for ownership marks, when Latour came slowly back down the uncarpeted stairs, holding an envelope which he passed over.

It contained a single sheet, stamped with what I assumed was the emblem of the French State, the name the Vichy regime had called itself. Intriguingly, where the bottom edge of the page had been torn, I could just make out what looked like the top of the eagle seal of the Third Reich itself.

I scanned the text - it appeared to be a preamble to an agreement on trade, dated December nineteen forty-four - so the right date for something issued at Sigmaringen, three months into their doomed sojourn.

'What is this?'

'It's proof that I do have material from Sigmaringen days. Come back with the money and you'll get the index and the summary of Freybourg's document. Pay me the balance that we're going to negotiate, and you'll get the rest. No copies, all original material.'

I waved the sheet at him. 'This is nothing. It's not a plan to rebuild Europe, it's an agreement on tariffs. I want to see an actual page from the manual.'

Latour had a strained look. I let the silence stretch out before letting him off the hook.

'Okay then, if this is what you want to use as proof to get the discussion started, I'll take it back to my professor and see what he says. But you must understand we are a small faculty, with no endowments, so nothing we can do will happen quickly.' I wanted to threaten him, but knew I had no plausible sanction to use whilst I was playing the role of a student.

His face now relaxed. 'If this is important, you'll make it happen. By the way, if this period of history is now suddenly of interest, maybe other people than your department might pay - and if artefacts go through the Iron Curtain, you can consider them gone forever.'

'Why would the Soviets know about the manual? And why would they be interested?'

He left the question unanswered. I would pay him back for that next time we met.

'Please be assured Monsieur Latour, my faculty will treat this with the seriousness it deserves - there can be no higher task than writing the correct version of history.'

'Do you really know what that is, young man? I presume you think your leader arrived up from the underworld and bewitched the entire population with a demonic charm? At least, that's what you may have been taught in school.'

My hackles rose, now would come the usual rant about how all Germans were equally guilty for what the Nazis did. I was right, but not in the way I'd expected.

'But did you also know that the Centre Party's von Papen, who was the Chancellor just before Hitler, ignored the Reichstag for two years and effectively also ruled as a dictator through Emergency Decree? You know that the Centre Party, in turn, learned that trick from the Social Democrats who governed in the same way all through nineteen twenty-four? Did you know that in that year the Social Democrats extended the term of their Chancellor Ebert simply by having the Weimar constitution altered?'

'What are you trying to say?'

'In nineteen thirty-three Hitler was just another prospective authoritarian Chancellor - at that time he still acted, to a degree, like the ones he was seeking to replace. The German people can't claim they were clueless about how he intended to behave in office, when they voted him into power.'

'I don't think they actually had the chance to vote freely. The brownshirts ran the streets, it wasn't a fair election.' Hamburg hadn't forgotten, it had given over half its votes to the Socialists and Communists. But that hadn't saved those same voters from being firebombed ten years later in a kind of pre-nuclear holocaust.

'Then ponder this - what do you think is happening in the Eastern bloc right now? It's merely a different expression of the idea, that, because of the Hitler experience, the people can no longer be trusted to make correct electoral choices, so any choice should therefore be limited? Put that in your doctorate thesis instead of tariff tables for metallurgical coal.'

Maybe he did have a liberal side after all.

Chapter Seven

Thursday, 13th March 1969

I'd got back to Brussels late the previous night after my meeting with Latour and not in the best of moods.

I hadn't really expected to find a long-lost file after a couple of days of searching but coming back with a half-page of text from an irrelevant document had left me somewhat flat. An account from Dupont of what also sounded like a completely different discussion in Sigmaringen to the one Freybourg and Latour had described didn't help my outlook either.

It felt like the investigation was already in danger of running out of steam. If Latour really did have the manual, then that might be as good as it was going to get. At least it would be some measure of success, but we hadn't even begun to track down Freybourg's 'blackmailer' as I thought of him.

Perhaps the document would contain further clues, Dupont's German sponsor with a 'boring' name was the only new lead on the horizon, but even if he had existed, neither Freybourg nor Latour seemed to have thought he was important enough to mention. That was the other thing, Freybourg had admitted his memory was no longer the best, and Dupont had seemed confused at times too.

It was time to face the music and tell von Barten and Kramer what I'd learned, scanty as it was.

Once more, the three of us were sitting around the same conference table in von Barten's office. Von Barten opened his notebook and smoothed it flat on the glass top.

He pushed out a couple of millimetres of lead from his silver propelling pencil and laid it down exactly in the centre of the page fold, waiting.

I waited for this little ritual to finish, licked my lips and began. 'I met with Freybourg's two contacts - Latour yesterday and Dupont the day before. Whatever discussions there had been at Sigmaringen, Dupont didn't seem to take them seriously. He said he'd contributed material to earn extra food rations, that a kind of manual had been put together, and that he'd taken a copy when he quit the castle and returned to France. However, he said that he'd burnt it there and then, as soon as he was across the border.'

I looked at Kramer. 'Does that sound reasonable, or plausible?'

'Possibly - it doesn't contradict anything which Freybourg told us, in substance.'

Von Barten started to make notes, I was surprised to see him doing his own written work for a change.

'But, when I met Latour, I heard something which sounded quite different - a serious attempt to work out plans for a European future, building upon the foundations of the wartime cooperation between Germany and France.'

Von Barten spoke up, 'What did he say they wrote down?'

'He was very coy at first, I'll explain in a minute. But he claims, like Freybourg, that there was a kind of manual written up - not just on how to rebuild the economy, but also on how to propagate their ideas, how to introduce them into the post-war structures.'

'So, it's as bad as we feared, eh Kramer?'

'Yes, unfortunately, it sounds just like what Freybourg described to Lenkeit and I last week.'

Von Barten ignored Kramer's platitude. 'What was Latour coy about?' he demanded.

I pushed over the single page from Latour, watching

them both as I did so. Von Barten put on his reading spectacles, raising an eyebrow as he scanned the sheet. Kramer was impassive.

'What is this?' von Barten asked sharply.

'He claims it's proof that he does possess documents from nineteen forty-four and 'forty-five. He says he'll sell us the index of Freybourg's manual for fifteen thousand French francs.'

'It's proof of nothing.' Von Barten stared at me, hard. 'If anything, it's proof he sniffs money and wants to buy time to go and type up something on some old stocks of wartime paper, which he can then sell to us. You may just have made the situation worse Lenkeit, by encouraging another aging chancer to create yet more noise around the Project.'

I reddened under his cold eyes. His suggestion had taken me by surprise, and I was annoyed I hadn't thought of it myself. I supposed that was what had got him to where he was today.

'What do we do now Kramer?'

Kramer cleared his throat. 'I think we go ahead and buy whatever he has. We need to know all we can about what we're dealing with.'

'Fifteen thousand francs, for a table of contents? It can come out of your budget Kramer.'

Kramer closed his eyes for a second or two.

'Let's send Lenkeit back to Strasbourg and see if he can get hold of the entire document for the same price. Use some encouragement if necessary, ditch the student act and put the frighteners on him.'

I didn't believe they were actually quibbling about the cash. Unless von Barten was one of those rich people who were preternaturally stingy when it came to any spending, even if it wasn't their own money. Listening to and watching them now, I began to see that Bernd's story about a bust-up three years ago maybe wasn't so unbelievable after all.

'Very well then Kramer, but let's not rush this, let's make this *Kerl* in Strasbourg wait and sweat a little. But not so long, so that he's got time to forge something, if he really doesn't already have a document in his possession.'

'What do you want me to do sir?' I interjected, before Kramer had a chance to reply. 'It's Thursday today. We could arrange it so that I drive Freybourg down there to review the document on Monday and see if it's genuine. We can be back here by Tuesday afternoon.'

Kramer didn't like my plan. 'No, we don't need Freybourg to go there in person. I'll authorise the cash, speak to my secretary and you can draw the money tomorrow. Although really,' he said, turning to von Barten, 'if we're going to do any more of these external confidential investigations, we'll need to create a new budget, or even set up a new department.'

He paused and von Barten didn't demur. Kramer continued, 'Anyway, for now, as I said, let's gather together all and any material out there and see if we can close this down quickly. Dupont destroyed his copy, Suffren's was presumably lost long ago, and I'm hoping we almost have our hands on Latour's.'

Von Barten's hand raced lightly over the page of his notebook as he caught up on his private record of the conversation.

He looked up, 'Yes, but what did the person who threatened Freybourg plan to reveal then? What if Suffren's copy wasn't lost and Dupont is lying to us or Latour is trying to sell his copy twice to two different parties?'

I added my contribution now. 'How do we even know Latour's papers are the only ones from that time. You know how much paperwork is generated in this building. Who's to say the same thing didn't happen back then, that there's something similar out there, authentically from that time, but entirely different to the document Freybourg was threatened over?'

Kramer ran his hands through his hair again. 'Let's just send Lenkeit and take a look at what he brings back.'

This seemed to finally satisfy von Barten. 'Very well then, let's see what Freybourg says. If they're not the right ones, Lenkeit will need to keep looking, though - he might need to rattle Dupont's cage too.'

As we got up to leave, von Barten said, 'Lenkeit, a moment please.'

Kramer disappeared down the corridor, and I turned, making to sit back down.

'Stay where you are and close the door.'

The panel was precisely engineered for its frame, beautifully made like everything else in the room. It closed with a solid clunk, shutting out all sound from the outside.

Von Barten closed his notebook and set it to one side with his pencil.

'What have you been doing all week? You met us last Tuesday and it's Thursday today.'

'Er ...'

'When I said this was of critical importance to the European project, did you think I was joking, or that this was some kind of game?'

His eyes bored into me. He was speaking in a normal voice, no shouting, which made it worse.

'Do you have any idea what our country went through after the war to get to where we are today? You stand there, living your soft life, like those students and their so-called protests last year, never really having had to struggle or fight for anything.'

I took a sharp intake of breath.

'Where is your report?' He stabbed the table-top with his forefinger on every word. 'You waltz up here, to the most senior French and to the most senior German official in the whole EEC, with this scrap in your hand?' He pointed to the page from Latour.

I didn't know what to say to fix the situation. I suspected that no matter what I said, it would be the wrong thing.

'Ah ...'

'Get out and be back with all the details of all your interviews to date, properly typed up, in two hours' time. I want everything, every word spoken, every address you visited.' He started stabbing again, this time towards my chest. 'Freybourg, Latour, Dupont - now.'

'Yes sir.' It was all I could think of.

I went back down and across the road to the Charlemagne and my shared office with Bernd. My ears were burning with shame, even though I knew his accusation was unfair. I could have spent time typing a report before I saw them both, but equally, I knew they had wanted to hear the results of my meetings, as soon as possible that morning. I didn't know how, but one day I would get him back for this.

It was the first time I'd seen Bernd in a week. Thankfully, for my state of mind, he was sympathetic.

'It's nonsense, he's just trying to unbalance you. I don't know what you got up to the past week and a bit, and I'm not going to ask. But you've only just got back from wherever you were. Don't forget, you have power here too, they're not going to run the interviews and take notes, they need you for that information.'

'I know, and that's why he now wants full details of everything I've found out to date.'

I glumly set up the paper in my Olympia and started bashing the keys one by one. I hadn't taken many notes during the conversations - I'd been trying to get the Frenchmen to open up. I summarised as best I could, typing directly from memory, adding a page with my travel itinerary to bulk out the report.

When I was done, I pondered how much I could tell Bernd - I really needed his counsel on what to do next. There wasn't a lot I could discuss though, not without having to explain the whole background, which was meant to be secret after all.

He put me on the spot before I'd decided. 'So, what can you tell me about the past week?'

'I'm not sure what I'm able to say. Don't know at this stage how sensitive it's all going to turn out to be. But before I go back up, do you have any tidbits on von Barten? What's he been up to this past week that I can bring into conversation?'

'No idea, I've mostly been doing vetting of new staff. But I did pull his personnel file when I was over in Records - did you know he's sixty-four this year? He must be thinking about when's the right time for him to retire, even though he's given no indication that his position is up for grabs - not as far as I know anyway.'

'I suppose the likely candidates are already assembling allies?'

'I'm sure they are - it's a fine judgement though, too soon could be seen as being ghoulish and backfire. Anyway, you'd better get back over there, otherwise he'll get really angry.' Bernd didn't elaborate as to what that might mean.

I laid the report, neatly stapled, on von Barten's desk. He pulled it over, licked a finger and leafed through it, sheet by sheet.

'This is much better, are all the details here?' He pointed to a section at random, on the meeting with Latour. 'You got this address correct?' I nodded. He flicked back a few pages and pointed again, 'Is this where you met Dupont?'

'Yes, at his house and then afterwards at my hotel.'

'Have a seat.' He pointed to the conference table again, closed my report and then rested his arms on his elbows, linking his fingers.

'Everything we see around us is potentially in jeopardy, all of the time. Politicians from the Six, and from other nations too, are always seeking to undermine the Project and subvert its supporters in the Berlaymont, every year. We provide them with solutions to one problem, like the question on national voting rights, and the next year something else comes up. Do you understand?'

'Yes, I get it.'

'Let's not pretend, after seventeen years of construction, that the whole edifice can now be brought down by a single piece of paper. If we, the supporters of the Project, are to carry on doing our work undisturbed though, it needs to be utterly above reproach or taint. Someone outside the EEC, even if they only intend to use the Sigmaringen document to make a personal attack, can't help but end up hurting us all.'

He paused to assure himself I was still following.

'Do not underestimate the determination and strength of will to make the EEC everything it should be. Every national politician on the outside attacking the Project is matched by people here on the inside, equally determined to stop them, by any means at our disposal. You will never see them or meet them, but I assure you Lenkeit, they are there.'

I kept nodding along.

'I need to know that you're fully on our side and trust that you're straining every sinew to complete this task. That's why I pushed you earlier. If you do a good job for the French, you can bank that for your future career. If you do an exceptional job for me and prove yourself a member of my circle of trust, you can go much further, in ways you can't yet imagine.'

I waited a few seconds - it seemed like his homily was over, so I got up to leave. 'Thank-you sir.' Inwardly, I wasn't so polite.

'I'd like to invite you to dinner on Saturday evening. Eight at my place. An intimate black-tie affair for a few of the younger up-and-coming EEC *fonctionnaires*. Bring a guest too, if you wish.'

I raised an eyebrow at this last-minute switch of the

stick for the carrot. 'Very kind of you sir, I'm sure.' I wondered how much von Barten already knew of my private life, and where I would find dinner wear at such short notice.

Chapter Eight

My taxi stopped at a quarter to eight outside the gates of von Barten's house on the edge of the Forêt de Soignes, to the south-east of Brussels, still just in the suburbs.

I crunched up the gravel drive under sombre trees, lit by yellow light spilling from an ornate ironwork conservatory at the side of the house where several guests were already sipping pre-dinner drinks together.

The house was more like a small mansion, three storeys with turrets steeply roofed in blue slate at each corner.

What really caught my eye, though, was the collection of expensive sports cars parked around the carriage circle outside the front door. I was glad I'd left the Volkswagen at my apartment - I didn't know who I was going to meet, but whoever they were, I would have died of embarrassment parking next to the Mercedes SL let alone the Maserati GT alongside it.

I was uncomfortable enough as it was, thanks to being squeezed into a borrowed jacket from Bernd. For a moment, I even thought of looking for a tradesman's entrance, so I could slip in quietly, but I squared my shoulders and rang the bell.

A waiter opened the front door onto a parqueted hallway, indicated a side room for coats and offered champagne from a silver tray.

As I looked round the empty coat room with its paintings of eighteenth century noblemen and -women and its marble figurines of Roman goddesses, I began to wonder how expensive the watercolour landscapes hanging in von Barten's office were, if this was what he displayed in a side room.

Von Barten caught sight of me through the doorway, excused himself from his companions in the hall, and came forward in greeting.

'Ah, there you are Lenkeit. When we say eight o'clock for dinner, that's taken to mean drinks from seven-thirty.'

I felt like I wanted to lift the parquet blocks with my fingernails, dig deep into the earth and bury my head far down.

'What do you think? The fruits of a lifetime's work in a good cause.' Von Barten waved his hand around the cloakroom with an air of utter self-assurance, like a Great War admiral signalling his subordinates by semaphore.

In the past week and a half I had got to know a different von Barten to the one I thought I had the measure of from my first few years at the EEC - more human, but still just as arrogant.

I took refuge in deference. 'You have a delightful home sir.'

'Come, let me introduce you to a few people of your own age. These social functions are where you get known on the circuit and where the real EEC business gets done.'

'Is this an official EEC function then?'

'Every time you meet colleagues in Brussels you're working. These dinners and drinks parties are perhaps the most important part of my calling at the EEC. I won't be around forever, and I won't get to see the Project to its conclusion - so I need to train apprentices, those who will light the way, so to speak, for the heavenly Europa in the decades to come.'

Whatever he'd been drinking earlier that evening, I needed some too. I took a sip, just in case it was the champagne.

'Do you have any idea of the infinite patience required to carefully deconstruct national allegiances and build up new loyalties? We need to challenge received histories, offer new, attractive foundation myths, and above all, make real connections of shared interest between nations at a personal level. And this is where it happens, with your generation.'

He tapped his glass with his long forefinger as he enunciated his points. 'But anyway, enough seriousness - do drink up your Veuve Clicquot, it's rather good...'

Von Barten steered me out of the cloakroom towards a group of other twenty- and thirty somethings, four men, and a young woman with plaited blond hair in a V-cut dress, whom they were trying to impress.

'Sophie, darling, make Lenkeit feel at home amongst these Latin poets, dreamers and occasional bandits.'

'Is that what they are? I thought they were your own private youth organisation. My uncle,' the girl said coolly. 'If you've met him, you must have seen straight through the old fraud.'

Von Barten drifted off, leaving me facing the girl alone, who was now standing slightly apart from the group. 'Your uncle, eh? Not quite what I expected tonight.'

'What isn't? Uncle Ernst isn't what you expected, or I'm not? You'll get used to his odd figures of speech if you come again. In some ways, though, he's completely transparent. People think he's just like one of those dissimulating politicians, but he's simply learnt the knack of hiding in plain sight.'

'And are you here tonight as family, or do you also work at the EEC?'

'Both of course - look, we've been placed next to each other at dinner, I'll tell you more then.'

She touched a loose hair back into place behind her ear and turned away to speak to one of the Italians.

Dinner was an impressive five-course affair, for what von Barten had implied was simply an elegant get-together for a few like-minded people. After her initial abruptness,

Sophie turned out to be an engaging dinner companion. She spoke freely of her work in Agriculture and of her professional relationship to von Barten - how he had eased her into a job for which I felt really needed many more years' experience. There was one question, however, that I had to ask, even if I didn't really want to, having half-guessed the answer.

'What exactly is your uncle's "youth organization"?'

She looked at me appraisingly. 'They aren't your sort of people, *Herr Polizist*. Just remember, that despite his little jokes about Latins, serious money truly knows no borders, thus making him quite liberal as regards recruiting his successors. The younger people he's developing are all old money, often the children of financiers and other businessmen he's known from long ago, people he believes he can form into good Greater Europeans.'

I was a little disorientated - she was talking with me, as if I was a special confidant of von Barten, or 'Ernst' as I might end up calling him one day, yet at the same time drawing a clear boundary between me and the inner circle of his bright young golden prospects.

Despite these occasional checks, as the wine flowed, I could feel myself become more and more uninhibited and had to start making a real effort to concentrate on her face, as opposed to looking elsewhere.

I mentally slapped myself and asked a question guaranteed to sober up the party atmosphere for any German. 'What did the von Bartens actually do during the war?'

'Well, I personally didn't do anything, the Denazification Law didn't affect Germans born in nineteen forty-six,' she grinned. 'There, I've told you something about myself, what will you tell me in return?'

I tried to read her and work out whether she was starting to flirt. 'Well, I was around during the war, but only in the womb, so it was my mother who had to be denazified.' As soon as I had said the words, I felt their crassness. Sophie, however, smoothed over my awkwardness, quickly diverting the conversation. She told me more about her childhood, of the schools she had attended, and of von Barten's wife, Anne, who now spent most her time back in Germany, having grown tired of playing the role of Brussels hostess. I was still lost as to Sophie's real intentions but was starting to enjoy the dinner in a way I didn't think I would.

'Now, unlike me, Uncle Ernst is someone who definitely has an interesting history. I think he has the nine lives of a cat, he would land on his feet regardless of what was happening in the world around him - and a lot did.'

'Want to tell me more?'

'You know that his job under Albert Speer was far more senior than he likes to advertise? He ended up coordinating almost the entirety of French and Belgian steel production for the war effort. At the same time, he managed to be close enough to the Kreisau-Zirkel, the anti-Nazi group, so as to end the war fully employable by the victors. Yet, during the war, he wasn't so close so as to be arrested after the attempt on Hitler's life in July nineteen forty-four.'

'That is news to me. So he's survived everything the twentieth century has thrown at him so far and stayed at the top of his tree? What does he really think of that whole sorry episode back then though?'

'Oh, that's not difficult - like I said earlier, he's always hidden in plain sight. He was completely and genuinely anti-Nazi - but principally because he thought they were just another flavour of Socialist pleb. He thinks that Germany was most effectively run when the Kaiser's word was law, but when those words were put in the Kaiser's mouth by the people who knew best for Germany - the big industrialists and the landowners. He sees the chaos of the Weimar Republic as proof, still in living memory, that democracy is best left in history books about Ancient Greece.'

'And you agree with him?'

'He's my uncle, I can say what I like to him and about him - he doesn't care anyway.'

She was too smart to be pinned down. I suddenly saw in her eyes a much more serious and thoughtful person, just under the surface.

'But given that the alternative is a dictatorship of the proletariat, does he still think that the current expression of democracy in the West is a mistake?

'Probably, but I imagine his EEC job keeps him fully occupied and away from philosophical reflections - unlike you, who's clearly spent too much time in smoke-filled cafes on the Rive Gauche. Anyway, Ernst isn't a politician, he can't really influence anything.' I thought this was a little naïve. Given that she'd been around so many of the EEC power players in past couple of years, she must know the plans they had for the future.

After the last meat course, just as coffee and desserts were about to be served, von Barten got to his feet at the head of the table and tapped his wine glass with the clean top-edge of his bread knife.

'As you know, at these dinners I normally invite one of you to say a short piece on a current affairs topic which I've given you beforehand. Tonight, Signor Rizzi will be pleased to hear that instead I want to take the opportunity to comment, very briefly, on the situation in France, and that we'll hear his views on last week's Sino-Soviet border clashes some other time.'

A smile lit up the face of one of Sophie's pre-dinner companions, an amiable young man in a soft silk shirt and elegantly knotted bow tie.

'As you know, de Gaulle and I haven't seen eye to eye over the years on the future direction of Europe – difficult, given that he's almost two metres tall,' titters rose up from all sides of the table, 'but I want to acknowledge, this evening, his strength of will and his adamant dedication to his interpretation of destiny of France. They are personal characteristics we should all cultivate.'

He looked around the room as he spoke, holding each person's eyes for a moment, even mine. That was also the excuse for the others to give me a good stare too.

'But de Gaulle's time is coming to an end - as it must do for every public figure eventually. Adenauer stayed on as West German Chancellor until the age of eighty-seven, six years ago - but he is exceptional in many ways, as I am sure you would agree.'

Von Barten pointed halfway down the table to a small man whose harsh voice had intruded on my conversation with Sophie at various times throughout the dinner.

'When does my favourite *Franzmann* here think de Gaulle's time will be up?' We all stared at him as he cleared his throat, buying time himself. Von Barten answered his own question.

'I'll tell you then. De Gaulle has said he will resign if the voters reject his proposed constitutional changes in next month's referendum. Why has he said this? After all, his party won the snap parliamentary election held after the protests last year. In my view, it's because he knows he will lose the next planned presidential election, in nineteen seventy-two, when he'll be over eighty. He wants to depart at some point soon, but on his own terms, so he can say he never lost a presidential election in a straight fight with another candidate. He can't bear the idea that, one day, history might record he was less popular with the French people than someone like Mitterand.' Von Barten looked around the table again, in a silent challenge to any thoughts of contradiction.

'He's loaded the gun of a confidence vote, handed it to French people and is daring them to use it - perhaps hoping sub-consciously, that the time is now.' The French guest folded and refolded his napkin, waiting on von Barten to finish. 'My view, is that after the chaos of the student protests and strikes in France last year, the voters will decide that this is their chance to send their seventy-eight-year-old President into retirement, regardless of the merits or otherwise of the proposals they are notionally voting for.'

He took a sip of wine. These people weren't apprentices, they were courtiers, nervous of a capricious king.

'Changes are coming, ladies and gentlemen. De Gaulle's departure will happen very soon, even if it doesn't come to pass next month. Inside our organisation, those currently sympathetic to de Gaulle's views on how the EEC should develop will then abandon their position. If he does go next month, we need to be ready so that we can start pushing for more integration, no later than a year from now. The next set of national powers that are ripe for plucking are obviously in the area of monetary union, where Pierre Werner has been working on proposals since the early years of this decade.'

The Italian, Rizzi, raised his hand and half-turned to the gravelly-voiced Frenchman.

'Why will the French change their attitude to the EEC just because de Gaulle is gone?'

The little guy now found his voice and rasped back, as if reciting his answer. 'Because France is going to find that it values its payments from Common Agricultural Policy funds too much to risk upsetting the other countries if they want to increase the areas of supranational decision-making.'

'Well said *Franzmann*. Sad but true, sometimes the dream of Europe needs financial encouragement to make it real. Anyway, enough from me this evening. Please enjoy yourselves, but, as always, do remember our rule that everything said here stays within these walls.'

This was the signal for the guests to rise from the table for after-dinner drinks and cigars, dispersing throughout the house in little clusters so that the networking could resume. I pulled Sophie's chair back from the table for her. She rose, unembarrassed by my gesture. Part of me strongly wanted to follow her into the next room, von Barten's study, to join her next conservation - but I also wondered if I shouldn't simply casually drift away and mingle with the other guests, so as not to appear too interested.

In the end, she made the decision for me, signalling me through the open doorway to fetch her a drink, then, when I offered her a balloon of brandy, patting the space next to her on the settee. I wasn't really sure why she continued to show interest, maybe my background made me somehow exotically different to the golden youth around her. We chatted some more and as the clock struck ten, she stretched her neck, slipped off her shoes and tucked her feet under her dress. She nursed the glass in her hands, keeping the spirit warm while she gazed into the fire. The gaps in the conversation now began to stretch out, and I excused myself for the bathroom, before the momentum was completely lost, intending to return and start afresh.

The house was designed for entertaining, next to the coat room there was a bathroom with two urinals. As I stood there, a hand clapped my shoulder and Rizzi installed himself next to me.

'A word of caution, my friend. You can look, but you can't touch.'

'Excuse me?' I laughed aggressively, shocked into anger.

'Oh, ha ha, very good! Oh my, that was too funny. No, I meant Sophie.' He turned and fixed his eyes on me.

'She weaves her magic on everyone, but it's not really meant for you especially. She is simply one of those girls who truly likes men, who prefers them as her real friends over women. But it's confusing when you first meet her. Before I came into von Barten's orbit, there were lots of false rumours on how she favoured us.'

He was swaying slightly now, slurring a little.

'But let me be very clear - she doesn't spend herself on anyone, if you know what I mean, at least, not at our level. She's more than our close friend, she's that one central person you find in every group, who binds it together. She's also von Barten's golden girl, the one whom we think he's truly serious about pushing up the ranks. We all know he wants one of his own in a position of real influence before he retires, which can't be far off.'

He shook himself down.

'So don't get any ideas about her. Even though she's rebuffed and frustrated each one of us at some point in time, we're all still fiercely loyal to her. I can't explain it, it's just the way it is.'

I left the bathroom and made my way back to Sophie, more determined than ever. On the way, though, von Barten shimmered out of an ante-room, his cold grey eyes bringing me back down to earth.

He grasped my elbow in a gesture of unwanted intimacy and steered me back into the room he'd just come from. We sat opposite each other in wingbacked chairs, the door to the hall open.

'So, any further thoughts on our problem over the weekend?'

I was glad, in a way, to be back with the office version of von Barten, I knew slightly better where I stood with this one.

'I'm meeting with Freybourg on Monday to review with him what we've learned so far. I also want to hear if he's been contacted again by this blackmailer, or if Latour or Dupont did so after my visits to them. After that interview, I'm driving down to Strasbourg again, to start the negotiation with Latour.'

I risked some honesty.

'This still a wild goose chase, a thin thread connects Freybourg, Latour and Dupont, and only a very thin thread connects Kramer with Freybourg.'

I paused and Von Barten nodded slowly. Out of the

corner of my eye I caught a flash of blond hair and long red dress as Sophie swept past the open doorway on Rizzo's arm. I carefully fixed my eyes on von Barten as he replied.

'Indeed, let's endeavour to find out what that last connection is, shall we? And keep it to ourselves of course.' von Barten lowered his eyes. 'By the way, my niece spoke warmly of you just a minute ago - I'm sure you can find an excuse to go over to Agriculture from time to time.' I stood up, keen to see if Sophie was still in the building.

'Thank you for dinner sir and good night.'

'I merely wanted to give you a taste of life in our little circle, many doors stand open from within it.'

I was almost hopping on my feet now. 'Thank-you again for the opportunity.' I would be as sycophantic as any courtier, if it would let me get away quickly.

In the hallway I asked, but Sophie had gone, and I wasn't even exactly sure which department of Agriculture she worked in. Nevertheless, I crunched back down the gravel drive with a firm purpose - a different person from when I had arrived.

Chapter Nine

Monday morning dawned, and I strode into our shared office at the Charlemagne. 'Off to any more fancy dinners or restaurants again for your "research"?' asked Bernd, who always seemed to get in first, no matter how early I came to the office. I didn't care - at that moment the question which consumed me was how many days I should leave it before casually visiting the Agriculture Directorate's office.

I still had a job to do today though. As I'd told von Barten, after seeing Freybourg I was going to drive down to Latour in Rosheim later this evening – but, despite the impression I'd given, this was unknown to Latour. I wanted to surprise him, knock on his door unannounced, shake him up and see what happened.

I'd also told von Barten on Saturday that I was going to meet Freybourg today to go over my interviews with Dupont and Latour. But I was as much interested in Freybourg himself. He'd hadn't made it clear the week before last, that he'd led the Sigmaringen effort for the French, or that it had been done under the direction of the Germans, as the other two had indicated. Given that Kramer hadn't wanted Freybourg to come with me to see Latour, I thought this was also a good reason to try to see him privately.

Freybourg was staying at the Hôtel Métropole where we'd first spoken. When I spoke to Kramer's secretary on the Friday as I collected two thick bundles of fifty-franc notes for Latour, it turned out that Freybourg was going to be there for as long we needed him in Brussels. Last thing that day, I'd sent a photocopy of my report for von Barten to the hotel by courier too.

Much as I enjoyed going to the Café Métropole, I wanted Freybourg to meet me on my ground - but first I needed to find somewhere out of the way. I agreed with Kramer that the EEC needed to be better organised for external investigations in the future, a future which I was determined would include me in a serious role, to impress Sophie.

As always, I turned to Bernd for ideas on how to get things done through the system. 'Where can I get a room, away from the Berlaymont, to meet with someone on my own?'

'Your weekend did go well, didn't it? Who did you meet at your dinner?'

I couldn't help a grin. 'You and your devious mind - it's for my lead - I want to get him away from Kramer.'

'Of course you do.' He tapped his teeth with his pencil for a moment. 'What's the difficulty? Just find the Chief of Staff at a Directorate or department which isn't based near here and say you're from Internal Affairs. No questions will be asked, it's a cheap favour that they can bank with you, to be repaid later with interest.'

It all came together, almost too neatly. After ringing around, by lunchtime I'd found an unused basement storeroom - Bernd had flashed me a couple of quizzical looks as I'd boldly demanded cooperation. By the early afternoon, I was sitting opposite Freybourg across a dusty table - and unbeknown to Sophie, three floors underneath her.

Freybourg was visibly more relaxed at the second meeting. He'd changed his suit from last time which made him look at least five years younger. Maybe Kramer had given him an expense allowance, so he could smarten himself up. He even led off the conversation, which didn't surprise me as much as it would have done last week, not now that I knew more of his role in Sigmaringen.

'Tell me how Latour and Dupont struck you - the last time I saw them was just before my capture by the Americans.'

'What's that story, if you don't mind?' I thought a couple minutes' reminiscence might put him further at ease.

'Tragi-comic at best. We'd known for months that Sigmaringen would be the prime target in Germany for de Gaulle's troops. They themselves were a mixed bag of army regulars who'd escaped in nineteen forty, Resistance fighters in uniform and even Senegalese colonial *tirailleurs*. Those were the ones we feared the most, as they were rumoured to behead prisoners.'

'So rather the *Amis* than the tender mercies of your own countrymen?'

'We went from village to village, following the sounds of gunfire, searching out the American soldiers we knew were somewhere to the north. Most of us had been in the trenches in the Great War, so a few rounds overhead from time to time didn't bother us.'

'Sounds like a story for another time perhaps, to do it justice?'

'As you wish - however, this time on the road north, so many German troops had already started to surrender, that a group of unarmed men, older than fighting age, dressed in a hodge-podge of civilian and cast-off military clothes and waving a white flag was no threat to them. They put us in the cage with the other prisoners-of-war, thinking we were Volksturm irregulars, but we were so loosely guarded in that first twenty-four hours that some of us, who had a pressing need to return, were able to break out and make it back to France on our own.'

Freybourg seemed to grow straighter in his chair as he spoke, remembering a time of action. I pondered - if he'd served in the Great War, was older than Dupont and therefore too old to have been entrusted with a copy of the manual, that would make him at least over seventy - he could have been my grandfather, whoever that was.

'It's instructive how different people react to captivity. Some of the most ardent, fire-breathing fascists were the first to turn, becoming more pro-Communist than the hate figures they had previously excoriated. There had been so much talk at Sigmaringen of continuing the resistance, but as the regime collapsed and with it the coercion that had kept us there, the folly of France-on-the-Danube was exposed to the cold light of day and the will to carry on evaporated.'

'How did Latour and Dupont react towards the end?'

'Dupont I liked at heart - I would still warm to him, despite his roguishness and what sounds like either profitable speculation or just simply talking himself back into his former position after the war - maybe a little of both. From what I understood, when reading your report though, Latour still smarts from defeat - his dreams of a new world order gone forever and now reduced to selling us the souvenirs of his former importance.'

It wasn't quite an answer to the question I'd asked, but maybe he couldn't really remember and didn't want to show it, embarrassed like the last time we met. Freybourg paused, 'Indeed it's surprising how predictable is a person's progress through life can be, even at an early age.'

'So what do you predict for me?'

'There's always an exception, maybe it's because we've never really spoken at length, or in German, but I find you hard to read. Inscrutable as the Chinese, or so we're told - maybe there's Eastern blood lurking in you somewhere, eh?'

I ignored this, took out the sheet which Latour had given me and passed it over.

'Looks plausible enough at first glance.' Freybourg fingered the embossed seal of what I now knew for certain to be the French State's, lost for a moment in thought. In the uneven light of the storeroom I thought I saw, for the first time, faint scars running underneath the wispy hair on the side of his head.

'However, as you've already noted, it appears to be the cover page of a trade agreement, not a blueprint for a new Europe – unless, of course, it was a cover sheet added afterwards, intended to disguise the underlying document. I think you'll need to make that return trip to Latour and fetch the rest to know for sure.'

'Would you come, to help verify the document which Latour wants to sell? After all, according to both of them, you were the one who directed the French compilers of the manual.'

'Is that how they put it?'

'Yes, and I politely request that you be more open with me from now on. I might miss the importance of something the other two say, if I don't know the full background. Who was your sponsor by the way?'

It couldn't hurt to ask the questions, even though Kramer had already said 'no' to him coming to Rosheim.

'Firstly, do you really think von Barten and Kramer are going to quibble over the price to bring this investigation to a quick close? Even one hundred thousand francs is cheap, if it makes their problem go away. They don't need me to verify any material, or perhaps they don't want me to, I case I don't verify it.'

'So you're not coming?'

'No, and as for the sponsor you talk about, you need to understand the nature of the relationship we had with our occupiers. Suffice to say, it was complex, and it changed over the four years. Someone that Dupont might call a sponsor, Latour might instead call a colleague.'

'So you're still saying this was a joint effort, as you did last week.'

'I'm the one being threatened here. I've no idea who or what is about to emerge from the mists of time. Monsieur Lenkeit, for my sake, you do need to force out of Latour everything still in his possession and everything still in his head - can you do that for me?'

I wondered if this was an answer to my request for openness.

'I understand. Tell me Monsieur Freybourg, could von Barten have any special, personal interest in this investigation?'

'You mean, how his job with the Nazi occupation forces in building an economic community in Northern France and Belgium was nominally the same as what he does today?'

That wasn't what I meant, but it was worth hearing how Freybourg answered his own question.

'Yes of course - that's his immediate concern here? That he's personally above any reproach for his conduct back then, right?'

Freybourg shook his head slightly. 'No, but since you've asked I'll paint you a picture and let you make up your own mind. Von Barten's position in Northern France and Belgium was leader – because all the Nazi titles contained that word - of the coordination committee which persuaded, cajoled and threatened steelmakers and coal miners to higher outputs. He was a combination of velvet glove diplomat and iron fist military governor.'

He paused, looking at me carefully. I'd really wanted to force the question as to whether von Barten himself had been the sponsor of the manual, but let him carry on.

'It wasn't easy at all - either for von Barten or his industrialists - to meet those quotas, given the transfer of workers to the Reich, aerial bombing, sabotage and the like - it needed a certain steeliness, if you'll pardon the pun. The customer in Germany was unforgiving, but it was a profitable business, all the same, for those firms which were awarded war production contracts - if they could avoid expropriation by the Reich.'

He hunched forward over the table and lowered his voice, even though we were quite alone.

'But think - how do you imagine the industrialists persuaded people like von Barten, put in charge of production, to give them contracts and let them keep the profits? Have you seen where he lives in Brussels? Do you know how many other houses he has?'

My heart sank somewhat. I already knew I wasn't in the social league of the von Bartens, but I suspected that I had no idea just how far outside I was.

'Now let me answer my earlier question to you. They say that when Jean Monnet was appointing staff to the precursor to the EEC, the European Coal and Steel Community, he asked for von Barten personally, because no one knew better where the skeletons were buried - who among their technocrat class had gone over the line from resentful into enthusiastic collaboration. Perhaps he asked for him too, because no one else was more motivated to make sure the past stayed hidden.'

He turned over the cover sheet from Latour to look at the back.

'Von Barten is EEC royalty based on Monnet's blessing alone. Regardless of the number of assets he accumulated during the war, or how he accumulated them, his Kreisau-Zirkel involvement makes him untouchable to anyone who might wish to dig up the past.'

'What happened there exactly?'

'Oh, by all accounts, he was genuinely brave, hiding fugitives on his estates after the failure of the twentieth of July assassination attempt. Although he made sure those people repaid their debt to him after the war, he's always made clear he truly hated and hates the Nazis.'

'H'mm, but how much I wonder. I wonder too, are there any wartime skeletons rattling in the cupboards of Monsieur Kramer, our own sponsor?' Freybourg tried to suppress a smile at this description.

'You must know that Kramer's anti-Nazi credentials are even better, even if he was only a very junior member of de Gaulle's administration in exile. In those early days, twenty-five-year-olds were writing ministerial decrees. Supporting de Gaulle was an uncertain bet until well into 'forty-two - at the start the Americans even recognised the Vichy regime as the legal continuation of the Third Republic - and de Gaulle wasn't the only Resistance leader setting himself up outside France. Self-belief was all de Gaulle had to offer in those early days. As Dupont indicated in your report, de Gaulle created his government in London out of thin air, simply by force of personality.

Freybourg passed the cover sheet back to me and started tracing the grain of the wood of the table top with his forefinger.

'The diplomatic minefields which Kramer helped de Gaulle to navigate between the English, the Americans and the Soviets were just as challenging as anything von Barten did, playing both sides in Germany - although not as dangerous, of course. But always remember this, Kramer is a wartime colleague of de Gaulle, one of the very first *hommes de Londres*, and that counts for way more right now than von Barten's credentials, making him the more serious player in the current game.'

'And what game is that?'

'The oldest one, of course, the struggle for power and influence. De Gaulle's vision for Europe has always been very different to that of von Barten and your country. Like a lever balancing on a fulcrum, de Gaulle wants to use Europe to multiply the power of France, but a France that is essentially independent. It was de Gaulle, after all, who started the French nuclear weapons programme and who decided to leave NATO three years ago. The EEC hierarchy though, right from the time of Jean Monnet, have been following a deeper strategy.'

'And how do you know all this? How do you know these details about von Barten and Kramer and the EEC?'

Freybourg spread his hands and shrugged slightly.

'My boy, I may have been away from politics for twenty-five years, but you forget, I was there at the time. I knew all these people, either directly or indirectly, when they were ambitious twenty- and thirty-year-olds, even von Barten. I read the newspapers, I read between the lines of the newspapers - and my advice is that you should cultivate the same scepticism.'

He slowly rose to his feet. 'Now you must excuse me, I chatter on in my dotage and have probably said too much.'

As he moved to leave he halted mid-turn. 'Please beware, Herr Lenkeit. Hard as you are to read, you seem too honourable for this affair, and my guess is this is one which will turn out very dishonourably before the end.'

Chapter Ten

I'd left Brussels later than I'd originally intended. The drive down to Strasbourg was a slog up over the Ardennes to the southern tip of Belgium, cutting down through Luxembourg, then back up again, over the Vosges and on to Rosheim.

As I left, black clouds were gathering over Brussels. Laden with rain, they followed me south into the gloom as the sun set, finally bursting as I passed through Dinant, the furthest point west reached by the SS in the winter of nineteen forty-four, during the Ardennes counteroffensive, which the Americans called the 'Battle of the Bulge'.

The rain sheeted down on the road and the traffic slowed to a crawl. I reflected, that despite spending the afternoon with Freybourg, I was still no closer to really knowing who he was, or what he'd done in 'forty-five.

Kramer or von Barten had described him as an 'overqualified fixer' for Marcel Déat, the one-time socialist politician turned arch-collaborator, latterly Minister for Labour in the Sigmaringen government. For sure, Freybourg would be a target for anyone seeking to clear up unfinished business from the time of the Liberation, but who would give him a warning about the release of his political testament for Europe and why? If he had truly reformed, as he claimed, then I was sorry for him that his past was catching up - but while driving through the rain to Rosheim to plug an embarrassing leak for the EEC would help Kramer and von Barten, I didn't see how it would help him, as he'd asked me to.

I pulled off the road for a sandwich and coffee at a lorry drivers' cafe. A French army truck pulled in after me, and I got to the counter, just before fifteen or twenty close-cropped conscripts arrived under the command of a sergeant. As I sat in the corner eating, I watched them place their orders. Like it or not, twenty-five years ago France and Germany had been in an alliance, until de Gaulle returned from England and said that they hadn't been. Now, as the story went, we were finally at peace, cooperating through the EEC for the first time since eighteen twelve when Napoleon and his German troops from that earlier puppet state, the Confederation of the Rhine, had invaded Russia.

Except that it wasn't true. Germans fight with the French, but almost hundred and thirty years later - for granted, with two wars in-between - French troops are again in Russia, fighting alongside Germans who are using French-manufactured trucks and self-propelled guns. If the Liberation was considered as the end of a French civil war, then from what point in time did peaceful cooperation between our two nations date from? - nineteen forty or the start of the EEC in nineteen fifty-seven? But three years ago, de Gaulle had taken France outside NATO and he'd also brought the EEC to a temporary standstill the year before that - so just where did the French stand today?

My head was even fuzzier as I arrived in Rosheim, just after eleven. I parked a couple of streets away from the main square, on the opposite side of the town to Latour's place and started walking - at least I'd left the rain behind in the Ardennes. The old moon was almost gone, its dying crescent lingering on, hanging directly above the street outside Latour's house. I watched from the deep shadows, until the footsteps of the late-night customers from the bar in the next street had faded away. The windows of the neighbours on either side were dark, but a soft yellow light glowed in Latour's downstairs room. I doubted he had company and wondered how often he'd re-read the philosophy books I'd seen on the shelves last time.

I stepped smartly across the cobbles and rapped on the door. After a long minute, I heard the bolts being withdrawn and the door opened a crack. Latour and I looked at one another silently for a moment. 'You again. Did you come here with money this time?' asked Latour, somewhat anxiously.

'First let me in and show me what you have to sell.'

'Do you have the money with you? Now?'

I pulled one of the bundles halfway out of my overcoat pocket and riffled the notes.

He unchained the door and opened it just enough to let me through.

I fixed him with a stare, we had both abandoned the pretence of any student research taking place. Latour broke first and disappeared upstairs with a grunt, returning with a leather document case, heavily worn at the corners. He brought out an unbound stack of yellowed sheets and fanned out the first few pages onto the table under the window of the front parlour. Then he sat down with his case on his lap, his hand resting just inside it.

I stooped over the table and pulled out a page at random from the middle of the array, it spoke of a split of patents between French and German chemical concerns. From near the front, I took another page, this time listing South American copper mines to be allocated to a Swiss corporation. Whatever it was, it wasn't a blueprint for a new European order - in fact it looked more like an agreement on how to divide and hide the spoils of conquest.

I drummed the table with my fingers, buying time to think. After driving over the mountains for six hours in the dark through a downpour, I'd had enough. I looked around the room and walked over to the chimney breast behind Latour.

He thought I was leaving and gave a cry of 'No!' as he half rose from his chair, feeling again for whatever was just inside the document case.

I swung round and brought the fire-iron down hard against the exposed wrist of his hidden hand with a dull crack. He yowled, releasing the case, clutching the forearm with his undamaged hand.

I kicked the case away and smacked him again with the metal bar, this time even harder on his thin upper arms, quick left, quick right, to make sure he got the message.

I picked the case off the floor and fished out a grimy Sauer 38H pistol. I recognised the model from the top shelf of long-unused weapons in the armoury at my old police station in Hamburg.

'Oh ho!' I said. 'That's not clever, threatening your customers.'

I walked over and pressed the muzzle deep into a cushion on the settle standing against the opposite wall. Without pausing, I pulled the trigger and heard a click. The safety catch was off, but I wouldn't have been surprised if there wasn't even a round in the chamber. I looked at the pistol again and remembered about the de-cocking lever, unique to the Sauer's design. Latour had obviously forgotten it too, probably never having fired the thing since the end of the war, if even then.

'What do you think you're doing? You've broken my wrist,' he whined.

'That I doubt, stop malingering.' I checked the magazine and reinserted it - I could see six of the expected eight shells, nothing in the chamber. I pulled back and released the slide to load a round. The action was still stiff, likely the lack of cleaning for twenty-five years, but solid - as you would expect from German engineering.

I looked up, and he glowered at me with hate-filled eyes. I supposed I was just another in a long line of Germans who'd disappointed him over the years, against his better judgement.

I held the Sauer loosely, finger on the outside of the trigger-guard and pointed with it to the papers on the table. 'I want the real stuff, the plans to subvert de Gaulle's victory and rebuild a Franco-German empire. Not this rubbish.'

Latour flinched as the muzzle waved back and forth. 'Why the obsession with something which never existed.'

'It existed in your head a week ago, you promised me material which would make every history professor in Europe envious.'

'You've mis-remembered,' he said urgently. 'Please, I need the money and I have to sell you something. This is still useful material, perhaps to someone trying to track down hidden Nazi assets.'

I was at a loss, he wasn't even attempting to suggest it was relevant to my original enquiry. He continued to watch me tensely. Latour was a man in distress, but I wasn't going to get any sensible answers by further use of brute force.

One the other hand, I had fifteen thousand francs in my overcoat pocket that he wanted very much, for which I had the documentation to disburse as I pleased.

'Very well, I want answers to new questions though. Every time you answer a question, and I think you're lying, I'll take off a thousand francs from whatever sum is in my head now. '

Latour's good hand was shaking now, I went and found two glasses and a dusty bottle of kirsch in the kitchen at back and poured him a generous measure.

'There, this is already more sociable, isn't it?'

He swallowed a mouthful of the fiery liquid, coughing a little. I sat down at the table, tilting the chair onto its back legs and began.

'I will ask you a series of questions. I want answers in one sentence unless I give you permission to speak for longer. The wrong answer, you'll lose a thousand. Do you understand?'

He nodded, slumped in his seat now.

'Who was Freybourg, really?'

'He was the leader of the French group writing the manual.'

'Have you met him since the war?'

'Twice, three months ago and then again last month.'

'What exactly did he ask you to do?'

Latour paused, almost imperceptibly. 'To meet with someone from Brussels, tell them all I could remember about Sigmaringen, but play hard to get when it came to any documentation - whilst making it clear that the trail ended with me.

'Did you agree with him what it was you were going to sell?' Again, a slight hesitation.

'He asked me what documents I might still have, and whether I would be prepared to part with them.'

'And what did you have?'

'Just this one I've shown you, I told you a lie the last time we met, I never was entrusted with the manual. There were many documents produced at the time, of all types. It was the only thing the Germans left us to do, running a paper empire. The pages here are genuine enough, if you keep searching you might find more like them.'

'But you told Freybourg you had the manual?'

'He asked me if I had a copy to sell, I told him what he wanted to hear.'

'Do you believe there's still a copy of the manual somewhere else out there?'

'Maybe in Germany, I can give you a name there. But I still need my payment, and then I want to be left alone, without any more trouble from anyone else.' He massaged his wrist, testing it gently.

'Whose idea was the fake document scam? Yours or Freybourg's? How did you agree to split the proceeds?' He remained silent.

'Give me the name and all the details you have to help

me find this person in Germany. I believe most of your answers so far, so I'll pay you three thousand francs and take this package of papers. I'll check out the name you give and if your lead takes me to this manual, you'll get another three.'

'Please, I need five thousand right now, I have no choice.'

'Why? What's pressing you? Did you borrow from Freybourg in anticipation of a payout?' I watched his expression carefully, but he was resolute.

'Very well then, four. I'm sure you can come to some arrangement for the other thousand with whoever you owe.'

He dolefully shook his head, I thought he was about to burst into tears. He opened and closed his mouth, as if uncertain whether to add something else.

'Go on,' I said, 'get writing.'

He resigned himself, laid the wrist he claimed was broken on the table and used a shaky left hand to write some lines on the back of one of the pages he'd brought down from upstairs.

'Here's the name, Julius Schmidt. He was another trade official, just like me. Before the war he was a banker, and before that he used to teach economics, maybe he does so again now. The last I had heard he ended up in the East, near Rostock.'

'In the East? You're joking, right? How am I going to find him there, and why would he have kept anything at all incriminating from the final months of the Nazi regime?'

'Perhaps because East Germany is more enlightened as to rehabilitation. To their way of thinking, everyone after the war needed reforming into good socialists, not just the out-and-out Nazis. They didn't persecute people, like me, who'd made genuine mistakes.'

I shook my head and got up to leave, thumbing out one hundred and twenty notes and wishing I'd asked for five-hundreds. As he watched, Latour spoke softly, gazing into the distance. Maybe his wrist really was broken.

'That manual, you know. It was a work of genius, a simple philosophy that took the best of what we had achieved and stripped out the references to the unpleasantness which a state of total war required of the economy.'

'That's "slave labour" to normal people.' He ignored me.

'It mapped a path for how we could build a new political unity for the benefit of the European peoples, a plan designed to work whether the eventual progress to that goal was fast or slow. We didn't know how the chips would fall after the war, but we were prepared to wait years or decades to make it happen.'

'I'm leaving you now, but I'm coming back, whether I find Schmidt or not. If it turns out you lied, or he'd dead, I'm going to lock you and Freybourg into a room for a month to rewrite your manual from memory, but with all the bits left out which might be damaging to the EEC.'

I drove through the night, stopping only once for a coffee and brandy at the same all-night transport cafe as on the way down. As I sat at the formica table at three in the morning, I slowly stirred my cup, half-drunk with tiredness, and tried to marshal my thoughts.

The pieces of this jigsaw weren't fitting together. I just didn't believe that Freybourg would have risked involving the SDECE in his document scam, not one where he hadn't already verified what Latour had in his possession and not for fifteen or even a hundred thousand francs. On the other hand, all that Latour had said so far was consistent with the story I'd been told over the past two weeks - there did seem to be such a document and maybe Schmidt was the boringly-named German sponsor who Dupont had referred to, backing up his story too.

Aside from running a scam, who were they really underneath, these people? If Latour had been German and in the Nazi Party, but hadn't been directly involved in any atrocities, under the denazification categories he would have probably been assessed as a Class Four - 'Fellow traveller'. Writing a paper on the theory of European union wouldn't have been a crime, not compared to the real crimes that had taken place at the time.

To my mind he was only mildly repentant, someone who probably believed in the general correctness of the direction of the Axis effort, able to mentally isolate the core ideas of European unity and anti-communism from the actions carried out in their name. I wondered how many such types were still were in positions of power and influence across the continent - including the EEC, as Dupont was sure of.

Dupont, I guessed, wasn't in on Freybourg's plan - he'd probably been added for verisimilitude. So far, the old ham was the only authentic actor in this whole play, as far as I could see.

As for Freybourg, he was much harder to read, just as he had claimed I was. He said at our first meeting he'd completely turned over a new leaf, and he seemed to have been away from public life for decades. Yet he had a level of knowledge and interest in current EEC affairs which seemed unnecessarily detailed for an aging Vichy civil servant. Maybe he'd been cooking up this scam for a while, but it had somehow gone wrong. Maybe I'd have to break his arm too, but that was probably just the double brandy talking.

Chapter Eleven

Tuesday & Wednesday, 18-19th March 1969

Driving fast, I finally got back to my apartment in Brussels at seven and dozed for an hour. Sleep wasn't going to happen, and I didn't want to waste any more of the day trying.

While I lay half-awake in my darkened room, a new set of suspicions crowded in, about Kramer this time. If even I, a junior employee of the EEC, was now wondering whether Freybourg had tried an elaborate con trick, threatening to smear the organisation - how diligently, then, had Kramer checked out Freybourg's story before turning the threat into official business? How committed was Kramer to the EEC, given that he was originally de Gaulle's man? Then again, von Barten's view was that de Gaulle's time in power was almost over - Kramer had a good fifteen years before his own retirement, why would he risk that for someone who might be soon gone? I dismissed the idea that Kramer was in on a money-making scam, whatever salary von Barten was drawing, Kramer was almost certainly doing just as well out of the EEC.

When I got to the office I asked Kramer's secretary for a time when I could meet with Kramer and von Barten together. I wanted to see both their reactions as I revealed my news, stage by stage.

The rain from yesterday was gone from Brussels too, but the sky outside von Barten's office window remained grey and cold. For this appointment, he'd locked the exterior door, which I'd never seen before at the

Berlaymont.

I sat at the head of the table this time, with each of them on a different side, and opened the discussion.

'Very early this morning I met Latour outside Strasbourg, as we had discussed.' I paused for effect, looking at both of them in turn. Von Barten was scarcely breathing, Kramer kept his eyes on me. Now came the moment I'd been rehearsing since the meeting had been confirmed earlier.

'He passed me a comprehensive document, outlining plans for a post-war period of consolidation and the rebuilding of a common European political entity.' The permanent creases on von Barten's forehead deepened. Kramer nodded slowly.

'But when I took a closer look at a sample of the pages, something didn't ring true.'

Now von Barten's eyes gleamed. I passed over the document, fanning out the sheets. Von Barten and Kramer both took a few each. Kramer was the first to speak.

'This isn't what Latour promised you. Did you actually pay fifteen thousand francs for this?' He could hardly get his words out fast enough.

'Give him time to explain,' cautioned von Barten. It was the only the second time I'd heard even a hint of friction between the two.

'Latour said he had lied previously and tried to sell me this Nazi-era document in its stead. He then admitted that he never had the "manual" as he called it.'

'And you didn't force him to prove that, slap him around even just a little bit, like a real policeman, to see if he was holding out on you?' asked Kramer.

'You were the one who told me that this job needed finesse - but I did enough.' I placed the Sauer on the table with a dull thud, von Barten raised an eyebrow. 'Now that is a genuine historical relic.' He stroked the grip with his finger, circling the maker's mark.

Kramer was not happy. 'So you went all the way to

France, twice, and came back with, what - an agreement on trade and the mergers of some long-defunct industrial corporations?' He rapped the table with his knuckles. Von Barten's eyes had glazed over though, lost in his memories.

'I did get a new name.' Von Barten came out of his reverie. 'Someone whom I think ultimately directed the writing of the manual, above Freybourg, and may well still have a copy. A German, who, if he is still alive is apparently living in the East.' Neither of them was reacting to this news - as far as I could tell, it seemed to be truly unexpected to them both.

'Gentlemen, we are at a decision point. If no one in the West has this material, but someone has threatened Freybourg into silence when it is released, what does that imply?'

'Don't patronise us,' snapped Kramer. 'You're not seriously suggesting this is an East German operation now, is that the best you have?'

A ghost of a smile flickered over von Barten's face. I suspected he was enjoying Kramer's discomfort, but now he made an effort to pour oil on troubled waters. 'Let's pause for a moment to consider what we've learned so far and the real nature of this threat.' He steepled his fingers.

'Monsieur Freybourg says that at Sigmaringen plans were made for a continuation of the European order by subverting the Allied post-war administrations. Dupont says that a practical "manual", as he so unflatteringly labels it, on cross-border cooperation was written to order, but thrown together in haste. Latour says it was a political testament, virtually a work of philosophy to inspire future generations. But it seems to me that if this so-called manual does exist, it will read as archaically as the papers before us. Of interest to historians in the future, but without any bearing on today.'

Kramer wasn't to be deflected though.

'Are you prepared to go to East Germany and chase down this lead, no matter how spurious it is? "*Doctor of*

Economics Schmidt, originally from Rostock".' He held up the page with Latour's notes. Von Barten pursed his lips grimly as I replied.

'You said that Freybourg walked into the SDECE to report the threats he'd received. You know that the EEC has no means of finding East Germans, seven hundred kilometres away from Brussels. But if your intelligence contacts in France can get me some leads I'll check them out for you, if I have a plausible cover story for being in the East.'

'You have family there, correct?' asked Kramer.

'Yes, but we've been estranged for years, whether by accident or design I don't know.'

'But if you were to arrange a visit, you could get permission to be there for a couple of weeks at least. You would have the excuse of being able to travel around, visiting different relatives.'

During this exchange von Barten had been silent, now he dropped a bombshell.

'Why don't we have my niece accompany you, she can play the role of the Western girlfriend or fiancée meeting her partner's family in the East for the first time. Women can be disarming to officialdom, less challenging to a male sense of pride, and thus less suspicious than a man travelling on his own.'

I couldn't believe my luck. On one hand, von Barten had presumably just thought of the idea so I gave him full marks for initiative, on the other, this also implied that Sophie had no idea what was planned for her, which was presumptuous of him, to say the least. Not that I was complaining, just as long as she didn't think I was the one who'd thought of it.

'So we have a plan? Are you agreed Kramer?' von Barten turned to his colleague.

Kramer threw up his hands and shrugged. 'Very well, let's do it. I'll find Schmidt, you organise the trip for your niece, and let's see what Lenkeit can dig up.'

I went back to my apartment and crashed out until late afternoon - I felt I was owed the time, having driven through the night. Later, I'd phoned Bernd to confirm our usual mid-week evening drinks in the centre of the old town. As we sat opposite one another over litre jugs of blond ale, Jan Stapel appeared, rapping the table in greeting. 'Hallo boys,' he said with a cheerful smile. 'What's troubling the police this evening? Whatever happened, I didn't do it.'

'Speaks a guilty conscience.' Bernd answered back jovially.

'Pull up a stool, Probationer Lenkeit here was just telling me about his upcoming trip to East Germany.'

'Really? And what takes you there, young man, work or pleasure?'

I hadn't told Bernd about von Barten's special twist, I wasn't in the mood for the ribbing.

'You've been there Jan, right? As a tourist or as a guest of the Democratic Republic?'

'The socialist struggle has required me to show solidarity with my brothers and sisters in the East by attending conferences on Marxist dialectical materialism, so yes to both.' He said this only half-jokingly.

'But in all seriousness, don't get into trouble over there. You have to register where you are staying, hand over any Western newspapers, convert a minimum amount of hard currency at the border into Ostmarks. You can only enter and exit at certain points, all sorts of restrictions. And the police probably know where you are at all times.'

He pulled on his beer. 'But if you like, I have some contacts who might be able to help you, if you do get into difficulties. Why are you going - more historical research?'

I pulled a face, I hadn't really told Bernd the details of the mislaid papers, but it couldn't hurt to open up a bit now.

'Yes, still searching for missing documents.'

'And who are you going to get them from over there?'

'We have some leads, but I can't say much. By the way, this is a question I haven't asked anyone yet. What will my Eastern relatives think of me?'

They alternated their replies, Bernd going first. 'How did your family come to the West?'

'My mother was pregnant, and I'm almost certain unmarried. As far as I know, it was simply the fortunes of war which took her West in 'forty-five.'

'Did she choose to leave her family in the East and flee to the West?'

'I don't know, we've never talked of it. She was a nurse in the German Red Cross, that's almost all I know.'

'And you said she's had no contact since?'

'It feels like she's tried to maintain a careful distance. Although she sends money and receives some family news by letter, she's shown no real desire to go there.'

Bernd and Jan were both silent for a time. Finally, Bernd spoke. 'It doesn't sound great, maybe she got on the wrong side of the Soviet occupation authorities and had to leave. Maybe she escaped before the Soviets got there. I suppose some refugees from the East feel guilty that they got out, but that others in their family didn't, maybe that's it.'

Jan added, 'There were twelve million refugees from the former German territories given to Poland and to the Soviets after the war, so there's twelve million different stories of why people left, whether willingly or unwillingly. But when you go, whatever you say, don't compare life in the West to the East, don't make them resentful of your wealth.'

'You must have drunk too much already - when you work for von Barten and Kramer, wealthy is the opposite of how you feel.'

That brought Sophie to mind again, although she was never very far below the surface of my thoughts. I had a strong suspicion she would, of course, take on the task of spying on me for von Barten, but be resentful of how it had been landed on her and of the role she was expected to play. I would let von Barten brief her and take the heat. I'd see her soon enough, and I didn't see the need to antagonise her any further.

The following morning, I called my mother at home from the office, on the off-chance she wasn't working her shift. I'd paid to have the line installed in her apartment when I moved to Brussels, and I still tried to send her money every month, as I'd been doing since police cadet training days.

'Mother, I've got some news - I need to go East for my work, and I'm planning to visit Aunt Hilde and my cousins.'

'This is a bit unexpected, why do you want to see them now?'

'Mother - I've never met them, they're my only living relatives apart from you.'

There was a long pause, the line hissed and crackled.

'Well, we were best friends as children. But I ended up doing my things and she hers. After the war, because she stayed behind, got married, and had her family over there, we grew apart - as you've guessed all these years.'

'Did you have some kind of falling out? Is that why you ended up with me in the West?' I didn't want to ask yet if it was over my father - it seemed all throughout my childhood that there was never a good time to speak of him

'The war was very difficult, families had choices thrust upon them which drove them apart, even without being physically separated. I left home to help with the resettlement of refugees in the early part of the war and was away again later to train as a nurse. We didn't see much of each other at all, especially not in the chaos of the last year of the war when the armies were on the move again.'

'How will she react if I turn up on her doorstep?'

The line hissed again.

'Must you, really?'

'I must actually, I need to write to her today to let her know. I have to visit under a family visa, so I've got to turn up at least once to prove my story. But I'll treat them with respect, I won't look for or expect any kind of approval - but if you had a falling out, I'd like to know what areas of conversation to avoid.'

'I don't know what to say to you. Just remember, everyone deserves a second chance - we're taught to forgive. Promise me you'll have the grace to give them that, no matter their reaction to you.'

'Very well mother.' I didn't sound convincing, as I wasn't any clearer as to what she meant. I had no choice but to ask that one question.

'Is it about my father?'

'Please don't go digging up the past, just try to make friends with them for my sake.'

Time to back off.

'Very well. What age are my cousins now, what do they like doing? - I need to know what presents to take them.'

'Karin is sixteen and Thomas thirteen. Take them something that won't raise any questions from their friends or neighbours, no books, tapes of Western pop music or jeans.'

It seemed like the personal side of the trip was going to be even more of a minefield than the professional.

Chapter Twelve

Friday-Saturday, 21st-22nd March 1969

I met Sophie at six in the morning on the platform at Brussels Central train station. I hadn't wanted to turn up in a car, even my Volkswagen, at my aunt's house and bring any more attention to her from her neighbours than necessary.

Von Barten's organisation of the trip over the past two days was impressive - he'd obtained tourist visas from the East German embassy within twenty-four hours and given me the names of a couple of COMECON officials he knew in Berlin who I could call on, if we got into difficulties. He'd also told me with a grin that he'd broken the news of the trip to Sophie and taken her into his confidence on the investigation. He didn't say how she'd reacted to the news she was to be my fiancée for the trip.

I found out as soon as I laid eyes on her - she was wearing a dark trouser suit and radiating a cold anger. We sat in the compartment on opposite banquettes, carefully saying nothing to each other beyond the bare minimum. That was going to have to change if our engagement was to be convincing. I had the sense though, that her anger wasn't actively directed at me - not yet - but I also knew that I was balancing on a knife edge and that a poorly chosen word could trigger her wrath anytime.

I really had no idea what we were heading into. I'd never been behind the Iron Curtain before, and I was taking on a family reunion at the same time as a search for someone who hadn't been heard of in the West since nineteen forty-five. Von Barten had rushed us off to the

East in double-time, but now we were alone and would have to use our own initiative to find Schmidt.

All that Kramer's people had been able to come up with was an economics faculty address. Apparently, our quarry, or at least another Doktor Julius Schmidt, was still on the books of Rostock University - gone back to teaching, as Latour had suspected. They suggested checking a telephone directory for a home address, given that his doctorate would appear in his title in the listings. I couldn't believe an espionage agency wouldn't have copies of something as basic as an East German phone book already, but maybe I was overestimating them. It painfully underlined how much effort and investment would be required, were the EEC to build up its own external investigative department.

This was going to be another long all-day trip, with changes at Cologne and Hamburg, before heading east to Wismar, the town where my aunt was now living.

Sophie remained with her head in a book, but as the hours passed, she could only keep up the frostiness for so long and passivity wasn't her thing. Just after we left Hamburg and neared the border the book closed with a snap, and she started to quiz me properly about the family I was to meet for the first time.

'Do you really only have two cousins?'

'Apparently, yes. I imagine we will be objects of curiosity to them too.'

'Hmph, I have at least eight close ones, if you count second and third cousins that is. So, do you know why your aunt ended up on the wrong side of the Wall?'

'I think it was more my mother who did, our family had been in the East for generations.'

'So had mine, my father and his brothers grew up on an estate in the far corner of East Prussia, now lost to the Russians. But Uncle Ernst salvaged enough from his war work for us all to get by on.'

'Is he really your uncle, or a kind of second cousin once removed?'

'Oh no, he's one of my father's three brothers. But I'm the only one of this generation who's joined him in Brussels. We lost some people during the war too of course. His favourite nephew was shot down over the Rhine.'

'And von Barten's wife, who you told me had given up on Brussels?'

'Anne? She and Ernst never had any children, that's why the nephews and nieces get the attention we do.'

'Just take it easy on my family, will you? Use your charm, let's do enough to be a plausible couple, so we can get on with finding Schmidt without raising suspicion as to why we're really over there. I have no idea where they stand politically, so let's assume they'll be wary of us.'

She snorted, but with a faint smile, 'Just as long as you remember that all this is make-believe.' She waved her ring hand at me.

At the Lübeck border crossing point we got out to have our papers processed and to convert the required number of Deutschmarks into Ostmarks, as Jan had described. The border guard grunted at our story and took a cursory glance at Sophie's modest diamond ring.

The first indicator of the gulf between the two Germanies was the whistle from the East German steam engine as it backed up to our train, the West German diesel locomotive and crew not being allowed across the border.

As the train lurched back into motion, I peered through the grimy window, noting the other differences. The architecture was familiar, even the concrete, obviously post-war, buildings sharing the same uninspiring style as on our side - but as we passed towns and villages it was obvious that fewer repairs and rebuilding had taken place since nineteen forty-five. In the West, gaps made by bombs in rows of houses were being progressively filled as the years went by, here, weed-grown spaces remained. What couldn't be hidden from the casual observer too, was the comparative dearth of cars on the roads.

My aunt lived in a suburb, on the edge of Wismar, and it was late afternoon by the time we boarded a bus for the last leg of the journey. I imagined it to be the first time Sophie had ever travelled on one - hopefully she'd look on it as a kind of adventure, getting down with the people. As we walked the last couple of streets to my aunt's address, despite my best intentions, we looked very out of place, dressed in our formal Western clothes and lugging our cases.

Thankfully, to spare any further embarrassment in front of Sophie, my aunt's house was much more substantial than my mother's apartment in Steilshoop. It was a detached house, which at some stage had been divided into two flats. Like many of the other buildings in the town, paint was peeling and there was the odd pane of missing glass boarded up with plywood.

In trepidation, I rang the bell and waited as steps approached down the hallway. If they hadn't got my letter already, sent two days ago, this call would be completely unexpected. As the time for the trip approached, I had been feeling increasingly guilty at using them in this way, but now it was too late to change the plan.

I had tried to imagine what my aunt would look like, but strangely, what caught me most by surprise when the door opened was that she was immediately recognisable as my mother's sister - a younger version with fewer gray hairs. She stood on the threshold as I removed my hat and extended my hand. Her grip trembled, then she withdrew her hand and crumpled into floods of inconsolable tears.

A man emerged behind her, laying a hand on her shoulder. 'What do you want with us?'

'Are you my uncle?'

'Ah, I see. We only got your letter this morning, come through.'

This wasn't the start I had hoped for. I supposed I should have been glad I wasn't doing this for real with a genuine fiancée, even though part of me wished that this was that moment. We assembled in the downstairs front room and, thankfully, Sophie now stepped up to playing the part written for her, thrusting out her hand, cooing, and giving a good impression of showing a heartfelt desire to get to know the family. My female cousin, Karin, shyly stroked the material of Sophie's suit, asked her about her lipstick, and became a friend for life when she saw Sophie's present, a make-up case. Meanwhile, I stared at the siblings with almost the same curiosity they had for me, looking back and forth between them and at my uncle and aunt, observing the family resemblances and traits. I began to understand why my mother might have wanted to avoid this meeting and wondered if, secretly, she was jealous of the family her sister had built.

We swapped stories and I began to learn the personalities behind the names I'd known for so long. My uncle worked at the shipyard in Wismar, where he'd been apprenticed. My aunt was secretary to an official of the trade union federation, part of the unofficial apparatus of the Party. Karin's real desire was to make clothes, but she'd probably end up in a textile plant. Thomas was a somewhat sullen teenager, edgy and uncommunicative. I'd brought him a hunting knife from Brussels that I'd found in a shop out in Saint-Gilles, but had no idea whether he'd make any good use of it.

After her initial upset on the doorstep my aunt had recovered, and then warmed up to us, especially Sophie, who had progressed to giving me affectionate glances as I explained my work at the EEC – the model of a dutiful fiancée. Von Barten was right about travelling with a female companion, or perhaps it was just that Sophie herself had a natural charm that worked to defuse awkward situations. Maybe to my aunt's eyes, the supposed engagement showed me to be my own person, independent from my mother and the falling-out that had divided them. I was glad she'd never find out that it was all a sham.

We had arrived with hardly any notice, but my aunt was expecting us to stay for dinner. The six of us crowded round a too-small table for a meal of potatoes, meatballs and mashed swede. The clink of cutlery filled the frequent pauses in conversation. After the initial, safe, exchange of personal details before dinner, there now remained too many forbidden areas of discussion to allow an easy uninterrupted flow.

I was going to have to take a risk, even if only for my mother's sake.

'Aunt Hilde, if I may,' I said quietly, laying down my knife and fork, 'how did you become separated from my mother at the end of the war?'

She looked at her husband, as if for approval.

'I was still living at home, my father - your grandfather - had been killed in an air-raid the previous year. We'd already moved westwards, to Wismar, away from East Prussia and the advancing Red Army. But your mother was serving in a field hospital, very close to the front line. She got caught up in the general evacuation to the West, we stayed behind.'

'And my father?'

'What have you been told?'

'I'd like to hear your story, she doesn't really talk about him at all, and I don't have anyone else to ask. Did she have a fiancé, a boyfriend? I was only told he had died in the war, same as the story told to a few of the other children in my class at school.'

My aunt glanced at her husband again. 'All I know us that something happened at the field hospital out East during one of the Russian offensives. The front lines were moving back and forth all the time, so we never got the full story.' Her eyes now flicked to Sophie's, holding them for a heartbeat.

'She was such a gentle person you know, an enthusiastic Party member, loyal to her oath.'

At this last jaw-dropping statement, delivered in deadpan tone, I carefully examined the corners of her eyes and mouth but found no trace of irony.

'Before she joined the German Red Cross she missed part of her final year of school to volunteer with the scouting movement, which we'd all been encouraged to join, the League of German Girls. She was a language teacher to ethnic German families relocated from the Baltics to the land we had taken in Poland in thirty-nine. Despite their ancient German surnames, some of them could hardly string a sentence together, having never used the language in everyday speech during the centuries they'd spent inside the Russian Empire.'

My frustration at drawing yet another blank on my origins was long forgotten in my shame. I flushed red and, above all, avoided Sophie's eyes. She had gone deadly quiet.

'Look, here's the photographs of your mother we were able to save when our house was bombed.'

From a nondescript book, tucked tightly alongside similar cloth-bound volumes on one of the shelves, my aunt drew a slim set of black and white photographs.

Amongst the shots of family holidays were three clearly taken at a League of German Girls camp. There was a picture of my mother singing round a campfire, running a race, and finally, giving the Hitler greeting to one of the female leaders. The enthusiasm in her eyes was clear across two decades and I felt sick. The very last print was a group shot with my mother in her German Red Cross uniform, sitting cross-legged on the lap of a soldier, her arm around his shoulders.

'Is that?'

'No - I'm sorry Oskar.' She paused, then continued

with her story.

'In the last two months of the war she simply cut us off - we feared at one point she was dead. We later assumed she'd left for the West, but we heard nothing from her at all, until an East Prussian refugee association based in West Germany found us and contacted me ten years ago. She couldn't have known where we'd moved to in East Germany, our original home in East Prussia was gone, and I'd got married and changed my name - and we too had no means of finding her either.'

It was a neat way to explain the breakdown in communications, but I had the sense it wasn't the full one. Maybe sometime in the late fifties my mother had been encouraged by people she knew in Hamburg to try to make contact with her sister.

'The war destroyed our family, as it did so many others.' The corners of her eyes now did well up. My uncle reached across the table and took my aunt's hand, as he glowered at me.

'How long are you staying in town?' He wasn't asking in an encouraging way.

'I don't want to impose on you. It's just that I know almost nothing about you, or myself,' I added quietly.

My aunt sniffed. 'I don't know what your plans are for tomorrow, but on Sunday we have a church excursion - a picnic in the forest. If you come with us you'll meet some people who were evacuated to Wismar with us, who knew your grandparents and your mother as a girl.'

It seemed like the right point to end the visit - it had been a long day, for everyone. We made our excuses and agreed a time and place to meet on Sunday, if we decided to take up their offer.

We rode back to the centre of Wismar on the bus, almost directly to the state-approved hotel, where we were registered on our entry documents. Sophie swayed as the bus bounced on the worst of the potholes, looking up at me from time to time, deep in thought.

There was no nightlife in the town, none we could easily blend in with anyway, and we'd both been up since before six. The evening was mild for March, so we ended the day sitting outside on the room's tiny balcony. There were two plastic chairs and a table on which stood a bottle of plum brandy we'd bought from the night-bar. She peered at me through the darkness.

I mused aloud. 'I want to go to their picnic, but we shouldn't really advertise ourselves here anymore than we need to. On the other hand, if we run into trouble on this trip I might not be allowed back into the country and I'll miss the opportunity to meet all these people at the same time again.'

Sophie chewed her lip. She leant over and added another fingerful of slivovitz to the tumblers we were using as schnapps glasses. 'Listen Oskar, there's something I've been thinking about. I don't really know how to say this in any way that makes it easy to hear, but I think your mother was raped, back in nineteen forty-five.'

For the second time that day, I felt like the floor had fallen out beneath me.

She furrowed her brow, but now that she had started she had to carry on. 'It happened far, far more than either West, or especially East Germany will admit. Not in West Germany, because of war guilt and the sense that we somehow deserved it after what we'd done to the Russians first. Not in the East, because the Russians are still their allies. I told you that my family had land in Prussia, we know just how brutal the Red Army were, when they burned through the countryside and towns, consuming everything and everyone in their path. It's seen as shameful, but it happened, and you're not the only child born as a result of that time Oskar.'

I didn't know where to start. She was silent now, folded back into her chair with a stillness and softness in her expression that I hadn't seen before.

'I don't believe you.' I eventually croaked. 'There's no evidence, it's just your supposition.'

'I've spoken to women who'd escaped to the West from our estates in the East, who my uncle helped find employment for after the war. Since I first heard those stories, I've searched out other refugees too.'

Sophie was emphatic now. 'Women talk to women, in a way they won't open up to a man. If you meet any German woman from the eastern territories who was over the age of fourteen in 'forty-five, especially if they were from East Prussia or Berlin, you should start with the assumption that they were raped.'

She took a sip from her glass. 'Your aunt didn't know if you'd been told, that's why she avoided the question. But I know what happened back then, and I know that no-one talks about it.'

Her face had hardened now, this was deadly serious for her, maybe more serious than the EEC games she was playing for von Barten.

'If she didn't have something to hide, she would have given you the usual story about doomed love, a fallen hero, and a child for the Führer.'

Anger mixed with shame was growing inside me, I had the sinking feeling in my heart that she was almost certainly speaking the truth. Even though I hadn't really given much thought to what had been done to women refugees in the east, the sense of loss and personal disaster was an undercurrent to my childhood. Our school atlas still showed those lost strips of the eastern territories and East Prussia as part of Germany, but in hatched shading with the annotation 'At this time under Polish administration' - however everyone knew, unspoken, that it was a fantasy they'd ever be restored.

I gulped down my glass in one, regardless of the burning, and snatched at the bottle to glug out a triple measure. I couldn't choose who I wanted to lash out at first - my mother, who had lied to me for years, my aunt, for being a coward and not telling what she knew, Kramer, for sending me here on a hopeless long-shot, and even Sophie, for interfering where she had no right to. I thought back to the day in *Grundschule*, when the class bully had called me 'Asiatic'. He hadn't used the expression again, because I'd thumped him good and hard. Given that I was one of the biggest kids in the class and didn't look particularly foreign in any way, the name hadn't stuck with the other children either - but I'd always wondered who'd given him the idea in the first place.

I slumped back in my chair as the night grew cold, pulling at the brandy to numb my senses. Sophie linked and unlinked her fingers, now unsure of herself. Eventually, she got up, came round and leaned down, stroking the corner of my eye. 'Never mind,' she tried to say lightly, 'I think your almond eyes give you a distinguished look.' She gave me a kiss on the temple, longer than a peck, perhaps for a couple of seconds, and went inside, closing the balcony door softly.

I kept pouring out and gulping down the brandy until the bottle was empty. An hour passed as I morbidly reflected on what my mother had gone through because of me, alone and in voluntary exile in the West from her shame at carrying a Russian baby. I reflected on the now ever-widening gulf between Sophie and me - every day since that dinner I seemed to learn of a new reason to diminish my chances. At best I'd have her pity, but no more than that.

I stumbled inside and collapsed on the spare mattress I'd laid on the floor when we'd first got to the hotel, seeking oblivion. Around three I woke with a raging thirst and headache. I got up to fetch water from the shared bathroom in the corridor and swallow some aspirin. When I came back into our room, I balefully looked for a while at Sophie lying on the bed, turned away from the door, facing the wall and seemingly sleeping soundly. As for me, it took hours to get back to sleep, just as the grey dawn light was seeping through the curtains.

When I finally woke it was already half nine, but I couldn't be bothered to get up. I just didn't care today - it was a Saturday anyway, why should I be working for von Barten or Kramer on their power-play games over my weekend?

Force of habit and a vestige of self-respect made me though. The first thing I saw when I lifted my throbbing head up from floor level was a note from Sophie propped on the desk. It said she had gone out to try to find Schmidt's address and would be back that evening. I was annoyed at the idea she'd ignored me and hadn't discussed her plan, thinking me incapacitated or perhaps worse, incapable, of doing my job. If she'd simply let me sleep out of sympathy at last night's news, I was resentful of that too.

This had to stop. I still had my mother, and she would still need me as much as ever. Our family situation was no different to yesterday, and I couldn't be regretful for a father that neither of us had known. Dupont's words over lunch that day, asking what sacrifices she'd made for me in those chaotic years before the creation of West Germany, now had a sharper meaning too. I refused to devalue her struggles and let her down now.

I was too late for breakfast at the hotel, and I didn't want to draw attention to the fact that Sophie had gone off on her own. As the morning slowly drained away I moped around the room for a while, before eventually going into the old town before lunch. I needed a walk anyway, because I was still drunk from the alcohol in my system from the night before. Apart from perhaps going to Rostock, an hour away by direct train, to look at phone directories at the post office there, I had no idea what Sophie planned to do. I hung around the station for a while, in the vague idea that she'd be coming back that way, but I also knew that I shouldn't loiter too long.

I found a bookshop and perused some school

textbooks for a little while. I was fascinated by how they portrayed both their state and West Germany. The grammar book for Thomas' school year even brought a smile to my lips for the first time that day. 'Identify the subjects in this sentence: Bernd's father is a member of the military unit of his factory. On many a Sunday he gets up early, puts on his uniform, and goes on exercise.'

My smile faded again, though, a little later in the same textbook. 'After the war, the soldiers of the Soviet Army helped the German population. They distributed food and the people thanked their liberators for this great assistance.'

I walked some more. How could I move things on with Sophie? She was a good actress, that was for sure, based on yesterday's performance at my aunt's. Even at dinner at von Barten's she hadn't really opened up, just given the impression of doing so. But given what she'd had the affront to tell me last night, surely I now had some kind of right to join her inner circle, especially if the next few days went well? My instincts were that she would require patience, an ambush at the right moment, not a frontal assault.

As soon as I could justify that it was time for dinner I found an out of the way cafe. The only main course on offer was an uninspiring slab of grey schnitzel for which I paid the same as for a decent meal in the West, thanks to the artificial official exchange rate. I was the sole diner, but the serving staff were as taciturn as I was, so I thankfully avoided any questions. Wismar's population might be poorer than Hamburg's, but life here didn't have to be drear. The joie de vivre you found in somewhere like Spain or Italy, countries of supposedly similar economic status to East Germany on a per capita basis, put the easterners to shame.

I made my way back to the hotel, picking up another bottle of brandy on the way, insurance against more misery tonight. There were no messages, either at the tiny reception, or in the room. I needed to start making plans to find Sophie and guessed I might well be ending up at the local police station, despite all my care to avoid attention during the day. A further hour or two passed, and just as I began to be genuinely concerned for her whereabouts, she flounced back into the room, triumphantly waving a piece of paper.

When I saw her shining eyes, brimful of pleasure, my annoyance faded in the face of her infectious exuberance.

'How did you do that?' I asked.

She smiled smugly, bringing von Barten back to mind. 'I pretended to be a student at Schmidt's university, said he had asked me to deliver an assignment to him at home, but that I'd lost his address.'

'Who did you find working there on a Saturday?'

Her face fell for a moment. 'Oh, I just walked around the corridors until I found another professor. Then I went over to Schmidt's apartment to scout it out.'

'Did you go in?'

'No, I thought you wanted us to visit him together?'

'Let's go tomorrow then, after the excursion with my aunt's church.'

'No, let's go first thing tomorrow, we mustn't lose any time.' She hadn't asked me once what I'd done this day just gone.

'If you've already found him, then we have some time to spare. Our visa isn't stamped for exit until Friday. Whether we see him in the morning or afternoon makes no difference.'

I felt compelled to meet these people from my mother's past. Throughout the day, as last night's revelation kept forcing its way back to the front of my mind, I had begun to resign myself to Sophie's theory. I wanted to make as much sense as I could of what my mother had done in the war, to discover the real person underneath the one I'd known all these years.

Sophie wasn't interested though, she wanted to push on with our task and didn't want to indulge me.

'We're not here for your benefit, we're here on assignment for my uncle. That's the only reason for acting at being a couple in front of your family. What do you think is going to happen tomorrow if we meet their church community? The lie will only spread further, and you'll not be able to put the genie back in the bottle if you do.'

'What other choice do I have? This is the cover story which von Barten gave us, I can't change it now.'

'What good does it do your family in East Germany, if they're caught spreading falsehoods? And he's Herr Doktor von Barten to you.'

I glowered at this put-down.

'I can't stop you from making a mistake, but I'm not staying stuck in here, pretending I've a headache. If you still want to go tomorrow, I'm not going to exert myself to play the loving fiancée - it will be at your risk.'

My heart sank again - I thought I'd been at the start of a good thing with her yesterday, and her success today had resolved me not to open the bottle tonight. But I remained resolved to go tomorrow and bear any consequences. As I already told her yesterday, this was likely my one chance to meet these people. After we returned to Brussels, I could always try to somehow patch things up with her.

There were to be no lingering kisses this evening, once in her bed, she wrapped the blankets tightly around herself and turned very deliberately towards the wall.

Chapter Thirteen

The following day dawned bright and a temporary truce was restored. We breakfasted at the hotel, then kicked our heels in town until noon - presumably the church excursion was taking place after their morning service had concluded. As we wandered around the partly-demolished Marienkirche next to the market, for want of anything else to discuss in the moment, I asked Sophie if her family were observant.

'Not really, my father and brothers were expected to attend church, as landowners, to make a demonstration to their tenants. But it was never discussed in our home in the West, and apart from Christmas, Easter, and confirmation, I never went.'

'My mother became religious when I was a teenager. She encouraged me to go but didn't make me. It was a small church near to the housing estate where we grew up - nothing fancy, no spire or stained-glass windows.'

'That's a shame, I like that kind of thing, especially the Catholic services I've had to go to - like weddings, where they have chants and incense. If I had to take religion seriously, I'd probably leave the Lutherans for them.'

She smiled for the first time that day and my hopes began to rise again, maybe she'd forgive me if we were successful in Rostock later.

'I'm sorry your uncle thought up this story of us being together. I was very embarrassed when he brought it up in front of Kramer. He shouldn't use people in that way.'

'But not that disappointed, I hope?' She grinned now.

'Anyway, I won't defend him for his conduct – he does it to everyone.'

I reddened, 'Just as long as you don't get the wrong idea about me being as presumptuous as your uncle.'

She'd opened the door to another question I badly wanted answered.

'Anyway, you've got lots of admirers already, like Signor Rizzi, from last Saturday.'

'Giorgio? He's just a dear friend.'

I had the feeling this was what she said about all of her male friends. If she eventually chose one of them to pair up with, it was going be on her timing and initiative and no one else's. Maybe Rizzi wasn't trying to put me off, but really had simply been trying to save me from frustration after all.

My aunt had billed it as an excursion to the woods for a picnic, but the plan had obviously changed, as it turned out to be a slightly grander affair. We met my family, strange as that phrase sounded to me now, outside their church and walked together a few streets to the allotment of one of the members of the congregation, where a barbeque had already been started. Neighbouring plot-holders were out too, enjoying the relative privacy of life outdoors, using their Sunday to improve their huts and chalets - the one piece of property here which they could almost claim as their own, according to Jan Stapel.

My aunt's friend's plot overlooked a field leading down to an artificial lake, with a cluster of trees hard up by the allotment boundary. Children played games whilst the women served food and the men conversed together in the thin shade of the budding branches.

Despite the earlier thaw between us, things slowly took a turn for the worse again. Neither of us had much, if anything, in common with anyone there. While she'd freely made small talk with my family two days ago, and while she still made an effort with my cousin Karin, as she'd warned me yesterday, she quickly stopped bothering with the new people we met. Church-going was definitely not encouraged in East Germany - it seemed to attract misfits and others who weren't going anywhere fast in life, at least not through the ranks of the regime. Sophie wanted to remind me she was still here unwillingly, and it began to be obvious to those around her too.

My aunt introduced us simply and without emotion to her other friends. We answered the questions about ourselves and especially about life in the West as noncommittally as possible. I received the odd enquiry about my mother, but only from some of the older women. When I started to ask them my own questions the mood changed, and they clammed up. No one passed me any messages to take back to my mother - it was almost as if she had passed on, not simply taken a train to Hamburg in 'forty-five.

The pastor of their church was equally odd. He was in his late middle age and trying to show concern for his flock as he circulated, but watching their responses, I could tell he wasn't really fitting in here either. I let him make his polite enquiries to us on how long we'd known each other and when we'd decided to get married, which soon turned to acute embarrassment, then real annoyance for Sophie.

Suddenly, she wasn't even pretending at civility any longer. She silently smouldered as I made up answers, as vague as I felt I could get away with. But when I strayed into adding embellishments here and there, about how we felt for each other, she frowned sourly, as if I was entirely guilty for the whole deception. Unsurprisingly, we weren't being convincing at all as a happy couple. I needed to divert the conversation and I did genuinely want to ask the pastor about my newly-discovered personal situation.

I took him to one side, away from everyone else. Sophie could fend for herself, I was done play-acting with her.

'Please Pastor, there's something I'd like to discuss in

confidence with you.'

'What's troubling you?'

'I found out on this trip, without anyone saying so explicitly, that I'm a Russian war baby.'

'I see. Has anyone ever treated you badly because they suspected that?'

'No, no, I can't say so - I don't think that anyone apart from my mother ever really knew for sure. At our church in Hamburg no-one ever mentioned it - and they were the ones most likely to have picked something up over the years.'

'So why would you think less of yourself? God doesn't.'

I squirmed. 'Why would he? I'm not a bad person. I look after my mother, I'm scrupulously honest at work, I treat all nationalities with respect.'

He shook his head sadly. 'In your eyes perhaps, but God is a God of absolutes - all of us are sinners, we all need to ask for his forgiveness. Just as we have to forgive those who've done us wrong.' I shivered, despite his earlier air of quiet helplessness in front of the barbeque guests, his eyes now had a steeliness I hadn't expected, pinning me to the spot where I stood.

'What are you saying? - that we're all so bad that it doesn't matter what we've done with our lives, or what's been done to us, God still condemns us - even my mother?'

As the words came out, the campsite photographs came into my head.

'I'm saying that God treats us all equally. He has the same expectations from us all, He offers us all the same gift of forgiveness leading to eternal life. We are simply asked to repent of our rebellion and accept that gift.'

I'd come for some mild words of comfort, not to have a window opened into my soul.

'Why did you come to the East?'

'Who told you that?'

'Your Schwabisch accent did, you're a long way from

Stuttgart.'

'It's hard to disguise - the locals here think I'm some kind of Western spy, which doesn't help my parishioners much. I even enrolled my children in the Free German Youth which upset the half of the congregation who hadn't, on grounds of principle.'

'So why put yourself through all this for these people? You could have found a nice church in the West, you didn't need to come here.'

'I have to take the message to where it's not being heard and to where I am called, not to where I want to go. I've left Swabia, and we've committed ourselves to become part of the society here.'

'Why would you give any kind of support to this regime?'

'Because it's the one which God has appointed for this land, at this time. Everyone needs to hear God's message, including the Communists, but they are more likely to hear it if they see that we're not out to undermine them.'

I raised my eyebrows.

'That's why my children are in the Free German Youth, my wife teaches maths at the local school, and we help our neighbours when they come to us with their troubles. The state has banned pan-German organisations, so the churches in the East agreed last year to split from their denominations in the West. We respect the law and because of our respect, we earn the right to criticize and tell the Party when their version of Socialism is immoral.'

I was confused, I didn't see how he and his wife were going to change anything fast, or why they should be supporting a regime that shot would-be escapees. It sounded like another justification for a bad decision, after the event - like others I'd heard recently.

'You think your life is going well right now, with your well-paid job in the West, and your fiancée by your side. But it can all change in an instant, nothing is certain, only God.'

It was Sophie who rescued me, shockingly rudely for her, by tapping her watch.

'My fiancée is saying that it's time we made our apologies and said goodbye.'

'You are welcome here anytime Oskar. Your aunt probably didn't tell you, but she arranged this barbeque at short notice for you.'

My cheeks burned with anger at Sophie's offhandedness.

I felt I owed it to my aunt to make a proper farewell, and when I went to find her I made Sophie come along too.

'Thank you for agreeing to meet me Aunt Hilde, we'll be in the East for a few more days, but we're travelling today to meet Sophie's relatives. I didn't know what I'd find here - I've never known a family apart from my mother before.'

My aunt smiled encouragingly. 'I've made my peace with my sister. Whatever happened back then wasn't your fault. Life moves on and takes us along with it, hopefully changing us for the better, if we let it. But I think that if my sister had really wanted to re-enter my life she would have come herself and before now. Maybe, now that we've met, she might think again.'

She kissed me and turned to embrace Sophie. 'And I am glad you have found happiness in each other. Remember that you'll have difficult days as well, but as long as you support one other faithfully you can do great things.'

Sophie returned her embrace, which, at least in that moment looked genuine. I couldn't believe von Barten had suggested this charade, and I felt a fool for agreeing to it. Sophie had warned me about deceiving my family, and surely this afternoon's farce had killed stone-dead any chance of even friendship between us. Maybe that was a kindness in disguise, though - better to know now there was no chance, than to allow myself to become yet another moth mesmerised by her flame.

We boarded the Sunday stopping train to Rostock an hour later. After the triumph of her last journey there, her mood on the return was icy. She'd bought a city atlas yesterday in Rostock when she went to find Schmidt's apartment and now held it tightly on her lap as she showed me the route she'd taken back to the train station.

She was obviously intending to take control, at least for this next part of the trip, and I couldn't really stop her. As I watched her trace the path through the streets with her finger I felt increasingly that I was here simply to give von Barten the excuse to send Sophie to the East under the cover of official EEC business. If it was the case that we were both effectively working under von Barten's direction, then she immediately outranked me.

As the train crawled through the suburbs toward the city centre I was glad it would soon be over, one way or another. I reckoned Schmidt's apartment was no more than a short walk a few blocks north of the railway station, then back again and the start of the journey home.

I didn't intend spending any more days in East Germany as a pawn of Kramer and von Barten if I could help it. Whether Schmidt had anything for us to either purchase or take by force today, I was done - we'd work out changing our exit visa dates at the border. This outcome was on her - she was insistent she'd found the university Schmidt, our only lead. No-one in Brussels knew what he looked like, so her word it would be, and I certainly wasn't going to chase any more wild geese – for her or anyone else.

We got out in silence and started walking, Sophie leading the way. As we left the centre and neared Schmidt's street the traffic grew quieter until it died away altogether. Rostock on a sleepy Sunday afternoon was as exciting as Rosheim.

Sophie marched up to the grey Wilhelmine apartment

block, but I stopped her before she could ring the bell. I pressed the button above the one next to Schmidt's name and waited. A voice asked querulously, 'Yes?'

'Herr Doktor Schmidt?'

'No, it's Herr Professor Doktor Schmidt you're looking for, the apartment on the floor below this one.'

So we were in the right place. I rang for Schmidt, but there was no reply, so I tried the first bell again.

'Yes?' This time somewhat impatiently.

'Please, I wish to leave a package for the Professor, but he's not in.'

'On the table in the hall, just before the stairs.' The door buzzed, and we slipped inside.

Without discussion, we quietly mounted the stairs, creeping past each landing until we reached Schmidt's floor. The hairs on my neck began to stand on end. We could try to talk our way out of here if we had to, but in a country as suspicious of strangers as East Germany, even honest mistakes notoriously got tourists into trouble.

Maybe Sophie knew better than me, but I wouldn't have pushed through the ajar door into Schmidt's apartment the way she did.

She called his name softly as we moved from room to room. His apartment was much more substantial inside than it appeared from the street. There was a hallway that opened into a lounge with desk in the corner, a kitchen, three bedrooms, privy, and a separate bathroom.

I had only seen two bodies of people killed violently in my time on the beat in Hamburg. The ones you would expect in a port city: a Bulgarian sailor stabbed in a bar fight - his femoral artery severed, and a drug pusher shot in the face just off the Reeperbahn.

But there was a lot more blood here, if that were possible - someone had made certain that the body lying in the tub was very dead.

Sophie blanched and quickly turned from the doorway to the room. What happened next, though, stunned me even more. She ran to the kitchen, grabbed a knife, then ran back to the lounge trying to hack open the locked drawer of Schmidt's desk.

'What are you doing, you madwoman? We have to go, now.'

'I've got to find it, this is a disaster,' she keened, on the edge of hysteria. I roughly grabbed her knife hand and tried to pull her out of the lounge into the hall. 'No!' she cried, almost shouting. 'Ten minutes, please, let me try.'

She dropped the knife, wriggled free of my grip and ran over to the bookcases, starting to pull books from the shelves.

I put my hands to my head in despair and ground my teeth. I knew I had to give her a moment or two to calm down, I couldn't simply frogmarch her out of here in this state.

'Five minutes, then I'm gone, regardless of who your uncle is.'

I drew breath and started to think through the possible explanations of what had just happened. Random killing and sheer coincidence? Dismissed. Theft of a document and silencing of a witness to prevent embarrassment to the EEC? Just possibly, but surely too heavy-handed for von Barten, and not by looking at Sophie's current performance. Securing historical material for use against the EEC at a later date? More likely, and it was obvious by whom.

We were about to find out for sure. Looking back, we had no chance really - I later surmised that the apartment block *Hausbuchbeauftrager*, the East German successor to the Nazi's *Blockwart* had been told to immediately report any visitors for Schmidt to the police. Either that, or the Stasi had already been watching the apartment block from the empty streets below.

I even somehow recognised the four agents when they burst into the hallway - maybe policemen the world over conform to the same few personality types.

The leader had done this a hundred times. He wasn't expecting any difficulties but didn't want any mistakes made to get him into trouble with his superiors. I even recognised myself, the youngest of the four, leaping forward with handcuffs, eager to show his diligence, or perhaps just happy that a long boring wait was over.

The photographer was a different touch, though. We were taken to the bathroom for shots with the corpse behind us, as if we'd been caught in the act.

Sophie was white, shocked into dumbness. In a way, I'd at least had been here before on occasion, even if those times I was the one wearing the uniform.

We said nothing to each other in the van on the way to our unknown destination. There was no story we could concoct together that would make it better, even if we hadn't been put into tiny individual cells once inside the vehicle.

I was surprisingly calm, the worst that could happen had happened. It was a set-up, and I expected there would be some kind of bargain to be made. This was international politics after all, how could there not be a deal to be done?

Chapter Fourteen

After three days of what I assumed was normal remand treatment in East Germany I was getting worried - that was probably why we, or at least I, had been given it.

The cells of the prison van waiting for us on the corner of the street, opposite Schmidt's apartment, were windowless. By my watch, we'd been driven fast for at least three hours, which could mean we'd ended up anywhere - from Berlin to the Polish border. I guessed we'd been taken to a special detention facility, but not to a regular prison, given that we'd been prodded out of the van in a gated car park of what otherwise looked like a typical office block.

Everything from that point, though, had the appearance of normality, if that was the correct word for it. We were separated before prisoner registration, and I was held in a single cell with glass blocks instead of a window but allowed regular hours of darkness and regular meals. Not that prison fare was anything to write home about, the vegetable broth and thin slices of bread spread with margarine only kept hunger at bay, and I began to understand why Dupont and his generation thought about food so much.

I had no idea what kind of coercion the secret police in this part of Germany used, but I obviously wasn't important enough to warrant it - yet. Only last month, the East Germans had traded no less than twenty-one political prisoners for one of the bloc's own, Heinz Felfe. Felfe was a Soviet double agent whose exposure in 'sixty-one had eventually brought down Reinhard Gehlen, the head of the West Germany's espionage agency, the BND. Allegedly, the affair had helped end the career of Chancellor Adenauer early too - although, as von Barten had said at the dinner, Adenauer was already eighty-seven when that happened, so the assertion was somewhat hard to prove.

My best guess was that I'd be in East Germany for a while, months, maybe even years if things went really badly. In Sophie's case, I presumed von Barten would do a deal and buy her back for a ransom. Whether on the surface you were dealing with a fascist or a communist regime, I now agreed with what Jan Stapel had said back in Brussels that day - underneath both of them were just organised crime rackets. All the killing they liked doing proved it, to me anyway.

If I did blame anyone so far, it was the pastor for putting the hex on me at the barbeque - with his talk of how well my life was going and how it could change with a snap of the fingers. Maybe he really was a prophet.

Of course, three days in my cell meant I had more than enough time to think about the case so far and try to finish the jigsaw puzzle that had first seriously troubled me on the journey back from Latour the second time, only last Tuesday week. I had to keep my mind focussed on something, even if it was a problem I was now unlikely to see through to completion.

I suspected more strongly now that Freybourg was running a play of some kind, principally with Kramer, rather than Latour, and that they'd set up a breadcrumb trail to be followed by me as Hansel, latterly with Gretel by my side.

Testing a counter-argument inside my head, though, I'd assumed that any Vichy documents would be bad for the German side, but that was based on the premise that the Vichy plans supported the kind of pan-Europe that von Barten was advocating. But what if a disclosure actually ended up being worse for France's image in the world?

What if I was overthinking it, and the French simply saw that something was about to surface which would look bad for France, so as far as possible should have German fingerprints on it too. That could still imply that Kramer and Freybourg were in marriage of convenience.

Or more wildly, what if the whole thing was some elaborate East German operation, of which our arrest was the final act? Latour had hinted at Eastern Bloc interest the first time we met. I really hoped in that case it was an East German scheme, not a Soviet one - I felt at least I could reason with other Germans, even though I supposed I had to start thinking of myself as half-Russian now too.

Jan Stapel's Marxism told him that history could be explained by a lust for wealth - maybe I should apply that to the people in this case too. Starting with the person with the motivations I felt most sure of, I decided that, above all, Latour was driven today by making money and that his story of Nazi plotting, whilst maybe still heartfelt, was to the support the sale of his material. This pointed to Freybourg as an extorter too - but I simply didn't know enough about his post-war career to prove if he was also in need of cash or not, so that line of thinking drew a blank.

Dupont didn't need to make money, or to protect a career, and his reputation wasn't going to be changed much either way, no matter what came out. I believed his story that, at the time, he and others had been put to work by their German protectors, for the benefit of those same Germans after the war. In a barter economy short of food, cigarette and bread rations were more valuable than money. I had the feeling that he hadn't been holding anything back from me – more that I hadn't been asking him the right questions. If I ever got out of here, I might take up his offer and satisfy my curiosity by going back to Saint-Valery to fill in the gaps.

Von Barten I guessed had a lot to lose financially from dark stories emerging from the past, but not if they were intended primarily as an EEC smear - only if they indirectly led to new questions as to how he acquired his wealth during the war.

Kramer, I presumed, had been well looked after financially by successive French governments as their trusted man in the Saarland and later in Brussels. Of course, if he compared himself to von Barten, he might well be tempted to make more money on the side too - if not from fake documents then maybe from some kind of political blackmail - but I couldn't see how.

I had a new theory too, as to the intended result of the investigation, at least, as intended until our arrest on Sunday. That expected outcome, I was going to bet, was why Sophie had been so insistent on searching the apartment of a man with no throat for a document she knew was going to be there.

My theory was, that whatever Latour had originally planned to sell to the EEC had disappeared between my first and last trips to him. Von Barten wanted Schmidt's version to be found, which must surely mean he'd arranged for Latour's to be taken off him. Which meant in turn that the copy due for collection from Schmidt was neutral for him and that Latour's was damaging.

No wonder he'd wanted full written details of my first trip to France, he'd stepped into the story that was being told to him in order to rewrite the ending. The only question left in my mind was - how close were Kramer and Freybourg really today? After all, they'd been mortal enemies on either side of the undeclared French civil war between nineteen forty and 'forty-four. Or had someone else put Freybourg up to this?

Still, it was only a theory, and I might be looking at the picture from entirely the wrong angle.

I was about to find out. It still felt like early morning - I no longer had my watch, but I guessed my breakfast of a single roll and a bitter cup of instant coffee had been around a couple of hours earlier.

The door was unlocked and after three long and boring days I was finally marched to an interview room containing just a plain wooden table and two chairs below a framed photograph of Walter Ulbricht - no manacles on the walls or two-way mirrors.

I was made to sit, then left alone for five minutes, no threats and no word of explanation either. It was more like waiting to be seen at the doctors' than being trapped on the wrong side of the frontline of the Cold War.

The banality of it all made the process more sinister than not - if it was designed to give prisoners the sense of being trapped in a faceless bureaucratic machine, then it was working on me at this moment.

The investigating officer entered with a bundle of files under his arm, which he set down on his side of the able. He was dressed in a plain grey suit, cleanly shaven, with slight wrinkles at the corners of his eyes. He would be completely unremarkable in a crowd of office workers leaving at the end of the day.

'My name is Major Johannes. I have been assigned to oversee the investigation of your case and recommend a decision on what to do with you.'

'What charge am I being held on?'

He raised his eyebrows and puffed his cheeks. '"Charges", not "charge". Espionage, torture and murder.'

I licked my lips. 'What is the deal?'

'There is no deal. We've already made contact with Herr von Barten in Brussels concerning the release of his niece - to tell him that she is also currently facing serious charges and to make the necessary arrangements - but no one is coming for you.'

My shoulders slumped, I had no reason to believe Johannes wasn't telling the truth.

'Depending on how soon we come to an agreement between von Barten and ourselves over his niece, you can expect your trial to start sometime in the next six to nine months. In East Germany, as you probably already know, yours are capital offences.' My anger flared at von Barten - now I had a far bigger reason to pay him back than merely being pulled up over an untyped report.

'So why do you need to decide what to do with me?' If I was to get out now I knew there would be a price to be paid - if not cash from the West or a prisoner exchange, then it would probably be my collaboration. But I wasn't going to humiliate myself further by offering them it to them unprompted.

'What were you doing in East Germany, aside from spying for the BND, as it says here in your confession?' He lifted an orange folder from the stack and placed it in the middle of the table, tapping it with his fingers.

'Given that you know I wasn't, what do you think?' A ghost of a smile appeared on Johannes' lips.

For answer, he pushed a thick document file across the table. 'Go on, don't be afraid - open it, it's not a bomb or something - or maybe it is?'

The folder was unbound and untitled. I dashed through the pages, skim-reading as I went. Although the cover was missing there was a table of contents, which referenced the key sections: a review of attempts at European unity to date, an explanation of how international cooperation on the war economy had developed, and an assessment of what had worked well, what hadn't, and why. The preamble talked about different post-war models for European government and proposals on resolving border disputes between Germany, France, Denmark, Holland and Belgium. The crown jewel, attached at the end of the file, was a precis from an official in the Ministry of Public Enlightenment and Propaganda of different approaches to selling the concepts contained in the rest of the document, each approach written depending on how the war might end.

Johannes saw me linger over that last section.

'Yes, remarkable isn't it? The distilled expertise from twelve years' practice at lying to the German people, harnessed in selling them the next new lie about their future.'

I raised my hands, palms up, in mock supplication. 'Where did you get this from and from whom?'

'It was in Comrade Professor Schmidt's possessions, he was a hoarder, felt compelled to squirrel everything away - but we found it in the end, we always do.'

He wagged his finger. 'But we'd never have known to look for it, if your people hadn't gone blundering around asking questions. You see, they're just not very good. It's a fault in the West, too much individualism within the agencies, too many petty rivalries between the agencies, and not enough focus on the common goal, if you people even know what it is that you all want.'

He punched one hand into the other a couple of times, just to show how much energy and enjoyment he got from achieving his goals.

'And speaking of focus, here's the deal for you. We want you to take this little time bomb back to Brussels and make sure it gets well used. You can even leave today, if we make a deal, you and me. You're to cause as much upset and disorganisation to that fast-growing bureaucratic empire, directed from the top floor of the Berlaymont building, as we judge is achievable.'

'And that's it? You then drop these false charges against me, against us?'

'No, you don't get to leave the birthplace of progressive socialism without signing your confession. If we were to let you go without signing, I have a vision of myself waving sadly goodbye to you at the Wall, knowing I'd never hear from you again.'

'Let me take a look.'

He extracted a slim envelope from his bundle of documents and slid them over.

Eight pages detailed how I had been recruited by the BND to spread subversion in East Germany and to assassinate key Party workers. It told the story of how I had approached Professor Schmidt to bribe him to spy for the BND too, and how he had resisted under torture until Sophie von Barten and I had killed him in his bath. The envelope contained the photographs of us in the bathroom, including one of the kitchen knife Sophie had used to try to break into Schmidt's desk, but with a bloodied blade, attached to a fingerprint report.

I pushed it back again.

'You know I can't sign this, it's not even plausibly close to what happened. I expected, I don't know, low-level espionage, estimating the distance between watchtowers at the border, that kind of thing.'

'You really are slow today. I told the guys over the past three days, soft treatment will get us nowhere - this customer is a tough nut - no food or sleep for seventy-two hours, that's what we need. But did they listen? No sir.' He grinned from the side of his mouth as he said it. He was becoming harder and harder to read.

'Very good, let's try again.' He puffed his cheeks out once more and laid out four files next to each other on his side of the table. His finger hovered over them, back and forth, before selecting the second from the left.

'Let's see now, Hilde Hofmann, née Lenkeit. July nineteen sixty-two. "*Frau Hofmann has been receiving packages from the West, from someone she claims is her sister. Her children have started saying that people in the West are kind and we shouldn't hate them.*"'

He tapped with a finger on the file next to it, a thicker file. He picked it up with relish and tutted out of the corner of his mouth.

'Oh dear, oh dear. Thomas Hofmann, born January eighteenth, nineteen fifty-six, age thirteen - same age as my own boy. Hear this from last summer, "*Pioneer Hofmann has shown insufficient zeal for the recent voluntary recycling drive to support our socialist brethren in the Democratic Republic of Vietnam*". And from two years previously, "*Thomas Hofmann has questioned the necessity of learning Russian at school, claiming he does not have any Russian friends.'"*

He closed the file. 'Really! I blame his parents. Didn't they teach him that on the far side of Poland he has two hundred and fifty million Russian-speaking friends?'

He shook his head sadly. 'It doesn't look good for them at all - politically suspect and harbouring Western spies on the very day they murdered the Comrade Professor. No, no, no.' He suddenly snapped his fingers.

'Let me embellish the story for you some more. We are the most professional espionage organisation in Europe, probably the world. We get asked to go to Moscow to give lectures to the KGB, we train half the secret police forces of the Communist bloc. You, on the other hand, work for the EEC's toy police force. You are, what, number three in a four-person department? Do this one job for us, learn from the best, see if you have a taste for more.'

'You're offering me employment? A chance for professional improvement?'

'Do you know why I called Internal Affairs a toy police force? It's because you're there to make sure the real crooks never get seriously investigated. It pains me to say,' here he placed his hand over his heart, 'that includes those people bribed and blackmailed by ourselves, and other governments too, of course, to influence trade negotiations and to send us interesting little details like the number of your colleagues.'

My heart rate slowed. All Bernd's petty struggles and strivings in office politics really were for nothing.

'You will belong to us, and we will pay you for your efforts. We always prefer willing recruits, but we don't have much time to develop you. I'm sure, though, you and I have lots in common and could be great friends one day, once we've had the chance to get to know one another.'

Here he nodded encouragingly. 'On the other hand, to help speed things up, I need to remind you about your cousins who might like to go to university one day, your uncle who might like to keep his foreman's position and your aunt's pastor who might like to avoid expulsion to the West, leaving his wife and children behind here. So it's nothing personal, but we do need you to sign the confession in the other envelope, just to make sure we stick together.'

'How many assignments to I have to do for you until I'm free?' I knew the answer as I was asking the question. Johannes didn't waste any time on it either.

'No one gives us enough credit for what we've done here. Stalin wanted to shoot one hundred thousand Wehrmacht officers in nineteen forty-five and turn our country back into a land of peasantry. But we've managed to tread the line between Russia and America and preserve a cultured, morally decent Germany. Not like your tainted version in the West, with its ex-Nazi Chancellor and war profiteer capitalists like Alfried Krupp, bribing their way to keep their ill-gotten gains.'

Despite myself, I nodded too. The problem was that I couldn't deny the last two facts.

'But if it's so cultured and decent, why are you keeping files on thirteen-year-old boys?'

'Because the price of freedom from fascism is constant vigilance against backsliding. We're simply encouraging the people to police their own thoughts and each other's - we don't really want to have to do it ourselves. In fact, in the main, the Ministry simply collects and processes denunciations, which, between you and me, is somewhat tedious. As a fellow policeman, an aversion to paperwork is something I'm sure you'll sympathise with.'

Again, amazingly, I found myself agreeing with him. The reports he'd quoted from the two files were so trivial that they had to be true. I could well imagine a life of drudgery in the lower ranks of the Stasi, generating endless reports that would change nothing of the fortunes of the State

'What assurances do I get that you'll protect my family in Wismar from harassment?'

'There's the beauty of the arrangement, you get to keep us honest too. If anything happens to your family, you're already in the West and can go and tell the BND, the CIA, the SDECE, whomever, about unreliable Major Johannes and how you no longer want to work for us.'

I knew the game was up. Johannes made it all sound so reasonable, a sensible solution worked out between adults. But I also knew that if I stuck it out, they would have a job to prove my guilt in any half-normal legal process and, that even if declared guilty, any death penalty was unlikely to be carried out. I had an easy way out or a hard one. The easy one I would pay for until I was no longer of use to them, maybe until I retired - the hard one might mean I lose the best years of my youth.

'I'll leave you alone to think about it for five minutes. As I do, a final reminder to take your young cousins and your fellow spy into consideration. Oh, and one more thing, in case we can't work anything out between us - only last year we changed how we carry out capital sentences. Now it's officially known as an "unexpected shot to the back of the head". Once convicted, you'll never know which day will be your last. "Lenkeit! Sit back in this dentist's chair for your regular examination" - then boom.'

He got up and left the room, leaving all his files and documents laid out on the table for me to look at, if I wished.

I put my head into my hands. *Gott, was soll ich tun?*

I looked at the confession again. It made clear that Sophie was at least equally guilty, more so if you counted her fingerprints on the knife. I looked at the ink marks of her fingertips on the report with sadness. If she got out now and I didn't, she'd for sure have found someone by the time of my release. But what if they made her sign too? – she'd be under their thumb as well Von Barten might pay to make the file disappear, but as in any blackmail, he would never really know when they might come back to ask for more.

Even if von Barten had originally imposed on her, she'd seemed happy enough to come and hunt down Schmidt. If she was here to help von Barten stalemate Kramer, then she was also here protecting her own career too. I would even be justified in pointing out that she was the one who'd held us back in the apartment for those few crucial minutes.

Despite all that, if there was a chance to protect her, I would. I knew I always would, no matter what bad-tempered words had passed between us those last two days.

'What is the deal with the von Barten girl?' I said, looking up at Johannes as he walked back in and stood under the picture of Ulbricht. He leaned against the wall, his thumbs hooked in his trouser pockets.

'Ah, the lovely Miss von Barten. I thought your lack of questions earlier was suspicious.'

'What if we do a deal? I'll sign a version which doesn't mention her as an accomplice at the apartment and makes it clear she was just my stooge to provide me with a cover story to be here in the East.'

He actually looked nonplussed for a moment or two. 'Really Lenkeit, you're quite the bourgeois gentleman.'

He smiled, 'But she's too important to let go that easily. Two birds landed in our laps on Sunday and you'll both sing for us. Without her confession, what hold do we have over von Barten? Herr Lenkeit, your confession will actually help her, as neither of you can go until you both sign.'

'I don't care. I don't care how long I end up here, I won't sign something that incriminates her.'

'But her prints are on the very knife used to cut the Comrade Professor's throat, and I promise you, she's going to sign anyway.' He smirked, 'You see, twenty years after the socialist revolution, it's now been a while since we had a real class enemy under lock and key, the daughter of capitalist landowners. There's a growing list of senior officers here who'd like the excuse to give her a special private interrogation, if she stays as our guest for much longer.'

'You bastard.'

'No, I strongly suspect you're the bastard.' He walked over and slammed a pen on the table. 'You sign, she signs, and you both go back West, without any unnecessary unpleasantness.'

I pulled the confession towards me with a heavy heart and scribbled my signature, as illegibly as I could make it.

Johannes smiled smugly, 'Well done, young man, you won't regret this.' He took the papers to the door and passed them to an unseen messenger and sat down opposite me again.

'Cigarette?' I shook my head. He lit up and exhaled slowly. Walter Ulbricht's face gazed at me paternally through a cloud of blue smoke.

'That wasn't so difficult, eh?'

'What happens next?'

'There is no normal procedure. Your train back to Brussels leaves Rostock at four - it's now just before midday. Everything now depends on what happens over there. We want a real stink, ambassadors summoned for meetings, late night crisis talks. We want see what the French and West Germans do when put under pressure and set at each other's throats.'

'We're still in Rostock then? We drove for hours.'

'Standard practice to confuse arrestees. We've lots to teach you when you next come for a visit.'

'Was this document plan yours all along?'

'We'll never say, one way or another. Just make sure that what I've described happens. As an agent, you need to be resourceful, creative, able to act independently to get the task in hand done. You've been in the army, you know what I'm talking about.'

'How will you get in touch with me in Brussels?'

He stretched out his arm to look at his watch. 'Later.

First, back to your cell to get properly dressed, then I'll take you out for lunch. We'll come back here afterwards to go over the detailed objectives.'

My mind was in a whirl as Johannes waited on the red light above the door changing to green, before admitting the warden who led me back to my cell. I'd started the day resigned to life on the inside and now seemed to have become the Stasi's newest recruit in the space of six hours, with an exciting, if possibly short, future ahead of me as a traitor to both West Germany and France at the same time.

My clothes were laid out for me, freshly laundered. My bags from the hotel in Wismar were standing beside my bed, with the shirts inside also newly washed and ironed. I went over to the sink and started to scrape away three days' growth with the razor from my washbag.

The cell door had been left unlocked behind me, with instructions to present myself at the end of the corridor when I was ready. I felt on top of the world when I shouldn't have done. A faint, treacherous inner voice was even starting to wonder if the Democratic Republic really was as evil as we were told it was in the West, or if they were just misunderstood and were simply trying to make the best of a bad hand.

Johannes picked me up and we went down a staircase with floor to ceiling railings to the carpark Sophie and I had arrived in.

'Where is Miss von Barten now?'

'You'll meet her at four, at the station. From now on you have to think of her as dangerous to you. No matter what relationship you had with her in the past, that's now over.'

We got into his Wartburg, which I was pleased to see was no more sophisticated than my Volkswagen and drove out. After his loquaciousness earlier, Johannes was silent on the way and didn't say where we were headed. He parked the car on a nearly empty plaza outside a nine-storey brutalist concrete block. Rain, with a tang of salt whipped up from the Baltic, stung my face as he led me across the plaza to the building, which turned out to be the Hotel Warnow, Rostock's Interhotel. The Hôtel Métropole in Brussels it was not.

The food at the hotel restaurant was more than decent, though. As we clinked glasses and relaxed, I felt myself wanting to open up, to justify my decision to him. Johannes looked at me over the rim of his glass, amused at my indecision.

'If in doubt, keep it to yourself, comrade. Consider yourself on duty, now and forever. Don't worry, you'll get used to it, though. Living the double life will become instinctive, such that telling the truth will seem positively unnatural.'

He told me about his family: his son, whom he'd mentioned earlier, his wife, who was a doctor - the highest rate of female employment in Europe according to Johannes - his daughter from his first marriage, who had joined the family firm and was a trainer at a Stasi academy. He described how she'd recently started running a course in agent handling for the Congolese secret police - as if she was simply a regular teacher switching classes at a normal school.

It was as alien as the Moon.

He got up to make a phone call at the bar and returned to our table with another bottle of wine. 'Your train isn't leaving until nine now. Let's make the most of the time.'

He poured for the both of us and kept my glass topped up as we spoke. But after two hours, the surrealness of a convivial lunch between recent prisoner and interrogator was starting to break through the veneer of contrived normality. The conversation was starting to drag anyway, and what I really wanted just then was to take a proper look at the document found at Schmidt's.

I suggested it was time to go back to his office and go over the plan for when I got to Brussels, and he assented with a sigh. On the way back, he was silent again, concentrating on the traffic - I wondered if he'd drunk more than I'd realised at lunch.

When we got there, he agreed that I could start by reviewing the manual more closely. I shifted a couple of chairs and spread the document out on a table in the corner, section by section, scanning the index to decide where to start first.

The file was actually a collection of other documents with commentary introducing each section. Sometimes the reference material was at the back and indexed in the main text, sometimes it was in the middle of the section in question.

I picked up the last section, on propaganda, which we'd already discussed back in the interrogation room and handed it to him.

'Does this read like something from the Ministry of Enlightenment, or what someone thinks they would have written?'

He shrugged and leafed through the pages. He wasn't forthcoming, so I tried to prompt a response. 'The problem with this section is that it's all simply common sense to us reading it now, it doesn't have a distinctive voice which marks it out as their work.'

All I got back was a 'perhaps.'

I wondered if that would be the case for the rest. I picked up a section on customs – it must have been written by a German, because it started with a lengthy explanation of the theory that import tariffs on raw materials ended up as a tax on that nation's own consumers of finished goods.

'How about this one?' I said as I handed it over. 'No idea,' he retorted, 'not something which we bother much about over here.'

I risked a question. 'But your people think this is a real

fascist-era document?'

'The forensics say so - ink composition, fibre structure of the paper - all agree it's something from that time.'

I looked again at the customs section, there was no author given, but it really did have a tariff table for metallurgical coal, along with other specialist items, just as Latour had said in one of his throwaway comments in Rosheim.

I wondered if there were other hidden signatures elsewhere. If I'd been Dupont and had been set a production target for the manual, I'd have recycled existing documents to speed things up. I chose another section on industrial labour relations, and there it was - in a list of author names at the end. 'Herr Doktor E v.B' jumped out. Either there were two officials in a similar area of work with the same initials, or von Barten had contributed to the manual. Of course, his section might have been used as reference material without his knowledge, but perhaps he was involved to a greater degree than he was prepared to admit. It wouldn't be any kind of war crime - but it would be surely damaging?

'Why didn't you bring my attention to this one earlier?' I held the section up for him to see. He shrugged. 'It's not proof of anything, we saw it and decided it would neither help nor hinder you. Let the people in Brussels make of it what they will.'

'Was this all the original material in this section?'

'Yes, why do you ask?'

If von Barten had really sent Sophie to bring back a less damaging version of the manual, and he knew about this section but was happy for it to stand, then he was an even cooler customer than I'd given him credit for. Maybe he took the view that a completely clean document would make it easier for the French to claim he'd switched versions.

I shook my head, I had to say something, even at the risk of them changing their minds about the operation.

'You realise there's no guarantee that this bomb will damage anyone when it goes off? Von Barten is a survivor above all else.'

'It doesn't matter, you've forgotten my exact words from earlier. You have to cause disruption, not that this document has to cause disruption. It's up to you whether you go back with claims you've discovered a French plot to smear him, or whether you suspect he's working for us. You work it out.'

'And how will you contact me?'

'We know where to find you, you'll hear from us when we decide.'

He reached down and rummaged in the cupboard under the desk and pulled out a bottle of korn and two glasses. 'Ah ha,' he surfaced again. 'Let's toast to your success.'

'This isn't your own office?'

'I work for the HVA in Berlin, the foreign intelligence branch of the Ministry. This room is our office, but it's not staffed all the time. We came down here especially for the interception.'

There was a single loud knock on the door and it was opened by a larger, older man, also in a grey suit, but with a shaven head and vice-like handshake.

'Are we done now?' asked Johannes.

'Yes,' he replied in a grating voice. 'All complete.' He gave the impression of coming from an older era of secret policeman, not averse to pulling out fingernails. I couldn't work out who was the more senior in rank. He fixed me with a cold stare as we shook hands, as if he was really mocking Johannes.

'All right then, time to get moving.' Johannes swallowed his drink in one and motioned to me to do the same.

I collected the manual back together, careful not to mix up the order of the sections. Johannes grabbed my suitcase, and we set off down the stairs again. He called up to his older colleague to leave it five minutes before coming after us.

Johannes swept through the gates in the Wartburg and got me to the station in a couple of minutes, this time driving at high speed. We swung round into the station forecourt and he brought the car to a stop. He turned to me with a serious expression to deliver his parting words.

'There are good Germans and bad Germans. Both are to be found on either side of the Wall, but remember that our people were fighting the fascists right from the very start. We are the ones who are really trying to free Germany from the prison of its past - follow your conscience and be suspicious of those who only pretend to be doing so.'

He passed me a ticket and my passport stamped with an exit visa, and with a final shake of the hand I got out and he was gone.

A minute later another nondescript Stasi car pulled up, and Sophie got out with her bags. She looked shell-shocked, pale, and uncharacteristically lost for words. I picked up her bag and led her into the station and a draughty, smoke-filled waiting room. For a moment or two I thought she was going be sick, but she pulled herself together.

We sat in silence, I fetched coffee and rolls for us both, and she drank and chewed mechanically - a broken parody of a young couple who'd just had a fight. The sky outside darkened as the evening drew on. After an age, our train pulled in and, in unspoken agreement, we quickly walked down the platform, searching for an unoccupied compartment to speak privately.

'Had you been drinking?' she asked with wide eyes, as soon as I'd slid the compartment door shut behind us.

'I had something while I was waiting, before you arrived, then I came out to the front to find you.'

She looked immediately suspicious. 'What did you sign back there?'

'They asked me to confess to spying for the West. And you?'

'I didn't sign anything.' My blood ran cold. I couldn't know for sure if she was telling the truth, but I suddenly knew in my heart I shouldn't have signed - I'd got carried away with the notion of being her protector.

Then, illogically, resentment flared in my heart against her and von Barten rather than Johannes. Just as I had recognised in the interrogation room, money could buy von Barten anything - including freedom from the Stasi for his family and had done so. By comparison, the Lenkeits, all of us – in the east and the west - never had a chance in life.

'They tried though,' she added soberly.

'What did they try to get you to sign?'

'The same as you, but I'm glad you didn't sign either Oskar.' Her tone sounded false, whether because she was lying, or because she thought I was, I couldn't tell.

'And we failed to get Uncle Ernst's document,' she added.

I merely nodded slightly. 'We did our best, let's see what might turn up elsewhere. But I assumed when you were briefed in Brussels he told you that the task was principally to find out whether or not these old copies still existed in the first place.'

Now I had multiple dilemmas - if I made the ticking bomb at the bottom of my bag disappear before we got back to Brussels I could start afresh with her, but there'd be no political crisis to please the Stasi. If I took the document back to von Barten and Kramer together, I might trigger a rupture, but she'd realise I'd just lied - I could plead the confidentiality of the assignment, but I'd have betrayed her trust. If I gave up the manual to von Barten alone it would disappear, again without a crisis, and again betraying her trust. It left me with no real option but to give it to Kramer privately in the hope that I'd guessed his intentions correctly and he'd find a discreet way to use it, with a cover story that it had turned up in the West. As the Americans might say, von Barten was going to become collateral damage, like napalming a South Vietnamese village to kill a single Viet Cong.

She was silent for a minute, then said quietly. 'They told me that they had a dossier of Uncle Ernst's business dealings in the war that they would leak to the Israelis.'

'What? I thought these guys were hostile to Israel?'

'But not above tricking them into doing their dirty work for them.'

'Sorry, "dirty work"? Does your uncle have anything to hide?'

'Of course not,' she snapped back, fierily now.

'What did they say the Israelis would do?'

'They said he would be on a plane to Tel Aviv within three years, sooner if they sent commandos to get him, as they did for Eichmann.'

'But that's ridiculous.' I lowered my voice again. 'How could they possibly fabricate a story that he was a war criminal stretching to that kind of treatment. Eichmann organised the Wannsee conference, for goodness sake.'

'The world is changing,' she replied. 'Things that were defensible back in nineteen fifty when Adenauer called a halt to denazification are no longer so.' She furrowed her brow. 'I think Uncle Ernst knows his time at the EEC is coming to an end, one way or another - if only through older age. That's why he's been a patron to the College of Europe graduates you met at dinner, to try to ensure his ideas survive him.'

She frowned. 'It wasn't the only crazy thing they said, though. They said that even if the Israelis didn't bite, the French would insist on my uncle being fired.'

'That was almost as crazy a claim as the other one. It also makes no sense for at least two immediate reasons. Firstly, Bernd and I have never known anyone to actually get dismissed, and in Internal Affairs we know just how much some people deserve it. Pushed to one side, promoted to a non-job without real power for sure, but fired? - no. Secondly, he's the *chef de mission*, he's Germany personified at the EEC, it would virtually be an act of war to ask for his removal.'

'So what made them let us go in the end?'

'I think your uncle paid a ransom. Or more likely, EEC money did.' I guessed that's why my train had been 'delayed' - they were finalising a transaction, checking the money had been wired to a Stasi account in somewhere like Switzerland or Luxembourg.

'What did they really do to you back there?'

She was silent, withdrawing into herself again. 'I got no sleep for maybe a day and a half.' she said at last. 'Kept upright in a chair, not allowed to lie down, Soviet jazz music, strip lights on the whole time. I'm surprised I lasted as long as I did.'

'When was this?'

'As soon as we were taken.' I silently ground my teeth. I felt insulted that they'd ignored me for three days and then hadn't seriously tried to ask me what we'd been doing East.

'What did you tell them?'

'I can't remember exactly now. I said we were here to meet your family and to collect a document from Schmidt, but that we found him dead when we arrived.'

I searched her face, it really did seem like she couldn't remember clearly the lines she'd fed them.

'The train crosses the border in an hour's time, you can sleep properly then if you like.'

'I'm tired beyond words.' She curled up along the banquette opposite me until Lübeck, when we had to get off to go through the exit procedure at the border post.

'Goodbye East Germany,' she said as the train pulled out of the station. 'I hope I never come back to this pigsty.'

As she lay back down again I wanted to say something along the lines of most of them being people in difficult circumstances too, simply trying to get on with their lives, but bit it back.

I switched off the main compartment light and stretched out myself but couldn't sleep. She'd as good as said she had come to East Germany as a messenger girl for von Barten, which meant he'd planned this, right from the day I got back from my trip to Latour and Dupont, once he'd guessed the shape of the danger he was in.

After a while, she started to snore softly. I smiled to myself, definitely not ladylike. I pulled out the manual again and re-read the section co-authored by 'E v. B'. As I turned the pages, the scent of typewriter oil and musty paper wafted up. Sophie stirred and turned over, her eyes still closed. I returned the manual to its folder and replaced it in my bag under the seat.

The night drew on, and around half past one I was eventually done for too. I tried to fight it, but I slept until we pulled back into Brussels Central at six with a crash of buffers.

I woke with a start, Sophie wasn't in the compartment, but her larger case was still on the rack. I stretched and waited, sure she would be back soon after her smoke. I got up to lean out of the carriage window at the passengers disgorging from the train, peering down the platform. For a moment I thought I caught a glimpse of blond hair tied back in a ponytail, but then it vanished. With a growing sense of unease, I pulled out my bag from under my seat. The manual was gone.

Chapter Fifteen

Friday, 28th March 1969

In frustration I grabbed my bags, kicked open the compartment door, and ran to the entrance of the station, scanning the platforms as I went. But I knew in my heart it was too late, along with the immediate knowledge that my story with Sophie was at a final, very terminal, end. However, that wasn't the only surprise which awaited me. Across the street from the station was a Citroën DS with Freybourg leaning nonchalantly against its passenger side. I could swear he looked younger every time I saw him. He waved me over.

'Welcome back, we thought you'd appreciate a lift home after your journey. Your fiancée Miss von Barten not accompanying us I see? - she did appear to leave in a great hurry five minutes ago.'

I grimaced, nothing I was going experience today would surprise me more than my arrival in Brussels. I slung my luggage in the back and made to get in the front passenger seat. Suddenly, from the driver's side, a short grim-faced man in a black leather jacket jumped out and came round to open the rear door for me with a neutral, appraising stare.

We drove in silence, I reckoned for almost fifty kilometres, probably almost halfway to the French border. Whatever theatre Freybourg had planned, I wasn't going to indulge him with questions. He sat, quite relaxed, in the front, occasionally opening his window to tap the ash from his cigarette. The driver stared stoically ahead, carefully keeping his distance from other cars, staying just below the speed limit. The Stasi hadn't bothered with overt violence this week, having refined their other techniques over the years - the French I wasn't so sure of, given their awful reputation in Algeria.

The journey took us through small towns alternating with woods and tidy fields, until we pulled off onto a side road, then down a long unmetalled drive - easily another kilometre - to a collection of farm buildings surrounded by trees. Through barn doors I saw a grey van tucked into the shadows and a long aerial leading from an upstairs window of the main house to the top of a chimney.

Kramer was waiting for me in the main room of the farmhouse, sitting at a long dark wooden table, dressed in a black polo neck sweater - reminiscent of the student protesters from Paris the previous year. A beaten-up pot of coffee stood in the centre, next to some cracked mugs.

I flopped down on a chair and raised my eyebrows at him.

He stared at me for a while, but I was still resolved not to be the one to break the silence.

'We heard that the Stasi lifted you. We need to know what you told them and what you found out over there.'

'Before I tell von Barten that is?'

'Von Barten isn't your friend, that I assure you.'

'Strange, everyone else wants to be.'

'Just answer the question.'

I shrugged my shoulders. 'Sophie von Barten tracked down Schmidt's address, so she claimed - it took her a few hours at most.' I tried not to grimace again as I spoke her name.

'Why didn't you manage to do that?'

'I was sick that day. She went out whilst I stayed in the hotel. Her story was that she'd be faster on her own because officials would be more likely to open up to a young woman than to the pair of us, or to me on my own.'

Freybourg and Kramer glanced at each other. 'Go on.'

'The Stasi were waiting for us around the corner at Schmidt's place. There was a body in the bath, conveniently easy to clean up afterwards, when I think about it now - perhaps it was Schmidt's apartment, but not Schmidt's body.'

'But no one knew you were coming, supposedly. That's why you had a week there, to give you plenty of time to find him.'

'They told me their alarms bells rang when someone, or some people, from the West made enquiries about Schmidt. They wanted to know why the enquiries were made and why we were there.'

'What story did you feed them?'

'I didn't, they didn't even ask me, because they'd already questioned Sophie von Barten first. They went straight to asking me to inform for them at the EEC, though. They read extracts from the Stasi files on my family in East Germany, and they made very clear the incriminating circumstances in which they had arrested us.'

'What did you say to that?'

'What could I say? What would you have said?'

'So you agreed to become a collaborator?' Freybourg sounded excited rather than disappointed - an Aesop's Fox With No Tail, given his own supposed wartime history.

'When did you find out we'd been arrested?'

Kramer replied. 'I got wind of it on Monday night when von Barten came to me to get access to the joint secret political fund - don't ask me any questions about that now. He was determined to finish this quickly, at any cost.'

'That timing could make sense, we were arrested on Sunday afternoon. Who did he say he was trying to ransom?'

'Even he wouldn't be so crass as to buy back his niece and leave a colleague behind.'

I shook my head. 'That's exactly what he would have wanted to do, even without the version of the manual he'd planted. He'd have had control of the story if she'd come back on her own. I'm guessing that's what he planned, right?'

They flashed a glance at each other, and I knew they thought so too. I rested my elbows on the table and covered my face with my hands momentarily. Looking up I asked, 'Do you think Schmidt was the German sponsor at Sigmaringen, Monsieur Freybourg - if that's who you really are?'

'Who do you think I am?'

'Against my better judgement - because I really didn't expect it of you, Monsieur Kramer, to be involved in something like this - I think that you, Freybourg, have been sent to carry out a political assassination on von Barten.'

'I won't respond to that last part,' replied Kramer, 'but why did you think this wasn't something for me?'

'Because I assumed that you had moved on from your Gaullist days and that the whole debate with the supranationalists had been settled four years ago. You do want to promote the Project, don't you?'

'Don't be so melodramatic,' he retorted. 'Do you think so much blood was spilled for France this century for us not to want to bind your country into an alliance? All we're doing now is making sure that the EEC project stays on the track we've designed for it and doesn't mutate into something that would jeopardise our hard-won freedom.'

I poured out some lukewarm coffee for myself, avoiding his eyes.

'From time to time we just need to give the occasional reminder to the supranational wing not to try to sneak their agenda back in and to respect the voting compromise.'

Freybourg interjected. 'That's all this is – you've made it in your mind into something it's not, something personal against von Barten.' I didn't believe him.

'I've only been at the EEC a short while, but even I can

see that this standoff isn't sustainable, not in the long run. There will be winners and losers, and if you want to stop full political federation, de Gaulle won't be around forever to protect you. But back to my question, was Schmidt the sponsor in Sigmaringen that Dupont mentioned?

'Possibly. The person who I think Dupont might have had in mind could well have changed his name and gone East.'

'But Latour knew a name.'

'That von Barten might have planted and then led us to,' said Freybourg.

'So if you were suspicious, why did you let me go to the East?'

'The same reason as von Barten did with his niece, to find what the other side was up to.'

'Then what is all this? The safe house, the secret agent radio set-up? Are you playing at spies, or just trying to relive your glory days in the Resistance? - because I now assume, Monsieur Freybourg, that you weren't within a hundred kilometres of Sigmaringen in nineteen forty-four and five?' Provoking him was worth a try.

Freybourg smiled. 'Oh, I was there alright, I really was Marcel Déat's fixer - but I'd been working for the Resistance since 'forty-three. Marcel wasn't the sharpest tool in the shed.'

I struggled to keep my temper, apparently, these days, most of France had also been members of the Resistance at some point during the Occupation, the number of formerly secret *résistants* only seeming to grow with each passing year. Latour must have been implicated deeply if he hadn't been able to claim the same. He should have taken a leaf from the book of the Paris Police who'd simply had to go on strike a few days before the Liberation to claim they'd been supporting de Gaulle all along.

'Déat had his own spies inside the Parti Communiste, which had a million members by 'forty-five. I ran that network, but fed the information it gave us, not only to

Déat, but also to the SDECE's predecessor. De Gaulle was insistent we found out who in the Party was following Moscow's line to cooperate with the provisional French government, and who from the Communist resistance movement was hiding their weapons for future use. I was at Sigmaringen to keep an eye on the Vichy traitors, to make sure we knew who was planning to run to Spain and elsewhere.'

'I don't care about your credentials. You secret service people have gone rogue - you did it in Algeria, and you're repeating it again now. What was your real plan, to bring this manual to light during a make-or-break referendum campaign for de Gaulle? Did you hope to force him into a denouncement or hope that he'd jump at the chance to proclaim himself as the saviour of France once again. I can't believe this was his idea.'

I was shocked to see that Kramer actually looked chastened, one of my shots must have hit the mark.

'How long have you sat on this for? Why hasn't the manual been brought to light and used before?' I answered my own question. 'Because you're desperate, that's why - things are going worse for your faction at the EEC than you're caring to admit. This is your last shot before de Gaulle's gone.'

I shook my head in apparent disappointment. 'Why should I help you now? What if I agree with von Barten's vision for Europe?'

'And do you?'

'Why do you think I'm working here in the first place? However, I don't particularly care about the details of what voting system gets used - yours or his. Thankfully for your sakes though, I'm coming round to the view that Europe shouldn't ultimately be run by the likes of von Barten.'

I was worried I'd been pushing them too far. Right now, as I'd realised on the train back from Rostock, working with the French was my only hope for creating a degree of disruption at the EEC to please Johannes. Time to toss them a bone.

'So what's the deal now? I think we all believe von Barten took the copy of the manual you'd left with Latour for me to find. He probably sanitised it and sent it to Schmidt for us to discover there. Or maybe Schmidt really was at Sigmaringen and had his own copy that he'd kept all these years - although that's unlikely.'

'And now the East Germans have von Barten's manual?' asked Freybourg.

'They must do,' replied Kramer.

I was silent - if only they knew.

'So why did they ask Lenkeit to inform?' he asked Freybourg.

Freybourg pulled a face. 'Sounds like a fishing trip on their part. But I confess I don't understand the effort to put a corpse in the bath to frame you for murder, when they already had your family as leverage. Maybe it was for Sophie von Barten's benefit - maybe they think she's a bigger fish, which we know she will be some day.'

I kept saying nothing.

'How were they going to contact you?'

'They said they would find me.'

'That makes no sense either.' Freybourg looked at me sharply, 'what aren't you telling us?'

'Just what I said. They knew why we were over there and wanted to me to tell them, from the inside, what happens next between France and Germany.'

Freybourg was still suspicious.

'Sounds like they don't trust you enough yet, not to be given any means at all of contacting them. Or else they think your information will be of such low value, that they can pick it up anytime.'

Or maybe there would be such an explosion it would be immediately seen from the HVA headquarters in Berlin.

'The manual in the hands of the Stasi changes everything, though. The East Germans are masters at deception, they'll recognise it for what it is,' said Kramer.

'We're stalemated,' replied Freybourg, 'if we carry on as we are, they can pull out their document and expose us.'

'But will they care?' I asked. 'They don't want the EEC turning into a stronger, more integrated bloc - as long as you aren't fingered as the source, you can carry on trying to take von Barten down a peg or two. If you give me cover from my national authorities, I can feed the HVA the right information to cover your tracks when they eventually contact me.'

'What are you asking Lenkeit? - you want to work for the SDECE?'

'I have to feed the Stasi some information for my family's sake in the East. If I do that, I want your protection if I'm found out, or if they choose to expose me. I also want you to sponsor their emigration to the West, if that's what they want.'

'You don't ask for much, do you? How do you realise it will look if the French are found running a German double agent from within Internal Affairs in the heart of Brussels? Whether or not we say it was only for good intentions, to deceive the Stasi, we'll be accused of endangering and undermining the EEC.'

'You could say the BND would have done the same, but that I came to you first because I didn't trust them, given that they're already riddled with Stasi agents, and couldn't risk my exposure as a double.'

'So what do you mean by "taking von Barten down a peg or two"?' asked Freybourg.

'After we were released, Sophie von Barten mentioned the Stasi had threatened to create a dossier of von Barten's wartime personal dealings and share it with the Israelis.'

'She said "create", not "release"?'

'The former, but I don't really know what they said to her, and we can't very easily ask her now.'

'Interesting, but hard to pull off in a short time.' Kramer drummed his fingers on the table, deep in thought. 'Freybourg, come with me.'

They left the room together, Freybourg's hand on Kramer's shoulder as they went through the door. After a couple of minutes, the Citroën's driver brought in cheese and baguettes which I wolfed down. Then he stood silently by the door, facing me with clasped hands. Slightly unnerved, I asked for hot coffee, the broken night's sleep catching up with me faster than I realised.

I waited and waited, eventually resting my head cushioned on my arms, stretched forward on the table. Finally, Freybourg came back alone.

'We're going ahead with our back-up plan to try to permanently take out von Barten, in a similar manner to the one your new Communist friends suggested.'

My immediate thought was that this was that the Stasi had wanted all along by mentioning it to Sophie. She and I had dismissed it on the train as being their naivety as to the workings of the EEC, but, through me, they had literally planted the idea into the heads of the SDECE.

'Then you truly have lost this new war for Europe, if you are reliant on the threat of Israeli commandos to push it in the direction you want. What do you think von Barten's been doing since before the start of the ECSC? In that time France has fought the Vietnamese, the Algerians, your own French nationals in Algeria and, last year, all of your students, when de Gaulle had to flee the country for a few hours.'

I glared at him, daring him to contradict. 'On the other hand, Germany had the exact same Chancellor from 'forty-nine to 'sixty-three, and von Barten has been quietly building up his retinue of followers here, conforming them to his ideas. I've seen it for myself - I've been at one of his "courts". He's thinking policy-making in terms of decades and lifespans. That's why he's diligently spent fifteen years planting seeds that will be germinating here, long after he's gone.'

Freybourg pursed his lips. I was in too deep now, I had

nothing to lose by laying it on the table for them.

'You've tried to replay the same deception games with fake documents that might have worked on the Vichy or the Nazis twenty-five years ago, but von Barten has seen through you and swatted you to one side. Did you really think a planted document is all it would take to make the supranationalists stop? Why not go the whole way in trying to taint them by throwing in a gold ingot stamped with the Nazi eagle, or a forwarding address for Martin Bormann in Argentina for good measure?'

That was enough though. I had to make a demonstration for Johannes, and Freybourg's plan was the only one on the table, even if I didn't believe in it.

My voice was calmer now. 'If you take von Barten out of active employment at the EEC, you'll for sure disrupt the network of patronage which his position affords him. But you won't kill the drift towards their vision for the EEC, and he'll still be in the background prompting and guiding his protégés. You might slow them down enough though, such that, if you're lucky, other events overtake their plans.'

'Oh I assure you, Kramer will manage it - he's been representing France at the EEC since 'fifty-seven, and he knows better than you what needs to be done. But just so you don't get any ideas, your fingerprints will be all over this effort too - unless you want us to expose you as a Stasi informant?'

'And if you do, Kramer comes down with me.'

'Enough. Here's the plan - you'll break into von Barten's house, stage a burglary. The Belgian Gendarmerie will discover some papers discarded by the robbers - evidently of no value to jewel thieves or the like - and then you and Kramer will confront von Barten with them.'

'Where will these papers come from?'

'We'll put our best forgers onto it right away.'

'So you don't actually have any evidence of him receiving bribes of cash and stock in return for assigning slaves and production orders to industrial concerns? Why not create an authenticable copy of the manual instead? You must have made one of Latour's version?'

'Without the true original we're not going to have enough credibility to cast suspicions on the deeper motivations of the supranationalists. But von Barten has his opponents, even within his own camp, people who want his job - either now or after he's retired.'

'Why didn't you secure Latour's document years ago if you knew about it? How long has this plan been active?'

Freybourg looked uncomfortable. 'There's no time to revisit the past now, what's done is done.'

'So be it. Who will do the actual break-in and when?'

'We'll find a night when von Barten and his wife are out of town, and one of Lebrun's men,' he pointed to the side door, through which my guard had gone when Freybourg returned, 'will bring his crew.'

'And this Monsieur Lebrun, is he to be trusted?'

'You can meet him yourself now and work out your part of the plan together - it was explained to him earlier, whilst we were out.'

Freybourg led me to the stables, next to the barn in which their van was hidden. At the back of the block there was an empty tack room which had been turned into an office. Lebrun was in his fifties, iron-grey hair and, to put it kindly, a face that could only be described as 'weather-beaten' at best. His grip was firm, though, and his eyes penetrating.

'Enchanted to make your acquaintance,' he said in guttural French.

I took a chance and switched to German. 'And likewise.'

He wasn't amused but replied in German too. 'Don't get any clever ideas smart arse.'

There was a stand-off for a few seconds. I switched back to French. 'How do you propose to make this look like a real robbery?'

'You're the ex-policeman, you know about these things.'

I had attended the scene of several break-ins, but nowhere as grand as von Barten's Brussels residence. I presumed it should look the same, but on a bigger scale.

'Find the safe and crack it, go through the bedroom drawers, pull down the books from the shelves. We need to make it look like we picked up some documents by mistake.'

Lebrun grunted. 'Are there live-in staff at this place?'

'I can't say for sure, maybe they go home when von Barten's out of town.'

'I'll have one of my guys take a look later today.' He turned to Freybourg. 'When do you want this to happen?'

'As soon as possible, but it only works if von Barten is out of town.'

I had a thought, if Sophie had fled from the train station, wasn't it possible she was with von Barten right now, also being debriefed outside Brussels?

'What if von Barten is lying low after Sophie von Barten's return and is also planning his next move?' I didn't want to explain in detail why that might be. 'We can stage a break-in this weekend and the papers can "turn up" in the hands of the Gendarmerie when you've created them.' I still thought that this scheme was going to backfire once von Barten called Kramer's bluff, and I wouldn't be surprised if it was Kramer who ended up on the chopping block instead. Johannes wouldn't care either way.

Lebrun broke in. 'If my guy is happy, once he's seen the place, let's go tonight. We have all the gear we need.'

'If we're going tonight, then I want to get back to my apartment now. I haven't slept properly for days and I need to change clothes.'

'Very well,' said Freybourg, 'let's not overplan this. "*Action Immédiate*", just like the helicopter commando raids we did in Algeria, eh Lebrun?' He slapped the other man's back. Lebrun smiled grimly.

We agreed that Lebrun would call me by seven in the evening and, if the job was on, we'd meet at ten, at a truckers' cafe in Halle, well outside Brussels. Lebrun's driver sidekick took me back into Brussels in Freybourg's Citroën.

On the way back, I wondered if von Barten and Sophie really were in conference, and if Sophie had told von Barten about the manual she'd stolen. Maybe she'd decided for herself that he'd misjudged the modern mood and that absolutely nothing should come to light. Only another von Barten would have the self-confidence to believe they knew better than the *chef de mission* himself, that Uncle Ernst was too out of touch for his own good in allowing the release of even a sanitised manual. If that was the case, I was about to try to change all that.

The other thought that was troubling me was, what if the Stasi had told her to find the manual in my bag? That would explain their poor preparation of me and Johannes' relative disinterestedness in the manual after lunch yesterday - although that could also have been from the wine he'd drunk.

Maybe I was only ever meant to play a role until the end of the train journey. What if, by losing the manual, they wanted to jolt the French into a personal attack, but on weak ground so it would fail? That in turn would mean that they had acted to help von Barten.

I shivered, what if he, fantastical as it sounded, was then already their man in Brussels? After all, he was the one who had the contacts in the East - Schmidt we presumed - as well as his professional contacts at COMECON. We'd all assumed his wealth came from his wartime dealings, favours granted by grateful French and Belgian industrialists to their German overseer and protector from the worst depredations of the Reich. But what if he really had been in the pay of the Stasi, or perhaps even the KGB, all along? Or what if he was KGB, but the Stasi wanted to weaken their Russian ally's influence at the EEC by damaging von Barten?

There were simply too many possibilities to consider - the French had to make their next move to shake the tree and see what fell out. Johannes had said to be inventive - the best I could do would be to help the French create a new, plausible, document for a more effective smear - and, once again, I had a good idea of who I could turn to for help.

I was dropped off a couple of blocks from my flat. I said farewell to the driver, getting a grunt for my trouble, walked on quickly, and went straight upstairs to put on a pot of the strongest coffee I could bear.

I fully extended the folding formica-topped table in the kitchenette and laid out the pages of research Jan had made on the IAR, the predecessor to the ECSC and thus in turn the EEC. I also dug out the worthless material which Latour had provided and started to make notes on a fresh sheet of paper on the content of Schmidt's manual - as much as I was able to recall from yesterday at the HVA office in Rostock and on the train back this morning.

When I was done, I paced up and down, buzzing with the caffeine in my system.

Sophie may have taken the manual prepared by Freybourg, but I was determined to rescue the situation. I had a hunch something could be put together which would work almost as well. At our first meeting, Latour had referred to Wernher von Braun, who'd presented the Americans with his missile plans at the end of the war and was currently leading the design effort for the Saturn rockets which were to fly men to the Moon later this year. He'd taken his war work and used it to get a position with the victors after war's end, and Latour hadn't rebutted my suggestion that the manual had been used for a similar purpose.

I was sure that von Barten had had access to the manual soon after its completion and was willing to bet he'd even used it himself, to prove his technical credentials to the Allies - now including the French - in the immediate post-war years before being appointed to the ECSC. I was relying, firstly, on the hope that he'd also reused the same material during that time, as the source for his own briefing and policy papers. I therefore hoped, secondly, that Jan Stapel would thus be able to find close derivatives of the original manual's contents still in the IAR and maybe even in the ECSC archives, wherever in Brussels they were now being held.

It was a long shot, with a chain of dependencies, but not completely implausible. My dilemma was how to convince Jan to do the work for me, although I did still have twelve thousand francs in our office safe in the Charlemagne building. I could also take a chance and hint that by helping me he'd be helping his socialist comrades in the East. As he'd gone to East Germany himself, there was even the outside possibility that the Stasi had already tried to recruit him too, but I wasn't going to push my luck too far.

I had limited confidence in the SDECE, and I didn't believe their creation of fictional documents implicating von Barten personally had a chance of working against a master of survival.

But it looked like I was locked into supporting the French - Sophie's theft of the manual had done that. And right now, no one else was offering to help me get free of my East German entanglement - the BND I couldn't trust, I was sure that Heinz Felfe hadn't been the last traitor there, and that they were still riddled with Stasi agents, as I'd claimed back at the safe house.

Maybe, as Latour had hinted, the material he'd given me on my second visit might be of interest in tracing hidden assets. While it wouldn't stand on its own, it might spice up the version of the manual I had in mind.

I swept all the papers into my document case, gulped down the remainder of the coffee and changed into jeans and a soft shirt.

On the way to Jan's faculty I called at my office to pick up the bundle of fifties from the safe, in case I needed to bribe Jan, either to do the work, or to keep quiet about it. Part of me had even been tempted to take along the Sauer from my apartment, but that way lay madness.

Jan was giving a tutorial in his office to a group of students when I arrived. I sat quietly out of sight around the corner of the corridor until I could hear them leave. As I sat, I realised that there was yet another parallel story, to Wernher von Braun's - that of Reinhard Gehlen himself. In the war he'd been a Wehrmacht Major-General, in charge of field intelligence on the Red Army. He'd made copies of his materials before the end of the war, ready to sell them to the highest bidder afterwards. But Gehlen had hit the jackpot - not only did the Americans buy his material, they created a spy organisation for him to run, which later became West Germany's BND.

I knocked on Jan's door and entered at his command.

'Well, well, well, so the prodigal son returns. Did your family accept you with open arms?'

'That part was good, all told.' I smiled, and I meant it, my aunt had accepted me for who I was, not where I'd come from. No matter what happened next, I'd found my wider family and, thanks to Johannes, now might even get to see them more than I'd thought possible.

'I wanted to return your notes on the IAR, I'm sorry I forgot to earlier.' He waved me away.

'I did have some questions, though, on some material I dug up in the course of my investigation.'

'Why I am not surprised?' He grinned back and raked his hands through his untidy hair. 'Hand over my folder and spill the beans.'

'I saw some original documents during the course of my enquiries but was only able to make notes. I'm wondering if the same document was re-issued by the IAR or perhaps the ECSC.'

'What was the topic, and who do you believe wrote it?'

'Labour supply across borders, how to incentivise workers to move to jobs available outside their own country.'

'Just like you guys from Hamburg coming here to take the jobs of Belgians.'

'Perhaps. I don't know who wrote the original, but I believe it could have been published or referenced by the current German EEC *chef de mission*, Ernst von Barten, during his time at the ECSC.'

'Let me see your notes.' I handed them over, keeping back Latour's material.

'There's a lot of topics here, more than just labour. In fact these notes refer to most of the relevant areas covered by the early EEC, not just the IAR and ECSC. This was all in one document?'

'Yes, a kind of manual.'

'Interesting. There's position and briefing papers in the ECSC archives, stuff from the European Movement and similar think-tanks, but nothing as comprehensive as this. And you had sight of the original?'

'I was given it to look at in East Germany but wasn't able to get it back over the Wall to Brussels. Do you think there's a chance you can find a later derivative of it in the archives here?'

'How old was this document?' he asked, suspicious now.

'From what I was told, it was from around the time of the Liberation.'

'So very early - I'd love to see it for myself.'

'Can you help me? I'd like to find the earliest documents from the archives on each topic listed here, so I can compare them to the manual I saw.'

'If it eventually leads me to a copy of that original somewhere in the West, sure. When do you want it by?'

I reddened, 'Don't take this the wrong way, but we can pay a consultant's fee.'

'I'll think about it,' he grinned. 'Tell you what, get them to pay me two thousand Belgian francs and I'll make a start today. Just to pull the earliest document on each area shouldn't take more than a few hours.'

'It might come in French francs,'

'Okay, two hundred and fifty French francs then.'

'That will be fine, it will help me a lot, I really appreciate it.'

'Now, now - no need to be so deferential - or I'll start to suspect that you're up to no good. Leave me your notes and I'll meet you later tonight for a drink.'

'Sorry, I have something on tonight. How about Saturday?'

'I'm meeting a girl in the evening. See you for lunch tomorrow?'

Espionage wasn't meant to be this easy.

I went back to my apartment and crashed out on the sofa for the rest of the afternoon - at some point soon I needed to call my mother, but not today, not until tonight's job was complete. Just before seven, the phone in my flat did ring - but it was Lebrun, as arranged - confirming we were on for tonight. I went to the cafe on the corner of my block for a quick meal and glass of red wine.

Before I drove out to the rendezvous, I went back to the apartment and got out Latour's Sauer from the back of my wardrobe. The thing was filthy, so I set to work to clean off the worst of the oily grime. Eventually, something like a sheen could be seen. The rounds were probably twenty-five years old - I couldn't imagine Latour had either fired or procured any since the war. I didn't have any gun oil to lubricate the action with, but reckoned I could get some and possibly fresh rounds too from

Lebrun - depending on his mood.

Shortly before ten I parked my Volkswagen and walked into the transport cafe. Lebrun was sitting in a corner alone, now also dressed in a black leather jacket, like the driver from this morning. He nodded curtly as I sat down. The waitress brought coffee, and then we were free to speak.

He drew slowly on his cigarette and gently exhaled in a long thin stream. 'We're all set, the client is away, as you guessed. The approach will be easy, it's some way back from the road, and my technical guy can get to work without worrying about the noise.'

'Alarms?'

'We'll cut the telephone lines, but I want to be in and out in ten minutes - there may well be a backup system that we can't easily find.'

'What's our chances of encountering the law?'

'Manageable, but we'll take precautions in case we find ourselves in a last resort situation. Drink up and let's get this over with.' He finished off his own drink and we left, unobtrusively, slipping through tables of the other diners.

As we walked to the far end of the parking lot, the adrenalin began to kick in, like it did before a night-club raid with the Hamburg police, or a live firing exercise during my conscription service.

We got into the back of the grey van which I had seen earlier that day at the SDECE safe house. He looked at me quizzically. 'Excited?'

'Maybe a little.'

He snorted, but didn't say anything.

The van pulled out onto Route Nationale Six and our careful driver from this morning coasted along the quiet roads into the centre once more, Lebrun's technical specialist sitting beside him up front.

The silence opened up and I felt compelled to fill it. 'Where do you come from originally Monsieur Lebrun?'

'None of your business.'

'What age are you, fifty, fifty-five?'

'What's all this to you?'

I didn't really know myself. I'd only learned a week ago of my likely origins, and now that I'd came across a former soldier, all the questions about the war and what we'd done in Russia that had been suppressed over the years were forcing themselves to the surface.

Lebrun was a direct person, so I gave him a brutally direct answer. 'I'm trying to understand what took place out East when you were serving there - I assume you were. My mother was a German Red Cross nurse, she was raped by a Russian soldier and I was born.'

'Shit start to life, almost as shit as mine.' He seemed to relent a little. 'So what do you want to know, what happened and why?'

'Something like that.'

'We did a lot of bad things in the East and not just to the Jews. When it was their turn to come for us they paid us back and then some. Rape was a basic right for Russian soldiers, like cigarettes or bread. Hard for the women who couldn't escape, but nothing can change that now.'

'So we were worse or were they worse?'

'It's just war, all sides are equally bad. After the war, in the fifties, I ended up fighting for the French Foreign Legion in Vietnam - and I tell you, boy, what the *Amis* are doing there now is no different to what we did try to pacify the yellow bastards, begging your pardon of course.'

He smiled at his choice of words. 'Your Papa could have been an upstanding eager young Wehrmacht captain, tragically killed by a single shot from a sniper. But you'd have been no better or worse off for it now, for all it matters.'

The van swayed through the night, the two agents in the front sat staring studiously ahead. Lebrun now rested his feet on my bench seat, across the centre of the vehicle from his own.

'Are you sure von Barten is away? It was a guess on my part.'

Lebrun looked at me shrewdly. 'Yes, silent as the tomb and all staff cleared out too. The only risk will be from the local cops, so you can stand guard whilst we do our stuff inside.'

'I have to be there too - I was a policeman, I know things too. To make this work we have to plunder through somewhere that documents might have been stored.'

Lebrun smiled softly. 'Very well kid, just stay out of our way when we enter and no heroics - just in case von Barten isn't as arrogant as he seems and has taken precautions we don't know about.'

He opened up a metal case, took out an Uzi sub-machine gun with a folding stock, and began to check it over. 'Do you have a cleaning kit?' I asked.

'Why?' he replied, as he threw a cloth roll of brushes with an oil bottle tucked inside to me across the van.

'For my historical collection,' I said, pulling out the Sauer from my waistband. Lebrun laughed, 'Where did you get that? Let me see.' I cleared the weapon then tossed it across.

Lebrun turned it over in his hands, 'Nice enough for a handgun, used as personal sidearms in the police, sometimes presented as ornamental weapons to Nazi officials.' He tossed it back, 'But it stays in your pocket when we go in.'

It was almost eleven when we reached von Barten's house. The driver turned in through the open gates, then stopped just out of sight of the road. His mate jumped down with a pair of wire cutters for the telephone line and jogged up the side of the drive, returning after five minutes.

We drove right up to von Barten's front door, then the driver swung around the carriage circle to point the nose of the van down the drive towards the exit.

'Let's go,' said Lebrun.

We all put on gloves, mine supplied by Lebrun, and jumped out. The driver's mate took out a locksmith's toolkit and the studded oak door swung open in under a minute.

Lebrun and his crew fanned out on the ground floor, searching for the safe. I stood for a moment in the hallway, remembering the first evening I'd met Sophie here. Despite any rational expectations, given my social status, things had started well enough between us. Travelling alone on a long trip with her should have been my chance to make real progress - she'd met my family, discerned my darkest personal secrets - but it had all evaporated into thin air. I knew in my heart I had been naïve all along – it should have been obvious that she had no real favourites and was no more thoughtful with me than with her other acquaintances – I'd simply chosen not to see it. My small consolation was that she clearly did care intensely for her career, and I knew that anyone who ended up close to her would always come second to that.

'We've found it.' Lebrun's voice cut through my reverie, 'In the study, at the rear.'

I went through to see the driver's mate knelt in front of ancient freestanding safe.

'I don't like it,' I said. 'It's too obvious a place.'

'It doesn't matter, we're only making a demonstration, not actually trying to find anything, and we only have ten minutes, remember.'

'I'm going upstairs anyway, to rip up the bedrooms.'

'I want you back down in five and waiting at the front door.'

I bounded up the carved wooden staircase two treads at a time. The master bedroom was obvious, and now for the first time I felt I was attacking von Barten personally. I went over to the desk and jemmied it open with a crowbar I had taken from the van, dumping the contents of the drawers over the bed, just as I had seen after real burglaries.

As I worked, I noticed a silver-framed photograph on the desk and stopped in my tracks. I had expected to see a family portrait, perhaps von Barten's own parents. But this showed four fighter aircraft in loose formation. They were in the middle distance, recognisable to me as Fw-190s from later on in the war, with the straight-sided crosses of the Nazi Luftwaffe faint but clear on the sides of their fuselages. The sun had shone brightly that day, the clouds were high and crisp, majestic as they tumbled earthwards, dwarfing the planes.

I carefully removed the photo from the frame and turned the print over, but there were no marks or writing to indicate when it was taken or who or what the subject was.

I replaced the print and propped it back up on the desk. That didn't seem right, so I swept the lot off onto the floor and trotted back downstairs.

Back in the study, the driver's mate was putting the final touches to an arrangement of plastic explosive and wires attached to the hinges of the safe. It would have taken a professional an hour to pick the lock properly, which we didn't have. We moved back to hall and whilst we were waiting on the fuse burning out, Lebrun laid a walnut box down on the side table.

'Look, I was right,' he said as he opened it up. 'Sauer 38H, just like yours, chrome-plated and engraved with von Barten's name, a gift from the Reichswerke Hermann Göring. Presented to high Nazi officials, as I said earlier. Your man has a past for sure.'

I gazed at the gun nestling on the red velvet liner of its presentation case.

'Where did you find it?'

'In the drawer of his desk in the study. You want to keep it?'

I shivered, this was the second piece of Nazi memorabilia I'd seen in five minutes.

'No, let's put it back where it came from. I couldn't keep it, even if I wanted to, it would link me to here.'

There was a dull thud and crack from inside the study, smoke appeared under the doorway. We all filed back in.

'Take it all,' Lebrun commanded, as his guys started to stuff their workman's holdalls with documents, share certificates and jewel cases. 'So he did keep the important stuff here after all?' I asked.

'Some of it, perhaps. But we're almost done here, we're not going to look elsewhere. Move it guys.'

With a loud zip the bags were closed and slung on backs.

'Okay boys, wheels roll!'

'For victory!' replied the driver.

'Nutcases. Is everyone here German then?' I asked.

Lebrun snorted, 'Tell you some other time, if we ever meet again.'

We filed back through the hallway, outside, and then back up into the van. The engine caught, and the driver accelerated away in a spurt of gravel to the gates and a left turn onto the public road. As we cruised down the avenue, I caught a glimpse of blue flashing lights half a kilometre behind us and was glad to be gone.

Chapter Sixteen

Saturday, 29th March 1969

Lebrun got the driver to drop me a hundred metres down the road from the transport cafe, then they drove on, back to their safe house.

I made my way up the road to the parking lot and walked smartly across to my Volkswagen, avoiding eye contact with the trucker and his mate who'd just got down from their DAF flatbed. Just as my watch showed midnight, I drove off, the hairs on the back of my neck still on end.

In the police I'd been told that the first twenty-four hours after a crime were the crucial ones for any investigation. After that, the memories of potential witnesses became confused.

I doubled back to Brussels and got to my apartment forty minutes later. I really was dead beat by this point, my last full night's sleep had been six hours in a Stasi holding cell on Wednesday, two days ago now.

When I woke, a faint sense of dread was hanging over me. Last night I'd crossed a line more serious than signing the confession in Rostock - because at that point I wasn't actually guilty of a crime. Now, I really was in the power of the French, my life in the West was over if they ever disclosed what I'd done for them, even if I brought down some of them with me. Not that that would be difficult - I was willing to bet that Lebrun had been SS, not Wehrmacht - why else then would he have spent his best years in the French Foreign Legion followed by the Service

Action? I'd even hazard a guess he'd originally been known as 'Braun', before he became 'Lebrun'.

I got up, did my domestic chores and made ready to meet Jan for lunch. As I walked to the bar, I wondered again about his real political beliefs under the mask.

Jan wasn't a conventional left-wing fellow traveller - that was for sure. The Lenin icon on his wall and his student protest marches were the facsimile of a European socialist agitator - but he was also clear and logical as to the faults of the Communist bloc and rational in his explanations to me of the way the world really worked.

To my mind, though, that made him potentially even more dangerous - someone who understood the flaws but still supported the system with eyes wide open.

He was sitting at our usual table, his curly head cupped in his hands, as if he too were deep in thought. His eyes were wary, in contrast to the happy-go-lucky dilettante I had come to like over the last year and a half, despite our differences of education and nationality.

We clinked glasses and he perked up somewhat. 'So how was it, really, in the East?'

'Truthfully, after the first few hours, I was surprised how normal it was. My family are simply ordinary working-class people, trying to get on with their lives, as far as they can. Not political, just living with politics around them. They made me jealous, me being a war orphan, of a kind.'

Jan's eyes now flickered alive. 'You've had an epiphany. You've seen that the system doesn't matter, as long as people are free to live their lives in peace.'

For someone so clever, he was actually very stupid. But I indulged him for a little while longer. 'Do you mean any system?'

'Think about the East - of course it's not a democracy like in the West, but does that really mean anything when you see how the Western countries behave? Look at France, with its dirty colonial wars, government turmoil, and new constitutions every fifteen years. Look at West

Germany with its cosy compromises with ex-Nazis - like the current Chancellor, for goodness sake.'

He fidgeted with his beermat. 'What matters is that the minority who actually care about the people get to create and defend a fair society. Democracy, as we understand it here, prevents that. Governments change and can change for much the worse as your country saw in nineteen thirty-three.'

I felt obliged to contradict him, remembering what Latour had told me that night. 'But Germany didn't have a functioning democracy back then, it had been entirely subverted, by all the political parties, who only seemed to give the constitution lip service.' I couldn't believe that I was actually arguing political science with a professor, even if he was just an associate one – not that it mattered, as a non-graduate, he'd never accept anything I'd say anyway.

'You're wrong Oskar, we need to evolve our political systems to ones where the voters' choices can be carefully channelled to select only the policies which are actually for their own benefit. Sure, the Russian communists have taken things too far, we all can see that. The Prague Spring last year was a disaster - they had the chance to give socialism the human face it needed to be finally adopted in the West, but blew it.' His eyes were burning now, this was the true believer behind the laconic mask he tried so hard to cultivate.

With a stab to my heart, I remembered what Sophie had told me at von Barten's dinner. 'It's like you're want to turn the clock back to the time of the Kaiser, where there was a Parliament with limited independence, used as a fig leaf to justify what Chancellor and Kaiser had already decided together. And look where that unchecked power took Europe, to the First World War. At least, with a western democracy, you can get rid of governments that don't work.'

Jan shook his head. 'That's a reactionary view of the world. This time it will be different. We can organise

society better and we will do it better, because we have to
– unguarded, the capitalists will always sneak back in and
subvert any government that's set up for the benefit of the
masses. A socialism of the peoples has a superior moral
foundation to a Western capitalist democracy - it therefore
deserves protection from poor choices by the electorate,
no matter if that looks superficially "undemocratic".'

He gripped the handle of his beer glass tightly. 'You're
one of the people - I know this is the system you want,
where the von Bartens of the world are put and, more
importantly, kept in their place. Work with us - you don't
need to march in demonstrations or plant bombs - but we
do need people in positions of influence, who're able to
help when they can.'

'Are you trying to recruit me to your cause?' I smiled,
finally feeling like the experienced one here. 'Let's just
agree for now that I've no desire to see von Barten and his
ilk run Europe, any more than you do.' This seemed to
satisfy Jan for now. He leant back and took a long draught
of his beer, licking the foam from his lips.

The sausages with *pomme-frites* we'd ordered arrived at
our table.

'So why all the serious questions? Did you get
anywhere with the research I suggested?'

'Very interesting.' He dipped a piece of sausage into the
mustard and popped it in his mouth, bending down below
the table to fetch a pile of papers.

'I'm not going to spread these out here, they're
originals - so don't get any greasy fingers on them. You
can borrow them for a day or two to make your own notes
from.'

My hopes rose.

'The sketch you gave me of the outline of an original
source document was uncanny. You couldn't have
imagined it yourself.' Always the unconscious little digs
with Jan.

'I limited myself to going through the proceedings of

conferences run by the IAR and ECSC between 'forty-nine and 'fifty-four. I found papers or references to all the topics you listed. And when I looked at the papers that were available, there were constant themes, the use of similar phrases in all of them.'

I raised my eyebrows. 'And who wrote these? Were they all from the same person?'

'Not so fast, I found papers on the same topics in your list, but the topics aren't that surprising - the usual you'd expect from a trade coordination body - customs tariffs, engineering standards for steel alloys, that kind of thing. There was always a political tinge to the content though, almost a given assumption that decisions should be made at a European level, based on pure technical merits alone, with no suggestion that there could be any national dissent or that the cause of European unity could permit anything other than uniformity in policy-making.'

'Okay, but that could just mean the group of people writing these submissions had the same political outlook.' It sounded promising, but not usable, yet.

'Assuming that the people contributing the papers had sometimes recycled earlier material, I scanned for discrepancies in the text. Occasionally I found nuggets of personal references to a possible original author or authors. "When I was working for Cockerill-Sambe on improved armour plating", that kind of thing. Occasionally something would be related that could only have happened some time before the IAR came into existence, generally wartime experiences from my reading.'

This was like chasing ghosts. With time, someone might forensically analyse the texts and identify groups of likely wartime documents with the same authors - but it was a tenuous link back to the manual.

'Could you say, definitely, if any of the papers had been written in their entirety during the war?'

'Many of the texts on pure technical issues could have been - but that's precisely because they were general texts, not commenting on current events.'

'But most of them had that political twist you mentioned?'

'Yes, that is a constant. I think you could say that half of the material there could have been written any time between nineteen forty and 'fifty.'

That was as good as it was going to get.

'Thanks Jan, great work - how long did you spend doing this?'

'Hey, it was fun. I never thought conference papers could contain a secret code.'

'Well, we don't know that for sure. I'll take these and read them to see if they match what I remember.'

'Let me know if it does, and if so, where I can get a copy of the original.' Jan polished off the rest of his sausage.

'Okay, I have to run, date tonight. By the way, what happened in the end with that girl we heard you were travelling with?'

'Painful subject that, don't feel like talking about it much. I thought we had something, but you know better than me how these things go.'

'Not to boast, but I probably don't.' He grinned. 'I'm the one who breaks it off, generally early on. It's safer that way with the undergraduates.'

'I know, I discovered that thin line between fun and fixation, when you introduced me to Brigitte last year.'

'Yes,' he said sheepishly, 'sorry about that one.'

I paid him three hundred and we left the bar together, the bundle under my arm. Jan turned left, and I went right, towards the Hôtel Métropole, in the off-chance of catching Freybourg, assuming he hadn't already shifted to the safe house.

I was in luck, apparently roughing it in the field wasn't Freybourg's thing these days. I didn't imagine that Algeria, or wherever else he'd been, had been a picnic, so maybe the French government owed him that.

I rang his room from reception, and he called me up.

For the first time, Freybourg looked older than when I'd seen him last. Today he looked like the sixty-seven-year-old he really was, as Lebrun had told me last night, on the drive back from von Barten's place.

He greeted me cordially, looking up from his desk where he was reading the newspaper. Even if his gang weren't as professional as the Stasi, they still had a certain humanity I could relate to.

'What do you have for me?'

'I did some thinking, we know the kinds of areas the manual was supposed to cover. What if it's still here in Brussels, but in parts, strewn throughout other, later documents which recycled the material?'

'Given that's how it was largely put together in the first place, I suppose it's possible.'

'Look, I have a friend at the Free University of Brussels, an associate professor in European history, a credible guy.'

'Well, what of it?'

'I gave him a sketch of what the manual might contain - all the topics which Dupont, Latour and yourself had mentioned and asked him to see what documents were in the IAR and ECSC archives that might actually have been written during the war. Look at what he found.'

'You told him there was a Vichy blueprint for a New Europe? What possessed you to do that?'

He was furious, slamming his hand on the desk. 'You're completely untrustworthy. You tell one academic, and you guarantee their entire cabal will know about it by this time next year. This was your chance to do something for us, to protect yourself from extradition to East Germany and a murder trial. Your naivety is criminal, Lenkeit.'

He was standing in front of me now, his greying teeth in my face.

'I swear, I'll have you on a plane to a desert prison in Chad before the week is out.'

'Calm down, Freybourg. Why always the melodrama with the French? Hear me out - he's a friend, he's intrigued by the idea of a single source document predating the IAR, but he doesn't know just how far back it might go – I assure you of that.'

I carefully parcelled out Jan's file on the unused bed of the twin room.

'These are originals, they have to go back to my contact, so please be careful with them.'

Freybourg began to leaf through the nearest pile.

'And why did he do this for you?'

'I asked him, and I paid him - he's an academic, three hundred francs for half a day's work isn't bad.'

'Do you trust him not to dig deeper? - he's not stupid, I'm sure.' Freybourg was already calming down as he moved onto the next pile.

'As much as anyone here. He already knows I was doing historical research for the EEC, "in the field" so to speak.'

Freybourg leafed through the pages until the end. His choler had fully subsided now, and he made a face.

'Well, there could be something here. Maybe better for us to pretend we have a derivative manual, than to create a story about wartime bribery from nothing.'

'We can do that too, perhaps. Remember the rubbish which Latour tried to foist on us? It's provable wartime material, and it's almost all about hiding assets - anonymous Swiss companies buying the freehold of land on which a steelworks is built, sale of copper mines in Yugoslavia to new owners in Spain.'

'Go on.'

'Just like with this replacement manual, it needs a ... dust cover, or a wrapper of some kind to turn the content inside into something else.'

'Maybe, let me think about it.'

He went over to the bedside table to place a call. As he dialled he half-turned to me.

'When can you keep the originals until without causing suspicion?'

I thought about Jan's untidy office.

'End of Monday, maybe Tuesday. He's haphazard, but when it comes to his original material, he's very protective.' As I should have been on the Thursday night train from Rostock.

'Agreed then. Yes, hello? One moment please.' He placed his hand over the receiver.

'Let's see what our guys can do over the rest of the weekend. We need to hit him when he's not expecting it. Come back to the farmhouse tomorrow mid-morning, and we'll decide how to proceed.'

My hopes rose, maybe this was going to be the way out of my Stasi predicament, and I'd be able to do just enough to please them. Time for a drink with Bernd, I'd neglected him for too long and was worried his suspicions and suppressed jealousy about my involvement in the investigation would grow the longer I left him. Before that though, I had to call my mother - I'd been putting off the time of reckoning for long enough.

At my apartment I poured a whiskey and then another - it was the only way I was going to get through this. I dialled the number in Steilshoop, and she answered some while after the usual three rings it took her to get to the hallway from the sitting room.

'Yes?'

'It's Oskar, Mother, I'm back.' There was a static crackle whilst she waited for me to continue.

'I met my Aunt Hilde,' my voice raised an octave. 'She's just like you, very kind. And my cousins too, really great kids.' I could hear her sobbing at the other end of the line. Any minute now, she was going to set me off too. 'I was so privileged to meet them, I wish you could have been there too.' Now I tried to make a joke of it. 'Twenty-four years was worth the wait.' She was in full floods of tears.

I laid the receiver upwards on the table and waited. Maybe it was the whiskey, but a great slow-burning rage was building inside me. Anger at the cruelty of the separation, at the naivety of apologists like Stapel, and at the smug self-satisfaction of people like von Barten, who thought they always knew best and always came out top, no matter the circumstances.

'Thank-you Oskar,' she said softly, when she had finally got herself under control. 'Tell me more about your cousins.'

I related the little I knew of their lives, mainly ordinary everyday things like my nephew's soccer team at school and my niece's camping trip with the Free German Youth – which reminded me of my mother's own youth organisation involvement.

'Mother, I spoke with Aunt Hilde, and I think I understand my own story now.'

The line hissed and popped again for another half-minute. I could hear her swallowing before taking a breath.

'I've always loved you Oskar. I thought my life was over when I got on that refugee train, but you gave it back to me, you helped change me from what I was.'

There was nothing I could say to that.

We ended the call and I sat in the gathering gloom, thinking ahead to a possible confrontation next week with von Barten. I wondered if there was any humanly possible way to avoid being directly implicated in the storm which the French were planning to whip up for him – but I knew that was simply the treacherous, futile hope of a reconciliation with Sophie whispering in my ear.

After a while, I picked up the phone again and dialled Bernd. It was Saturday night, not our usual evening to go out and there was no reply. I left it, Monday would be time enough to talk to him.

I wondered again where Sophie was right now. Had she showed the manual to von Barten? Were they having a laugh at my expense, holed up at one of his other properties in Germany? Or maybe she'd burned it already, just like Dupont all those years ago - a document full of ideas which should never be written down, in case the very act of writing killed them through exposure to the light of day.

I turned in and waited for tomorrow.

Chapter Seventeen

I made a couple of wrong turnings on the drive out to the SDECE safe house. After an age, I found the lane and pulled up alongside Freybourg's Citroën, but only by eleven.

Kramer and Freybourg were sitting at the long table with the same ancient pewter coffee pot between them. The new file was spread out down the length of the table. Kramer looked up. 'At last, there you are.'

'You're well-hidden out here. Let me see.'

I picked up the front of the new file. To my eye, it looked like a masterpiece of deception. The front cover was plain, without the too-obvious seal that had been on Latour's trade document cover page. The text was roughly typed, as if done in a hurry, with a worn-out machine and drying ribbon. For the first time the manual had its own title, 'Discussions on the war economy of the Hitler regime and lessons for a post-war New European Order'.

'Who wrote this?' I held up the new preamble text and table of contents

'I did,' replied Freybourg. 'That much I did remember, given how much time we'd spent discussing the purpose of the document back in Sigmaringen on the top floor of the castle being buzzed by low-flying Allied aircraft. In the end, we got more done in the cellars.'

Reading the introduction to the first reference document of Jan's, I was impressed again. The manual I'd inspected with Johannes' was what a Fourth Reich conspiracy document would be expected to read like -

technocratic for sure, but peppered with juicy political references to a securing a European homeland against bolshevism. Plus the killer section, now sadly missing, the advice from Goebbels' Propaganda Ministry on how to sell the ideas.

The new file, which Freybourg had woven out of the material found by Jan, had an altogether different quality of rawness. It read more like a sales pitch to the Allies for the achievements of its authors, without any recognition of the irony that they were selling to people whom they'd just been fighting against. It didn't have von Barten's signature under the title, but as far as I was concerned, every page could have borne his imprint - having heard Jan's unwitting indirect description of von Barten's world-view yesterday.

'It's good, but it's not enough. You've assembled this as if it's a post-war document.'

'Correct, but the linking text makes clear where the original material comes from. It's supposedly come from von Barten's safe - we're exposing him as a Nazi-era plotter, betrayed by his nostalgia, holding onto his blueprint for a New Europe.'

'But you know that won't work either - he was no Nazi.'

Kramer broke into the exchange. 'You're not understanding what really went on then.'

He stood up and went over to lean up against the window, folding his arms and turning to Freybourg and I, his head visible in silhouette only.

'Our first idea was to undermine von Barten by using a flagrantly compromising manual, full of Nazi language. But as you know, the pan-Europeans long predated the Nazis. In fact the most enthusiastic promoters of the New European Order during the war were Vichy, not the Germans, because Hitler wasn't interested in sharing his conquests with anyone else.'

Freybourg nodded along.

'The truth is, that it wasn't the Nazis hoping to subvert a post-war world, in nineteen forty it was firstly the pan-Europeans trying to subvert the Nazis, to try to get them to remake Hitler's Europe along pan-European lines. When the war was clearly lost, they evolved their position and worked to secure the continued support of particular Germans, who they knew were still going to be influential after the war, to promote their pan-European ideas to a new set of rulers.'

Something was troubling me, but Freybourg spoke before I could form it into words, 'Sponsors like Schmidt didn't use us in Sigmaringen, we used them.'

The idea that had been on the tip of my tongue a moment ago slipped away. 'So all this effort in the past month, to try to demonstrate that some of the Nazis tried to co-opt the Vichy French to disseminate their post-war plans for a European national homeland, has been for nothing? And you knew it all along?'

'It's not at all been a wasted effort, it was always a two-way street for some of those people. We know that von Barten is worried, precisely because the roles were never clear when he got mixed up in it back then, and now we know the lengths he's prepared to go to, in order to protect his reputation. His Kreisau-Zirkel group did debate various plans for a post-war Germany, but if he happened to exchange ideas with what's now the wrong set of people, he's in trouble. The boundaries of that circle weren't precisely drawn.'

I gave a deep sigh. 'You've still not got anything that will really stick on him. What did you do with Latour's pages of material?'

Freybourg answered, 'I think we hold them back. Ideally we want to do a proper job and actually trace his property and stock holdings back to the war and only then fabricate some transfer agreements to show he had sticky fingers - but not so many that he can challenge them in detail and deny the lot.'

I nodded, there was such a thing as too much evidence.

'But we're meant to be handed discarded documents from the robbery by the Gendarmerie all at the same time. If you don't use them now you never can.'

Then an idea came to me.

'Surely you agree then, that this still isn't enough. We need something to cause him an almighty headache from an unexpected direction.'

'What do you mean?'

'No-one has ever been able to pin suspect wartime activities or dealings on him - more likely, no-one's ever really tried or thought to try. But you recall I told you, the day I came back to Brussels, that the Stasi revealed to Sophie von Barten they did have an idea of something they would threaten to release to the Israelis.'

'Go on.'

'What if von Barten is already known to the Stasi in a different way. What if, by making the suggestion of wartime wrongdoing, they want the EEC to launch an investigation into his affairs, precisely because they know there's nothing left to find?'

'It seems tenuous,' said Freybourg.

Kramer spoke too, 'How would that help them? If a valid EEC investigation clears him, then his position here is even stronger - he ends up with a badge of honour because the Stasi smeared him, and he survived.'

Now it was my turn, 'Yes, but what if he really is a Stasi informer, even if not an actual agent as such - just like they asked me to be - and what if they plan a smear simply as a ruse, with the objective of actually strengthening his position, in the way you've just described.'

'It's a pure fabrication Lenkeit - there's no basis for it.'

'Who cares? Feed the story I've just made up to the BND through your own SDECE channels. Let's threaten him with a BND treason investigation.'

'I understand, but again, this is a confection on your part. He'll just brush it all off, and we will be the ones worse off in the longer run.'

I admitted to myself that it was still pretty thin.

'Then sharpen up the document, add some extra provenance, add some suggestion it's connected to an earlier war crime investigation. Tell him he's being reported to the BND as a suspected Stasi informer. Pile it all onto him, and let's see if one of the accusations sticks. All you want is to encourage him to leave the EEC faster than he would have done.'

Freybourg retorted, 'But even then, he'll still be around. He won't have any patronage to offer, but he can pull strings for his network of so-called apprentices behind the scenes. He can push his agenda in many ways, like getting himself a position at the College of Europe. If he's going to leave, it needs to be under a cloud so toxic no one will associate themselves with him ever again.'

Kramer poured himself a coffee, then filled another cup and pushed it in my direction.

'What do you mean by "war crimes" investigation?'

'All the industrial plants which von Barten managed, or directed the output of, used slave labour to different degrees. The voluntary compensation payments which some German corporations have made to date are surely only the start of a new phase of enquiries and lawsuits in the coming years.'

Freybourg spoke up. 'Nazi-era documents seized by the Allies for use in war crime investigations were held in the Berlin Document Centre. We could create a BDC cover slip for the whole file, maybe include the pages from Dupont to make a suggestion of guilt by association.'

'But how would von Barten supposedly have got access to a BDC file?' Kramer countered.

'Because he used his position at the ECSC to have the file permanently removed from the BDC records and then kept it for sentimental, or some kind of obsessive hoarding reasons, as you suggested earlier.'

I carried on, 'You want to shock von Barten into

retirement, to make sure no-one wants to be associated with him or his ideas again? Then go further and really do what the East Germans suggested - tell him you're going to the Israelis with the material, and that you're starting our own investigation into his finances. Hint at the BND. Finesse the Gendarmerie story, say that you've managed to hush up the local police - I know how that's done - on the condition he leaves the EEC.'

'It's not enough to simply tell him all this, something needs to leak too,' said Kramer.

'We'll pretend to start the financial investigation, but I can do it carelessly, so that people get to hear it's going to happen.'

Kramer furrowed his brow, looking down at his feet for a minute. He raised his head, finally decided. 'It's a plan, and it's not going to get any better by waiting. I'm going to bring this forward - we'll ambush him at the end of the day tomorrow.'

I leant back in my chair. That had been hard work the past two days, steering them away from a premature narrow personal attack on von Barten. Of all of the players, I had the strongest reason for it to succeed. No one else had their family hostage in one of the world's most pervasive police states.

'Will you stay for a bite?' asked Freybourg.

'Very well, but before I go back to Brussels I need to speak with Lebrun again.'

'Go and find him, he's in the stables.'

I trotted across the courtyard and went through to the tack room at the back. Lebrun was flicking through a magazine, I guessed long periods of waiting around were to be expected in his job. I pulled out the Sauer and asked Lebrun if he had any rounds which would fit. He extracted the magazine and took a look.

'Where were these rounds stored? Do you realise how old they are? There's nineteen forty-five headstamps on the casings.'

'I don't know. In the magazine all those years, I presume.'

'They're probably fine, you can try a single shot at the far end of the stable wall. Here's a box of twenty-four anyway, but fire the ones in the magazine off first, unless you want them as souvenirs.'

I thanked the old soldier and pocketed the box. He followed me outside into the main body of the stable and put the bar across the doors.

'Go on then, let's see if it still fires.'

Slightly self-consciously I took the stance, pulled back the slide, released the safety and raised my arm. It had been three or four years since I'd done this last. Arm up, breathe out, and arm down again to the aiming point.

The gun gave a kick and the bullet struck the wall about a metre from the hook I'd been shooting for.

'It's a useless weapon at range,' said Lebrun, 'but you know that already. Lots of rounds close up is what you need. That's why I switched to the Uzi. Just don't fire that thing towards me any time, in case you hit me by accident.'

I grunted, the smell of gunpowder brought back memories of days on the range with the army and the police.

Lebrun unbarred the door and I went back to the main house to say my farewells to Kramer and Freybourg. I'd decided I'd had enough of their company for one day and excused myself from eating with them.

I got back to my apartment at two and poured myself a whiskey. I had the rest of the day to kill before the meeting tomorrow. Filling the time, I morosely wondered what would happen the next time I came across Sophie at the EEC.

We both knew that I'd hidden the manual from her, and we both knew that she'd stolen it off me. She would have realised that I'd been given it by the Stasi, which meant that not only was everything which I'd told her waiting in the station at Rostock and on the train a lie, but also that I was now working for them. On the other hand, the bigger picture was that it was potentially damaging to her uncle, that the EEC had asked me to find it, and that she'd taken it out of circulation – so she wasn't entirely honourable either.

Whatever dealings I was going to have with her in the future, at least I wouldn't just be another of her 'dear friends' - I certainly stood out from the gaggle of her admirers now.

I kneaded my temples in my hands.

If I was to have a future in the EEC, she would have the Stasi connection to hold over me, unless I pretended it had been the plan all along of one of the Western intelligence agencies to infiltrate a double agent into the HVA. But if I really claimed that, I would come across as fantastical at best, deranged at worst.

Whether the attack on von Barten came off or not, she would suspect me faster than the speed of light, even if Kramer fronted the entire thing. If it succeeded, she'd be wounded, but would fight on. If it failed, she'd not need anything from me again, apart from to keep tabs on me, so she could expose my Stasi connection one day. There was always the chance the East Germans would do that themselves of course, in an act of vindictiveness, if Johannes didn't get his result.

I poured another whiskey - I just didn't see a way ahead. I didn't really know why I was wasting time speculating about her, I supposed that I was living in hope of turning the clock back, and that it was just human nature not to give up.

Where was she now? I'd guessed she was still lying low, having gone straight to one of von Barten's other houses, and I wondered how much planning they were putting into their next move. I wondered too if some of von Barten's 'court' would be there as well - my guess was that it had been the '*Franzmann*' who'd put the frighteners on Latour and taken his copy of the manual.

My mood darkened, the green-eyed monster of jealousy awakening and baring its teeth. They would be having dinner again - wine in cut glasses, Cuban cigars afterwards, the princes and princesses of modern Europe. I thought of my mother, struggling to raise a child on her own on a nurse's salary, and even my peasant Russian father, as I imagined him, probably even poorer.

This obsession with Sophie had to stop - she had opened a door of possibility, of acceptance by their circle, but I knew I would never belong there - not unless I reached a level in the EEC way beyond where my current level of patronage was going to take me.

My hand went to the Sauer in my jacket pocket and gripped it tightly. With its seven rounds, it was a popgun in a new world of widely available automatic weapons. But it was my popgun, I had won it from an adversary, and holding it gave me a sense of secret power. I would take it with me tomorrow, because I had no real idea how the day would pan out and I was determined to be ready for any eventuality, any crazy trick which Kramer might have up his sleeve.

I really needed to see Bernd to hear about his cases and take my mind off the whole affair, but that too would need to wait until the morning.

Chapter Eighteen

Monday, 31st March 1969

The day dawned in a blaze of orange framed by black clouds, rolling slowly across the sky. I walked a different route to the Agriculture building than normal and found a cafe I'd never been in before. I sat by a high counter, looking out onto the street. I propped De Morgen, the Flemish language morning paper, up on the window glass for privacy and idly scanned it to pass the time whilst I ate my croissant. I had found that if I read the Dutch slowly, consciously speaking the words aloud in my head, I could understand most of what was written. However, the boring article on the upcoming election of the Yugoslav Socio-Political Council defeated me. I doubted it would make any more sense in my native language and guessed that was precisely the Yugoslav government's point - give the people a fiction of a democracy to make them believe they had a say, whilst Tito carried on as usual.

Something else was dawning on me, on the edge of understanding, but again I couldn't grasp hold of it. I shook my head and returned to thinking about the meeting ahead.

I wasn't late, but Freybourg and Kramer were already in the basement room, a cloud of blue smoke above their heads. Kramer stubbed out his Gaulois and pushed the final version of the file across the table for last look. The BDC insert slip was cleverly done, with a back story of how the file had been acquired and from whom.

According to the text which Freybourg had drafted, the

document had been presented to the British occupation administration by Herr Doktor von Barten, seeking employment as an adviser. The file had been forwarded to the Allied Control Council, which was how it had ended up in the BDC. To twist the knife, Freybourg's story said that von Barten's name had been added to the CROWCASS list of suspected war criminals and persons of interest.

'That's going to hit him between the eyes,' I said.

'We think so too. Now to the reveal. We have a contact in the Belgian Sûreté - it would be plausible that the Police Locale or the Gendarmerie would take this file there first. We'll tell von Barten I called in a favour and that the file was given to me discreetly. You won't be involved, apart as a witness to the meeting.'

This was a small comfort – in my delusion, if I wasn't the one actually wielding the knife there was that sliver of a chance that Sophie might one day be convinced my involvement hadn't been intentionally malign. As far as Johannes was concerned, he would assume that any document which surfaced implicating von Barten would have been the one he gave me.

'Okay then.'

'Let's do it, let do it now. Von Barten arrived back in Brussels last night - we don't know if he'd been told about the break-in before he got here, so let's hit him right away, in case he's still surprised.'

'Just like the Liberation, eh Kramer?' Freybourg said animatedly. 'Trucks rolling up at dawn, collaborators pulled from their beds, shot whilst trying to escape.'

'We're both getting too old for this.' Kramer pointed at me. 'Let's make this one an honorary Frenchman and retire in ten years.'

'I don't smoke your filthy high tar cigarettes.'

'Here's the drill - you wait in your office, I'll call you up to von Barten's room when I'm ready. Freybourg will wait along the corridor in my office, just in case we need him.'

We left separately for the Berlaymont building. Bernd was going to have a ton of questions about the past two weeks, which would take my mind off the coming confrontation with von Barten.

I squeezed my Sauer one last time inside my jacket pocket and pushed open our office door.

'So, the long-lost wanderer returns! So kind of you to grace us with your presence and perhaps do some actual work.'

'Very funny.'

'What have you been up to? And more importantly, what's the story with you going to the East with Sophie von Barten?'

'Nothing happened over there.'

'I bet you wish something had, you sly devil. Anyway, you've got bigger problems now - people have been making all kinds of enquiries about you: how you came to Brussels, what kind of car you drive, how big is your apartment.'

'You mean the standard questions we ask when investigating unearned income? What people were these?'

'From departments even I've never heard of. Human Resources Research, Special Commission for Ethics.'

That was von Barten sending me a signal, I was sure. 'And when did this start, a couple of days after I left for the East I suppose?' Bernd pointed his finger at me, thumb cocked back, like he was a cowboy shooting a gun. 'You got it, partner.'

Kramer and Freybourg's plan had better work I thought.

'Okay then, can you do me a favour? Keep a track of any more enquiries - I think this is political again, to do with the people upstairs.'

'You mean they're threatening to investigate you for something? It's absurd, you're the most honest person I know.'

'Well thanks, but be a buddy and stay on top of this, will you? Maybe try to do a little digging yourself, let's see who's behind this.' I had assumed it would be von Barten, but it might be Kramer - in this game, you never really knew where you stood.

My telephone rang twice, I lifted the receiver. 'Come up please Lenkeit,' said Kramer.

It was time. The same bars of light ran over the walls of the lift, as I had seen that day when I was called up to Kramer's office for the first time. The sun didn't care what happened in our foolish little lives, it kept on shining just the same.

I straightened my tie and entered von Barten's office.

'Yes sir, you asked to see me?' I addressed Kramer.

'Sit down Lenkeit and get your notebook out.'

I raised an eyebrow. Von Barten was impassive on the opposite side of the table to Kramer.

'Firstly, tell Herr von Barten in your own words what you found out in the East.'

'Sir, your niece discovered where Schmidt was living, we went there together to see what he knew of any documents put together at the end of the war. When we got to his apartment, we found him dead and then the East German police found us. They held us for a few days, but didn't have anything on us, so we were eventually released.'

Von Barten looked at me coolly, the smoke rising straight up from the cigarette he held steady in his hand. He cleared his throat. 'So, nothing then? There never were any secret Nazi plans to take over Europe by stealth?'

I couldn't help swallowing. 'Nothing genuine that the past weeks of this investigation have uncovered - there may well be crackpots inventing material to try to sell, but I don't believe anything real is going to surface now after all these years.'

Von Barten looked at me and gave a sigh of what sounded more like relief that I was playing along with

Sophie's game, than anything else.

'This failed investigation, though, doesn't take away the fact that these plans were drawn up at one point,' said Kramer. Von Barten turned towards him suspiciously. 'I think, even without evidence, there is a moral case to answer for.'

'What on earth to you mean Kramer? This is not how the Community works. We don't drag up the past, we move forward.'

'But not everyone does, not those outside Europe.' Now Kramer lit the fuse. 'It's very simple. Last night, I had a disturbing call from my SDECE contact. He said he'd been passed a document from his man at the Belgian Sûreté, which I ought to have. It pertained to you, von Barten. Apparently, the local cops were called to investigate a break-in at your house here, which took place sometime over the weekend.'

I turned to Kramer, frowning in feigned surprise. Von Barten raised an eyebrow, Kramer ploughed on. 'Half a kilometre down the road they discovered a holdall with items the thieves had discarded as of being no value. It had this inside.' He slapped the file on the table between them. Kramer licked his forefinger and opened the file, sliding out the cover slip and stabbing at von Barten's typewritten name. 'It's over Herr Doktor.'

Von Barten picked up the slip to scan it, then flicked through the document. He silently stretched his arms above his head and got up, going over to the picture window overlooking the Parc du Cinquantenaire. He stood there for half a minute, gazing at the Triumphal Arch, then turned to us and started to slowly clap his hands.

He leaned down on the table, arms wide apart, fingers out-splayed. He spoke softly, almost breathing the words, 'No, you're finished Kramer.' He picked up his suit jacket from behind his chair, swung it around onto his shoulders and made to go. Kramer almost shouted after him, 'And we have contacts in the Mossad too. Quit now, while you still can.'

Von Barten turned and smiled sweetly at me. 'Lenkeit, if you would be so kind, come with me. There's a burglary I need to have investigated.' He turned back around, heading for the door, and said in a raised voice, directed to Kramer behind him, 'By my own people.'

If he thought that, then surely Sophie hadn't told him about her copy of the manual?

I glanced at Kramer, who nodded his head ever so slightly. I hurried after von Barten - he was already at an open lift. We rode down in silence to the garage level, and walked over to his car. He threw me the keys of the Mercedes and got in the back. 'You know how to drive to my house?'

'I remember from the evening of the dinner.'

I carefully swung out of the car park, the lunchtime roads were clear, and we were at his house in fifteen minutes. The whole time von Barten was silent. The couple of times when I glanced in the rear-view mirror, he was staring out of the window.

When we arrived at the house, I wondered if he wanted me to open his door, like a chauffeur, but he got out himself and went up to the front door pushing it open, still unlocked from the night before last.

I followed him into the ground floor study, the acrid smell from the explosive used to crack the safe still lingering. He sat down at the desk and lit a cigarillo, but didn't offer me one. Propped on the desk was the photo frame from upstairs, the one with the formation of fighter planes. The glass must have been smashed when I swept it off his desk in the bedroom. He pointed to it now.

'Of all the things they could have stolen or damaged, this was the worst which Kramer's men did.' He looked at me carefully. 'Do you know what it's a picture of? Dreams that vanish with the morning. Hans was my brother's eldest boy, but I loved him as if he were my own son. He was my heir, he would have inherited everything.' He pointed around the room, gazing into the middle distance.

'His plane is in that photograph. He's forever flying there, high up in the clouds, in the bright sunshine of eternal youth.' My heart missed a beat, a moistness shone in the corner of von Barten's eye.

He turned to look full at me now, his voice bitter. 'You know who put him there - up in the heavens?' I shook my head.

'It wasn't the French or the Americans, the Tommies or the Ivans. It was the German people. They were the ones who put the crazies into power - forget the myth about how evil Nazis led the people astray - it's their guilt, theirs alone.' He balled his hands into fists and gently thumped the table in rhythm with his points. 'And I promise you Lenkeit, nothing, nothing which that *Franzmann* has planned will divert me or my people from the task of ensuring that no European is ever offered that chance again, to vote unlimited power to the wrong sort.'

He rocked back onto the hind legs of his chair. 'Do you understand Lenkeit, do you really understand what we are doing here at the EEC?' He looked at me accusingly.

I opened my mouth a couple of times, trying to form the right words. 'You're building something that will take real power away from the nations, piece by piece, decade by decade – that we all know. But instead of the body which this power goes to, one day being elected by the people, you want to ensure it remains immune from the democratic process, forever.'

'Well, well, well - not bad for a high school graduate. Think about it - it's what the people really want isn't it? They just want to be left alone to live their unimportant little lives, without being troubled with the hard decisions.' He pulled on his cigarillo. 'And the tide of history is with us. No matter what amateur plot Kramer has cooked up, it's still going to happen because the people who can see it, and who know better, are too lazy to do anything to stop it.' He was warming to his theme, 'And the plebs of

Europe don't deserve a second chance at their experiment in popular democracy, not after what they did in Germany in nineteen thirty-three.'

'But what if the technocrats get it wrong, how then can they be stopped? You were one, you actually worked for the regime to help them fight their war.'

'Nonsense, I was resisting the system from within.'

'And getting well paid for it.' I was getting angry now. 'It's all the same with you aristos, you always have a justification for why you should get what you want, at the expense of other people. Maybe if your lot had actually tried to make the pre-war system work, instead of subverting it we would have never got into this mess. Those are Latour's words paraphrased, and he was in even deeper than you.'

'No - now you're speaking like one of your Eastern socialist friends.' He gave a nasty smirk. 'You have a choice Lenkeit, you join us wholeheartedly and work against Kramer and his crew, and we'll expose his plot together. But if you don't, I will terminate your career here and anywhere else in the Six you try to find work,' he grinned some more. 'And I will make sure your mother is never employed in the German medical profession again.'

I shook my head and smiled at his arrogance, 'That's the benefit of being a little person. Sometimes you might want us to do something for you, as if we have a choice which you can bend to your will. But what if someone more powerful has got to us first? Then literally nothing you say will work on us.'

Now it was my turn to get really angry. 'And who appointed you to take away the choices of half a continent on deciding who rules them? What makes your future EEC any different from Yugoslavia, or Romania or the other soft-line Communists?'

I pounded the table, 'Do you have any concept of how many lives the industrialists wrecked, of the depth of pain and suffering because of your conspiracy of silence before the war? You signed a pact with the devil when you turned a blind eye to the way the Nazis manipulated political life - all in exchange for suppressing the trade unions and getting rearmament contracts.' Jan Stapel the socialist couldn't have put it better himself.

My hand went to my pocket to grip the Sauer.

'You cannot and will not pin the rise of the Nazis on the *Junker* class, not on me anyway - in nineteen thirty-three I was hardly older than you are now.' Now he was shouting too. 'My God, Lenkeit, you little, pathetic, pointless … creature.'

'Did you really say that? Did you really almost say *Untermensch*?'

'I know what happened over there,' he smiled sickeningly, 'my niece laughed as she told me. "It seems like Lenkeit and his mother both got fucked by the Communists." And guess what, you both deserved it.'

The red mist fell, an animal cry rose from deep within me, erupting in a harsh scream. I jumped to my feet, whipped the Sauer out of my pocket, placed it up against his teeth and fired.

The adrenalin surged through me as he toppled back on his chair, very dead. I went dizzy and lost balance momentarily, dropping the Sauer and putting my hands flat on the desk to steady myself. I sucked in deeply, hyperventilating. I couldn't think, my brain seemed to have shut down. I saw myself from outside my body, as if I was hovering near the ceiling, like a ghost, already dead myself.

Gott vergib mir. Gott vergib mir.

Then my instincts kicked in, shockingly fast. I felt deadly cold, detached, as a plan formed unbidden inside my head. I searched the room for the presentation case Lebrun had found the other evening. There it was, tossed onto the sofa. Von Barten's Sauer was highly chromed, engraved with spidery script. I dropped it into my jacket pocket. Now I had to get powder residue on von Barten's hand and his fingerprints onto the ejected shell casing. I scrabbled on the floor, desperate to find it. I ducked lower down still, laying my cheek on the parquet, and saw it winking at me from underneath the settee where I'd sat with Sophie. Losing it would have been disastrous. Retrieving the casing, I polished it with my handkerchief as I walked round to von Barten's side of the desk, almost gagging when I got there, in spite of my shock. I focused on his outstretched right hand, was he right or left-handed? I stuck with the right, hoping, and pressed his fingers tightly onto the casing, before placing it on the floor by the window, as if it had skittered there when he took his own life. It wasn't a foolproof plan, just the obvious one.

I looked around the room again, I needed to find something to fire the gun into, but where I could dispose of the spent bullet? The adrenalin was wearing off a little and I was coming down from the high. My best idea was a log from the basket by the grate. There obviously hadn't been a fire for a couple of weeks, at least, and I was hoping there wouldn't be another one any time soon, not now that spring was here and von Barten was dead.

I went over and found a piece that looked long and wide enough, shook off the dust and loose bark and carried it back round the desk. I wiped down my Sauer, placed it in von Barten's now cooling hand and fired it for him into the log, making sure I cupped the slide with my free hand to trap the ejected casing, which then went into my pocket. The log split nearly all the way down the middle on impact, and I was able to pull it fully apart to retrieve the bullet embedded in its groove, my first piece of luck.

I wasn't completely sure about leaving the gun in his hand - would it have stayed in his dying grip if he'd shot himself? But I was only painting a picture here for the police. I even had the presence of mind to bury the split log at the bottom of the basket and wipe down the steering wheel, car keys, gear stick and driver's door handle of the

Mercedes.

Then it was time to go, before the enormity of what I had done hit me, I lost my cool, and made a serious mistake. I was halfway down the drive when I realised von Barten's prints would still be on the passenger door. Damn it. I went back and finished the job, now in a cold sweat, shivering slightly.

For all my care, I knew my fate was in the hands of Kramer. He knew I had gone to von Barten's house, and I had no alibi, not unless he chose to provide me one. I wasn't too worried about an attack of conscience on his part – given the hints Freybourg kept dropping as to how they'd run other operations in the past, at the Liberation, in Algeria, and maybe Vietnam too, for all I knew.

I thought I had done enough in setting up the scene as a suicide to convince him that it was safe to protect me, but maybe it was time to reveal Johannes' instructions to me as well, to show my value in the East and thus to Freybourg as a useful double. Johannes had sent me with a document to stir trouble inside the EEC and now here was potentially the biggest trouble of all. Even if von Barten's death was accepted officially as suicide, I'd given Kramer his best chance to finish off von Barten's patronage network and reignite the battle for ideas and influence inside the EEC.

I had to get back to Kramer as soon as possible, to warn him before von Barten was discovered. Once more, I trotted back down the side of the driveway and along the avenue as fast as I could, but without suspicious haste. It was the middle of the day, and as I got closer to Brussels the suburban streets were clear - both a blessing and a curse, as I would stand out in the memories of any observers who happened to be there.

I found a public telephone booth and dialled the direct line to Kramer's inner office, avoiding his secretary. There was no reply. I waited a minute and tried again, but without luck.

I had no option but to get back to the Berlaymont and find him. To anyone else who asked I would say I'd been to the basement at Agriculture. I agonised over whether to take a bus, or to carry on walking. In the end I reckoned it wouldn't matter and got on a STIB at the Boulevard de Triomphe, which struck me as particularly inappropriately named, given what I'd just done. By the time I got to the Berlaymont I was sweating noticeably, especially for the gentle spring sunshine.

Kramer wasn't there - his secretary said he'd left early as he was going to France that evening. My panic was rising, I couldn't decide whether to put my head round Bernd's door, so I could at least be placed at the Berlaymont that afternoon. But that would risk having to spend time completing my story about the East and worse, arousing his policeman's suspicions, given my current state of mind.

I decided I had no option but to try the safe house one more time. I eased the Volkswagen through the afternoon rush-hour traffic as the offices of the EEC emptied early. The excuse doubtless was the upcoming April session of the European Parliament in Strasbourg and the winding down of business in Brussels for the next two weeks. To me, it was a symptom of the abuse of power von Barten had represented - sounding strange when I said it to myself in the past tense. I knew I was still in denial about what had taken place, and I guessed I'd pay for it later.

When I got to the farm, only Lebrun was home, in the main farmhouse building. He came out into the courtyard, closing the front door fast behind him. I reckoned he might have some tools I could use to file off the serial number of von Barten's Sauer and allow me to get to work on the engraving, but I wasn't about to start telling the world what I'd done. He was the first person I'd spoken to properly since the shooting.

'Where can I find Kramer?'

'It's Kramer you want? Not Freybourg?'

'No, no, it has to be Kramer first.'

'What's got you then? What have you been up to? And who said you could just turn up here as you feel like it?' His short-cropped grey hair shone in the sun.

'Do you have any way of getting hold of Kramer, please?'

'I can radio his driver, they're on their way back to France,' he glanced at his watch, 'about to cross the border - but this had better be important.'

By this stage, I might have well as confessed to Lebrun, but I stubbornly held on. 'I assure you, this call is one he does want to take.' I ventured a smile, but it felt false.

'Okay then, wait a minute.' He took me through the house to the kitchen where a radio sat on the large wooden table. He fiddled with some dials and picked up a walkie-talkie handset. After a few brief words, he handed me the handset, watching me all the time.

'Kramer, it's Lenkeit.'

'What happened at the other place?' I glanced at Lebrun and wilted a little.

'Prepare yourself. He took that file really badly. He's shot himself.' The silence at the other end opened up like a void, I resisted the temptation to fill it. Eventually, Kramer asked, 'Shot himself, as in shot dead?' Lebrun's eyes were impassive.

'Yes, I need to see you now Kramer, to discuss what happens next.'

'That I can't do, I need to set other wheels in motion. You need to get back to Brussels and start telling people about the investigation.'

'How does that matter now?'

'It matters ten times more than it did before.' He paused, and then continued in a cynical tone, 'People need to be convinced he really did have a good reason to … do what he did.'

I wasn't going to agree an alibi over the radio. 'When are you back in Brussels?'

'My friend will tell you.' With that, the line went dead. I handed the receiver back to Lebrun.

'Well?' I asked.

'What the fuck has just happened?' was his reply. 'No explanation?' I shook my head. 'Alright then, play it your way. Kramer's coming back early tomorrow morning, he'll call in here first and will be back in Brussels by the start of the working day. I can leave a message for you.'

'Trust me, Kramer needs to hear this from me first. Tell him to meet me at the Cafe Metropole at nine.'

'You don't half attract trouble, do you? You'd better clear out now then and quickly.'

My face fell, I was hollowed out by the anti-climax of not being able to get hold of Kramer and now having to wait another twenty-four hours to even start trying to straighten out this mess. I was still at the stage of seeing it as a temporary problem I would be able to solve.

I said a cursory goodbye to Lebrun, turned my car around and headed back to the city. I was determined to get rid of the Sauer as soon as possible, so took a detour to buy a metal file at a general goods and hardware store in one of the villages off the Route Nationale. Turning off onto the next forest track I came to, I stopped at a passing place where I got straight to work. It was a crude job, the file kept slipping on the polished surface, but by brute force I managed to score out all of the engraved names, and most of the rest. If the gun was ever found, though, the unusual chrome finish alone might be enough to link it to von Barten.

A few kilometres on, the Sauer and the second casing ended up in the middle of the channel of the Scheldt, after I'd made sure there were no barges facing my way as I tossed them in from the bank. Hopefully, I was still far enough away from Brussels such that, if by bad luck, the weapon was ever dredged up, the connection with von Barten would be long broken.

My head was still in turmoil when I got back to my apartment. Instinctively, I knew I had to quickly get used to lying smoothly about today. I needed to put the events of the past eight hours deep down into a compartment of my mind and lock it tightly.

The best people to start practising with were my regular drinking buddies. I called Bernd from the apartment, but didn't get an answer, so Jan it was. Thankfully there were no European politics this evening. We did our usual circuit of a couple of bars and, unusually for us, a restaurant, because I was famished. Jan told me about the next protest outside the American embassy which his latest student girlfriend was planning for them to attend. The reasons given seemed to be a fortnightly carousel of Vietnam, nuclear disarmament and black civil rights, but to me it sounded more like a pleasant afternoon's walk through the city with friends and the added frisson of danger from baiting the US Marines who acted as the embassy's guards. I reckoned some of the Marines could have served in South-East Asia themselves and might take the insults badly - but that connection seemed to have passed Jan by.

Chapter Nineteen

After coming back from the evening out I immediately felt better. I even slept the whole night through. On waking, the whole incident with von Barten yesterday morning seemed surreal - like it had happened in a dream, or to someone else that I knew.

As I got up and moved about, getting ready for the day, a new wave of depression set in at the thought of having to explain it all to Kramer and of being at his mercy. I supposed if the negotiations with him went badly later today, then I'd be in the hands of the Gendarmerie that evening, unless I made a break for the East German border.

I'd asked Kramer to meet me at the Cafe Metropole instead of his office or the Agriculture building basement. I wanted to stay as far away from the EEC as possible this morning until I at least knew my chances of being in the clear. I got there well before nine and took the same corner booth where we'd first met with Freybourg.

Once again I scanned De Morgen, hard to believe it had only been a day since I'd last read it, now wishing desperately I could turn back the clock. There was no mention that I could see of a shooting, which didn't surprise me. I began to wonder if it would be family who found him - his wife or even Sophie - and the dark clouds of guilt started to close in. I tried telling myself that, between us, Kramer and I had only dealt out to him what he deserved for his probable nefarious wartime activities, but for which he otherwise would never have paid.

I hoped Kramer had got the message and was going to show. Instead it was Freybourg. This wasn't a good sign I thought - Kramer hedging his bets, waiting to hear my story before deciding whether to protect me or wash his hands of me - whilst all the time benefiting from the fallout. After all, this was a German on German killing which he could plausibly deny close involvement with. In fact, whatever happened to me, both Johannes and Kramer were going to do well out of my moment of madness.

Freybourg laid his hands on the table, leaning forward slightly. 'Tell me what happened yesterday morning,' he asked in a low voice.

'I went back to his house - he still thought I was one of his people, but I think he wanted to make sure. I think he also wanted to work out his next moves with me.'

Freybourg looked sceptical at that last claim, so I carried on. 'As regards the investigation of course. Then there was an argument, and a … a shot was fired.'

Freybourg cleared his throat. 'Go on.'

'I need Kramer to cover for me, if it comes to that. No one else links me to von Barten.'

'You stupid boy.' he said quietly. A burning sensation suffused up my cheeks to the tips of my ears. It felt like they were glowing bright red for all the world to see.

'What do you think happens next? This whole delicate confection has been blown sky high by your idiocy.'

'Not if you support the story that he shot himself in shame. I made sure it looked just right.'

'Powder burns on his hand, a single shell casing left behind?'

'Yes, all of that. Second round used to create the power burn, that bullet dug out and removed, all other prints wiped. They will buy the story, I think.'

Freybourg sat back in his chair and shook his head in dismay. Now was the time to play my last card.

'What happened yesterday will be heard in the East, I will have built up goodwill over there that I can cash in on for months, maybe years to come.'

'Who are you to be able to judge their reaction? They only asked you for information, as I recall.'

My ears went red again. 'They asked me to stir up trouble.'

'With what? You told us you came back empty-handed.'

'I did, because they gave me Schmidt's manual in Rostock, but then it was stolen by Sophie von Barten just before we arrived in Brussels.'

Freybourg held his head in his hands. '*Putain.*'

Then he slowly made fists and gently thumped the table to make his points.

'Anything else you care to tell us? You need make up your mind, right now, which side to choose, and you'd better stick with it, because the prison in Chad isn't an idle threat – it might be our best option to hush all this up.'

'It's been chosen for me, I need Kramer's alibi. You'll always have that hanging over me.' They wouldn't though, because then Kramer have been conspiring to cover up the death too.

'When you say "goodwill" in the East, how does that help us?'

'If they trust me, they may let me play a more active role in their organisation over here. Haven't I passed the highest test of loyalty, like when men join the Mafia?' I leaned forward 'Isn't someone connected to an ally of the Soviets and to the SDECE, but unknown to your colleagues back in France of value to you? I pointed. 'Do you know where the Eastern Bloc moles inside your shop are hiding?'

Freybourg drummed his fingers on the table, thinking.

'What do we do with you? Let you carry on at Internal Affairs?'

'Get Kramer to sponsor the creation of a counter-espionage unit at the EEC. It doesn't have to do much, it would just be bait for the people in the East and for anyone else, like the von Barten circle who'd want to join it, thinking it's a position of influence in the overall direction of the EEC.'

Freybourg nodded at me. 'You're a sneaky one, aren't you? – even for us.' He nodded some more. 'That I can try to sell to Kramer.'

I slumped back. It had gone better than I had hoped for, or deserved. Now the anti-climax washed over me and the worm of guilt began wriggling again.

Freybourg gave me a ghost of a smile. 'It will get easier, you know. The second time, that is. We've all had to learn to live with memories we didn't choose to have thrust upon us. If you stay in this game it will probably happen again at some point, so get used to the idea.'

I guessed I had no choice.

I made my own way back to the Charlemagne. I needed to test myself in front of Bernd - I was as ready to face him now as I would ever be.

He was at his desk, typing a report, and beckoned me in with a wave of the hand.

'At last. Do you actually plan on working here anymore? Or shall we just get you the office between von Barten's and Kramer's?'

I grinned, the first time I'd felt like smiling since yesterday morning.

'Don't worry, you'll have lots of my company soon. I think the main investigation into the missing documents is done.'

'Oh really?'

'Yes, but keep this strictly to yourself, here's the big news. We're shortly going to be asked by Kramer to formally start an investigation into von Barten's wartime finances.'

He stopped typing and got to his feet, eyes as wide as

saucers.

'Kramer's certifiably crazy. This will not end well. It doesn't matter what von Barten did or didn't do back then, the antibodies will respond to protect von Barten and attack Kramer instead.'

'Really? I think Kramer must be pretty certain there's something on von Barten financially. I can't really say more, but the wartime documents on European policy that we found didn't make great reading for him either.'

'Is that what it was really all about? I'm still astounded by Kramer, though. You understand that this puts us in a difficult position? If we, as Germans, go after von Barten, then our careers are over too - who's going to protect us?'

'As I said, keep it quiet for now.'

'I'm sorry, but I don't like it, not one little bit. I just hope that because of your earlier involvement they give this enquiry to someone else in the department independent of us.'

'What else are you working on right now? What can I do this week, if there's going to be a pause before the von Barten affair gets going again?'

'You can help me test some of these expense claims, to see if they can be backed up. So far I've found a four-thousand Belgian franc bottle of vintage cognac recorded under "midday meal" at a conference in Bonn.'

'There's no point in drinking the cheap stuff, that's a crime in itself.'

He passed me a stack of claims and went back to his report. We worked companionably for a while, before deciding it was time for lunch ourselves.

As soon as we got to the cafeteria in the Charlemagne I could sense a change in the air. In the queue, as we waited with our trays, the person ahead of us suddenly turned around and whispered, 'Is it true, that von Barten committed suicide yesterday?'

I turned to Bernd, whose eyes were saucers again.

'What?' he said sharply, 'Who told you that?'

'It's been going around for the past hour and a half. Apparently, he didn't show for a meeting this morning, so his secretary went to his house and called the police when she didn't get a reply to her knock.'

'We've heard nothing so far,' I replied.

'Let's go,' said Bernd, 'I want to go over the road and see what's going on.'

I tagged along, playing the part of an ant whose nest has just been turned over by the spade of the gardener.

We rode to the top floor and Bernd called in at the office of our boss's own superior. He wasn't there, but his secretary was gossiping with two of her friends from the same floor. They looked up at us with the disdain that was their due - we merely worked for the top floor - they were the top floor. However, the desire to spread bad news was too tempting to pass up. Yes, it was true that von Barten had shot himself, no the police weren't giving more details, but Kramer had been recalled from France, as he was the last person von Barten had met with. No, there was no suggestion from the police that Kramer was involved, but they had argued before.

As we left, I knew I had to make a quick decision. Surely it would be more suspicious to Bernd if I didn't mention that I'd been at the same meeting as Kramer, but then it came out later?

On the way back down, I introduced it gradually.

'Would we get involved in the police investigation?' I asked Bernd.

'Not unless EEC confidential information was involved.'

'It puts a stop to Kramer's financial audit of von Barten, though. You know, I'm pretty sure I was at that last meeting with the two of them - that's when Kramer announced it.'

'What? Why didn't you say so earlier?' he asked sharply, suspicious for the first time.

'I don't know for sure - we met him mid-morning.'

'What did you do afterwards?'

'I went over to the Agriculture basement room, then left to meet one of Kramer's contacts in private, outside Brussels.'

'You realise the Gendarmerie will question you too, Oskar?'

'For sure, standard procedure.'

'Did von Barten give any indication that he might end it all?'

'He was seriously angry at Kramer, as you would expect. Kramer effectively told him that his career was over.'

'Whatever did Kramer have on him? I'm sorry, but you're going to have to tell me properly - the investigation is over now anyway. I suppose von Barten might have been angry when first told, but when he got home and thought about it, he changed his mind? Really? - this is von Barten we're talking about.'

'Okay then, but the next piece is obvious when you think about it.' I told Bernd of what I'd thought Jan had indirectly suggested and Freybourg less so, how von Barten may – probably - had taken pay-offs from the companies he oversaw during the war, to ensure they received their allocations of forced labour and raw materials, and not rivals.

'Staring us in the face the whole time,' he replied. 'Maybe von Barten did it as a last act of defiance at Kramer. Better for him to go that way, knowing that it would also kill the investigation, and prevent his legacy being sullied.'

Bernd nodded to himself some more as the lift reached the ground floor and we left the Berlaymont, through the crowd of lunchtime workers, crossing back over the road again to the Charlemagne.

I was feeling alive again, I sensed I was going to get away with it. But the out of body experience I'd felt in von

Barten's house now returned to a degree – what if the price I'd pay was never to be completely myself again.

I gave Bernd's idea some encouragement, to take root in his mind. 'You remember I went to that dinner of his, the other week?'

Bernd pursed his lips.

'Well, it was the strangest thing. There they all were - the up and coming department chiefs of staff and associate director-generals - they all sat round that table, as if they were at the court of King Charlemagne himself. They hung off his words, fearful of being spoken to, in case he made them look foolish in front of their rivals.'

Bernd raised his eyebrows, the jealousy ebbing away.

'But if he were to be involved in a scandal, it's not just his legacy, his supporters would be also tainted by association. By killing himself he knew it would all be hushed up, and he might even come to be regarded as a kind of martyr for his cause.'

'I think you're pushing it now Oskar, that's all a bit too far-fetched for me. But on the other hand, I'm just happy we're no longer going to be putting our necks on the line in an EEC civil war.'

We arrived back at our office and settled back down to our tasks until the end of the day. My hopes began to rise irrationally, that the police would simply forget about me, hidden away in the Charlemagne, and that they'd never call me, even to speak informally with them.

Chapter Twenty

The call I'd been secretly expecting came through at eleven the following morning. I was in our office, continuing to work through the expense reports. I was beginning to wonder though, if keeping my head down was a mistake, and if I should rather be badgering Kramer - spending time on the top floor to make sure his name was linked to mine.

My ability to act a role was now going to be tested to the limit - I was about to find out just how successfully, under examination, I could suppress the memory of what I'd done. If I could pass this test, I'd probably be able to carry on doing so - the guilt I'd deal with later.

The meeting was in Kramer's office, on his home ground, and my spirits began to rise with the confidence that he would come through and protect me.

Two men in plain suits, from what I assumed were the Gendarmerie, sat around Kramer's low meeting table, speaking with Kramer in French as I entered. The three of them stood up, made introductions, and shook hands.

We sat back down on the same innocent sofas, stirring coffee with the same reassuringly solid silver spoons that I'd seen on that very first day, almost a month ago now.

The senior of the two opened the conversation.

'Do you speak French well enough to understand and answer our questions?'

'Yes, I think so.'

'This isn't a formal interview, not yet anyway. We're

talking to everyone who was with Herr von Barten in the twenty-four hours before his death.'

'Very well.'

'You met with Herr von Barten and Monsieur Kramer late yesterday morning? What did you talk about?'

I looked at Kramer for confirmation, he nodded quickly.

'I work in Internal Affairs, as Monsieur Kramer will have explained to you. A month ago, I was engaged by both Herr von Barten and Monsieur Kramer to try to locate some wartime documents which we believed were to be used in a blackmail attempt.'

Kramer winced. The junior of the two Gendarmes stared at him. Kramer spun his forefinger, directing me to roll on.

'To cut a long story short, yesterday, the investigation effectively concluded, when we showed these same documents to von Barten. We'd found out that many of the early planning documents of the predecessor organisations to the EEC had actually been written before the end of the war, by Vichy and Nazi economic administration officials.'

The jaws of both the Gendarmes went slack and they looked at each other.

'It was a political scandal you see. Von Barten had worked as part of the Nazi war effort - for years the story had been this was to give him cover for his activities in the German Resistance - but these documents hinted that he'd mainly done so out of pure self-interest, enriching himself along the way.'

There was no point holding back now. 'Then, to add insult to injury, he'd taken his wartime experience and used it as his professional and technical credentials to accelerate his career at the ECSC and here too.'

'Very good Lenkeit,' interjected Kramer. 'Gentlemen, what my colleague is trying to say is that the investigation was not just political, but high political - ambassadorial-level political. On Monday, after we confronted von Barten, if that is the appropriate word, I left immediately for France to brief the Minister of Foreign Affairs and only got back yesterday.' His visitors were stunned into silence.

'As you have grasped for yourselves,' here he nodded confidingly at them, 'these were profound implications. Although the results were genuine enough, they may never have been acted on, as the judgement would probably have been that the murky past of one person shouldn't upset the balance between our six nations.'

He paused to let the Gendarmes come to their own conclusions. The senior one spoke again.

'So what you're saying, is that he was in deep personal trouble, and may or may not have known how public this bad news was going to become?'

'He was an experienced operator. He knew that even if the immediate decision was to suppress the truth, eventually these things do leak,' replied Kramer smoothly. He opened his mouth briefly, as if about to add something else, but then thought better of it. I wondered if he had been going to link back to the blackmail story.

The junior turned to me now. 'What was von Barten's reaction when he was told the outcome of your investigation?'

'He was angry, stormed out of the office. But I suppose people react to bad news in stages.'

'Who saw him afterwards? When did he go home?'

Now was the moment of truth, or rather lie. Relief surged through me as Kramer went first.

'He left the office straight away, as far as I could tell. When I spoke with his secretary later that day, just before I left myself, she didn't know where he had gone to.'

'And you, Herr Lenkeit?'

'I went to the Agriculture building, where I'd been working the case privately the past few weeks, given the confidentiality of the issues in question. I did some clearing out - my regular office is in the Charlemagne, over there.' I pointed, hoping a little misdirection would help.

'So it looks like he took himself home, a black mood came over him, and he decided to end it,' said the senior.

'Have either of you been to his house before?'

I hesitated for a moment. 'I went there a couple of weeks ago, for a dinner with some other *fonctionnaires*.'

'Wasn't that a little odd, given that you were investigating him?'

'We were investigating a suspected blackmail using these old documents, which were still unknown to us all at the time. We didn't realise von Barten himself would be caught up in it, and I suppose he didn't anticipate it either.'

'A shotgun makes a real mess of a person's face.' The junior looked at me closely as he said it. I balanced on the edge of surprise, keeping my eyes on him, trying hard to judge the correct timing of my response.

'Nasty way to go,' I replied.

'H'mm,' said his boss. 'Very well, seems like there's not a lot to go on for now. We don't want to be involved in anything political, but he has a family who need to be convinced it was suicide.'

Kramer and I nodded sagely in agreement.

'Of course,' Kramer replied. 'Let us know what you need, and we'll help where we can.'

'If this becomes a murder investigation you may have no choice,' said the junior. His boss looked at him sharply, deliberately pausing before speaking.

'Thank-you Monsieur Kramer, Herr Lenkeit. Be assured of the Gendarmerie's discretion.'

They left together, Kramer and I stayed behind.

'They must know about Article Twelve,' I said.

'Of course they do,' retorted Kramer. 'How many times has it got people here out of trouble? The right of *fonctionnaires* to be *"immune from legal proceedings in respect of acts performed by them in their official capacity, including their words spoken or written."* The nineteen sixty-five protocol on the privileges and immunities of the European Communities - best work we ever did, writing that,' he concluded smugly.

'Okay, make yourself scarce now Lenkeit.'

'I told my colleague about the financial investigation, like you said to.'

'That's enough extra information to be scattering around for now. Let's wait on the Gendarmes concluding their enquiries. If they get suspicious, you're on your own of course.'

With those words of comfort in my ears, I went back to the Charlemagne.

'Well, what did *les flics* want with you?' said Bernd.

'How did you know?'

'I didn't, I guessed they would. Did they give you any details of what happened?'

'No, apart from that he used a shotgun.'

'Awkward to shoot yourself with one, but quite likely that he'd have had one or two about the house.'

'What, to shoot squirrels in the Forêt de Soignes with from his window?'

'Don't be flippant you ghoul. I bet he was shooting pigeons with his friends on their estates every other weekend. Do you really think he did it?'

'Yes, I do. He was mightily angry when he walked out on Monday, he was so furious, to the edge of reason, that I'm not surprised he flipped out when he went home that day.'

Towards the end of our day the phone rang again. It was the junior Gendarme from earlier.

'Herr Lenkeit, it's Lieutenant Bonfils. There's a couple more things we found at von Barten's place I'd like to discuss with you.'

My alarm bells rang once more.

'How can I help?'

'Can we meet, perhaps this evening after you're finished work for the day?'

'If it's important I can meet now.' He sounded a little taken aback, but I wasn't in the mood for mind games, I wanted this over and done with.

'Can you come to the *poste de gendarmerie* on the Rue Royale?'

'No, but I'll meet you in the centre of town in an hour for a beer with my colleague, we're both ex-local police in Hamburg, you can ask us what you like then.'

Bernd was intrigued, to say the least. We discussed the case as we walked to the Rue du Midi.

'So he's got some doubts as to whether it really was suicide?'

'I just don't know, but he's going to have to be open with the details if they want our help.' I was surprised at my own brazenness, but also worried that I really was losing my mind, in the truest sense of the word - that I couldn't trust the words coming out of my own mouth and being spoken in my own head, even when I wasn't lying.

We entered the bar and waved at Bonfils. He was sitting up at the bar, his tie loosened, a half-drunk beer in his hand.

We pulled up stools and ordered.

'No one told me you were ex-police.'

Bernd replied for us. 'It makes sense if you think about it.'

'How did you get the job at the EEC? You happy with the pay?'

'I got a recommendation from Bernd, he got one from someone else. The pay is fair, but don't believe the stories of gold-plated salaries.'

'What did you do in Hamburg?'

Bernd looked at me, I carried on. 'We were uniformed *Landespolizei*: street patrol, traffic, drunks, domestic arguments - that kind of thing.'

'But not detectives?' he looked disappointed, everyone seemed to be, once they found out.

'Well, we worked with detectives, spoke with them when we did jobs together - so we've seen investigations up close.'

'And that's what you do here in Brussels?'

'Yes, we're really the glorified extended arm of Personnel.'

He smiled at this. 'Very good. I wanted to ask you a couple of questions, Herr Lenkeit - a couple of odd things turned up.'

'Please, "Oskar".' He was hardly older than me.

'Very well then, "Oskar". If you had a choice of shooting yourself would you go for a shotgun or a pistol?'

'Me? I suppose a pistol would be better, higher chance of it working, so to speak. Why do you ask?'

'So you weren't surprised when we told you earlier he'd been shot with a shotgun? You for sure looked surprised.'

This was weak stuff and a public place wasn't the location to put the pressure on - they must really have nothing. I looked at Bernd.

'No, not so much. We expected he'd have a shotgun in the house, for hunting parties, that kind of thing.' Bernd nodded in support.

'So here's the odd thing I wanted to ask you about.' I had to admire his doggedness.

'He was actually shot with a pistol, an old wartime piece that apparently had come from a presentation case. But the problem is that the pistol is nothing special, it's an ordinary ex-police weapon - and it doesn't match the case.'

'How do you mean, it doesn't match?' asked Bernd.

'It was a plain weapon and more scratched than you would expect it to be, having sat in a presentation case for twenty-five years.'

'Why would von Barten have had it anyway?' I asked deliberately. But I was worried now, that I'd forgotten to wipe down some hard-to-reach surface of the gun.

'We don't know, it's a reasonably common weapon, a couple hundred thousand were manufactured.'

'Was he a sports shooter?' I asked.

'We'll need to ask his family.'

I was faced with another dilemma, if I didn't mention my trip East with Sophie now, it would look strange later. Yet I wanted nothing more than to get this all laid to rest and to avoid giving him new lines of enquiry.

'I worked with his niece on the blackmail case, we went to East Germany together to do some research.'

'Really?' Bonfils face lit up, I'd just made his evening worthwhile.

'Yes, but it's not that surprising, the circle of people who could know had to be very limited. She works at the EEC too, so he decided to take her into his confidence, so she could help with contacts over there. Have all the family been told now?'

'Yes, but they're not convinced it was suicide.' I sensed that the word 'either' had been on the tip of his tongue.

Bernd took a long draught of beer.

'Why do they say that?' he asked.

Bonfils thought for a while, before cautiously replying. 'They don't believe the evidence that you, Lenkeit, presented to him on Monday was credible.'

The ice was cracking under my feet. I'd guessed that Sophie must have kept her stolen copy of the manual secret from von Barten - but surely she couldn't bring it out now, if she hadn't already destroyed it, and demand a comparison with our replacement version? That would only create more noise to tarnish his reputation, and weaken their network further. The story we'd have to stick to, would be that whatever von Barten had seen on Monday, it had been enough for him to pull the trigger.

'They didn't see or hear the conclusions we presented to him, so their claim implies he must have told them something after he left us. Did he do so?'

Bonfils deflated a little – Sophie had made a speculative shot in the dark – but maybe she'd only got the Gendarmerie to test the story, to give the family some comfort, if it could be so-called, that it wasn't murder. It didn't put my mind at rest, though. For my conscience's sake, part of me secretly wanted her to know the truth.

'I suppose it does sound like they are in denial.'

'Well, here's to a clean end to your inquiry,' said Bernd, as he clinked glasses with Bonfils. 'You know as well as we do, how at some point with these things you just have to say "enough".'

Bonfils shifted on his bar stool, looking at me over the rim of his glass as he emptied it. 'Well, thanks for meeting me,' he said finally. 'Anytime,' I replied, 'let's meet again after this is over. It's always good to make new friends in the police. We always like to hear how other forces do things.'

Bonfils' mouth turned up into a faint smile, 'For sure, Lenkeit, for sure.'

Maybe we'd win him round eventually to the side of the ex-policemen.

Chapter Twenty-One

I woke with a sense that a corner had been turned and that the suspicions over von Barten's death were going to lose momentum with every day that passed. It was time to lock down the French and secure their long-term protection.

Through his secretary, Kramer was playing hard to get in the morning, but I eventually pinned him down at three, after lunch.

I sat facing him at his desk, the mood colder - no cosy chat over coffee on his sofa this time.

I opened by asking after Freybourg.

'Gone back to France and shortly to a well-deserved retirement, I should imagine. You can only play his game for so long before your opposite numbers get to recognise your strategies and anticipate your moves. He'd come out of semi-retirement as a consultant to the SDECE for this one - his last field mission.'

'What happens now, here in Brussels?'

'This particular gamble is over, we can't reopen the inquiry now. But we're assuming the determined supranationalists will have been knocked back with von Barten's departure from the scene. We'll watch them, think of something else when we have to. If de Gaulle had come out strongly in response to a scandal, we might have been able to encourage him to again challenge the supranational nature of the treaties, try once more for a clear and definite change of direction for the EEC.'

'Von Barten said something to me, earlier. He said that he blamed the German people themselves for what had happened to us and to Europe. He said we should never allow the voters to give unlimited power to the wrong people again. That effectively, we had to restrict their choices to what was acceptable to the likes of von Barten.'

'Did you think he was wrong to say so?'

I hesitated, searching for the right answer.

'I understand his point, I think, but I don't believe democratic France would support that.'

'Let me be direct Lenkeit. Say that the Germans do get their way and build a technocracy which gives the EEC control over all the key areas of national decision-making, why wouldn't a patriotic Frenchman still want to capture the institutions and make use of those levers to extend our influence throughout Europe?'

'The monster eventually turned on Frankenstein. Best to kill it now, whilst it's still on the slab.'

'It hasn't happened yet, but you've agreed to help us keep your country in check in the meantime. What do you propose?'

Now the thing that had been hovering at the edge of my mind back at the safe house resolved itself into a form. 'It's not the Germans you need to worry about. If de Gaulle goes and the political pendulum swings the other way, then everything associated with him - his *Europe de patries* - will be a target for his opponents. Out of a simple spirit of revenge, the anti-Gaullists in France will adopt supranationalism as their own idea and unknowingly deliver the final victory to Vichy.'

Kramer growled in disagreement, I quickly moved on. 'What to do next? I told Freybourg already - create an "External Affairs" department - billed as a counter-espionage unit, so it can be below the radar. But use it as an internal secret police force, use it to find out things people would rather keep hidden, use those secrets to clip the wings of *fonctionnaires* who're becoming a threat to you.'

'Freybourg said you were devious.'

'If I join such a department, then the Stasi will already

have their man inside and won't try to insert anyone else. We'll know exactly who can be trusted and who's suspect. Think what you can do with it externally too - spy on foreign trade missions, or as you choose, either disrupt or accelerate the accession of the countries outside the Six who're seeking to join.'

'Now you're thinking like someone who belongs here.' He stared out of the window, looking over the Parc du Cinquantenaire.

I waited on him finishing his contemplation of the Triumphal Arch, just as von Barten had done, only on Monday.

'If we do this, you're our man first - no matter what the Stasi threaten you with. If we ever suspect you're playing a double game against us, then not only will I go back to the Gendarmerie, but the Stasi will get to hear that you were a foreign agent of the SDECE. You'll have nowhere to run to, either in the East or the West.'

He raised his eyebrows, seeking confirmation I'd understood.

'Yes, I get it.' He didn't though, if he threatened to tell the Stasi that the SDECE were running an agent inside the EEC's counter-espionage service, my first port of call would be West Germany's BND.

'Leave it with me. We're done now, for the next few weeks. Go back to working your regular job and be patient.'

I sat back in my chair. I was done in, suddenly sick of the whole thing.

'Thank-you, Monsieur Kramer.' I might be a murderer, but at least my mother had taught me to be a polite one.

I called in with my boss at the Charlemagne, told him how I'd been released from the Kramer special assignment, and that I wanted to take on as many new tasks as possible. I knew I'd need a distraction from what was about to crash over me in the next few days.

Thankfully, Bernd was out of the office for the rest of the day. I knew too, that a transfer to a new department was going to mean a break with him. He was only human, after all - he was the one who'd recruited me to help his career – and he was going to see this as me overtaking him.

When I got home, I received the other call I'd been expecting since Tuesday morning. I was told to go to a German bar, Am Karlshof, in Stalingrad, which I supposed was the Stasi's idea of a joke.

My contact was dressed in a studded leather jacket and jeans. He looked more like a gangland thug than the Third Military Attaché, or whatever his official title at the embassy was. He nodded to me as I entered, and the thought crossed my mind that I some point I ought to get another gun.

'I've been told all about you. The friend that you met in Rostock sends his greetings.'

'What does we want from me now?'

'Cheer up, he really means it, you're his newest and brightest star.'

'And who are you?'

'I'm just the messenger, mostly. Sometimes the muscle, but always just following orders.'

'That makes two of us then.'

'I'm Paul. You get to choose your own name, in case you didn't know'

I raised an eyebrow. 'What's it to be?' he demanded. I looked around the bar for inspiration. I might as well choose one I could live with, I was going to be stuck with it.

'Thomas.'

If Bible names were allowed, I would be the doubting apostle, as my private reminder of which side I was really on.

'Here's your first payment.' He pushed across an

envelope. Inside was a photocopy of a forty-eight hour exit visa for my aunt.

'You trust her to go back afterwards?'

'They always do, the ones who have families.'

Chapter Twenty-Two

Sunday, 27th April 1969

The past three weeks had been very difficult. The nightmares started a couple of days after meeting my Stasi handler, on Easter Sunday to be precise.

I would wake up with an oppressive sense of impending doom around two or three in the morning and that would be it for sleep for the rest of the night. I was drinking more in the evening too, before going to bed, to try to dull those waking senses, but without success. Both Bernd and Jan had noticed my general detachment from life, they tried to probe the reasons why and tried hard to cheer me up.

To his credit as a friend, Bernd hadn't made a fuss in the end, when I'd been appointed to the secret External Affairs department. I'd moved out of our office to join my new partner Willem, two floors above in the Charlemagne, where we were still based for now. We were both officially employed by Internal Affairs as our cover, so I tried to suggest to Bernd that occasionally there were bound to be some cases he and I would be working on together. Recently however, he'd gone quiet - maybe I'd finally used up his store of goodwill.

Jan's solution to my problems was shallow. For all his philosophy, all his belief in Marxist dialectical materialism, his only practical offer of help was weed. I tried it three or four evenings, but it made no difference, I still woke feeling guilty. Strangely, in the last week, I'd started feeling more guilt about beating Latour and breaking his wrist, than blasting von Barten's brains out the back of his head.

Maybe it was simply because what I'd done to Latour had been premeditated.

The worst day of the past three weeks was that of von Barten's funeral. It was a private ceremony, back in Germany. No one that I knew had attended, nor did I hear any reports about the day. That made it worse in some ways, because my mind then filled in the blanks. I imagined Sophie, wrapped in black, perhaps supported by Rizzo, tossing earth on the coffin. I wondered if any old colleagues from his wartime days working for Speer had been there. Had Speer been there himself? He'd finally been released from jail three years ago at the end of his sentence, the Soviets having withheld their consent for parole for decades. Probably not, though - von Barten might have been Speer's protégé, but the most famous living person from the Nazi leadership would have been the last person von Barten's supranationalists wanted in attendance. I wondered too, if he had really been well-enough known inside the Kreisau-Zirkel resistance movement for some of them to attend. Or maybe membership of the two groups overlapped, just like von Barten had himself.

I knew that at some point my path would cross with Sophie's again, but the Berlaymont and rest of the EEC estate seemed to provide plenty of opportunity to avoid people you didn't want to meet. One week she'd added me to the distribution list of a memo on Agricultural Policy payments fraud, even though it wasn't an Internal Affairs competence. I was newly resolved to stop jumping to conclusions about her – I'd simply signed to acknowledge I'd read it and passed it on without comment. But I had been right about External Affairs - the person appointed to what they thought was the tempting prize of director was someone close to von Barten and Sophie, but who had no idea I was reporting on them back to Kramer every week.

Since the day of the funeral, I had slowly shrugged off

the events of March - I supposed the human spirit would always eventually bounce back, given time. The one person I still couldn't face, though, was my mother, especially not after I'd told her about the trick which Sophie and I had played on her sister. Johannes had been as good as his word, and my aunt had wasted no time in arranging her trip to Hamburg - that was why this weekend I was here in Saint-Valery, using the excuse of work as a reason to stay away.

Dupont, I was sure, had never expected me to call in the favour of a return visit, and would never have guessed I'd decided to do so from inside an East German prison. He got company and I had my chance of a break from Brussels in the hope that I might finally clear my head.

I was out of ideas in that regard though. I knew I had done wrong, committed a grievous crime - a sin even - and I had no way to make recompense. Even if I walked into Bonfils' *poste de gendarmerie* and confessed, it wouldn't undo what had been done. Although I resisted it, I did know what I ought to do - but I didn't want to give Aunt Hilde's pastor the satisfaction of being right. I'd prayed for forgiveness in the moments after I'd pulled the trigger, but it had been an instinctive reaction. I wanted peace, but I wasn't prepared to undergo the humiliation of any kind of act of repentance. I still felt, to a degree, that von Barten deserved what I done to him - that was the best rationalisation I could come up with.

I'd spent the previous day with Dupont: walking his dog on the promenade, dining at the restaurant of the Hôtel du Somme, ending in the day in his study overlooking the sea, smoking a companionable cigar as the evening drew in.

Today was Sunday, the day of the constitutional referendum which von Barten had referred to during his dinner, all those weeks ago.

Earlier today, I'd walked with Dupont to the voting

booth in the Marie. The mood there was mixed, for some it clearly felt like the end of an era - the last gasp of the political leaders of the Resistance generation. But equally, or perhaps even predominantly, I got the sense that the mood of others was relief that the country was finally moving on, drawing a line under the disturbances of the previous summer, and de Gaulle's imperious reign of the past eleven years.

We were now sitting together again in the gathering gloom of his study upstairs, the radio softly on in the background, speaking of his days in the Vichy government. On my first visit, Dupont had brushed off the capitulation as simply being a final act of appeasement, but now he explained how the ground had shifted under the feet of the Third Republic, long before nineteen forty. He spoke of the early influence of the Saint-Simonian movement and of a later constellation of politicians and economists, writers and philosophers. They had all contributed to a growing belief, that technology and technocrats alone could solve the problems of the world which the politicians of nineteen fourteen had created. He went further back, to the Dreyfus Affair, straddling the turn of the century, telling the story of how the uneasy contract between the forces of Catholic reaction and Republicanism was first put under strain.

As I lit the lamps in his study, only now at the end did I begin to realise what von Barten's real story had been. He'd probably seen the Nazi takeover as the excuse for his class to get close to and subvert the Party, thereby recovering the power they'd lost with the uncertain birth of the Weimar Republic. Then, when the full awfulness of the disaster the regime had inflicted on Europe had become clear, he'd changed tack, getting close to the German resisters to give him cover, but also making allies with the French believers in a New Europe too, as further insurance for an unknown post-war world.

I knew he wasn't a narrow-minded German nationalist

- he simply believed that he and his kind knew best, not just for Germany, but for all Europe. In his arrogance, he didn't blame the German political and industrial establishment for the outcome of war, but instead projected it backwards in time onto the people themselves, not quite half of whom had voted for the Nazis in nineteen thirty-three, after fourteen years of Weimar turmoil.

Whatever punishment was to be visited by the Allies on Germany's sense of national identity, he was quite happy for it also to be meted out in turn to the other European countries too, whether they deserved it or not. His self-appointed role at the EEC, shepherding the College of Europe graduates, encouraging them to believe in the necessity of erasing the national identities held onto by the plebs, and building a sense of Greater Europeanness, was simply the progression of his life's work.

I was sickened, when I thought back to what Jan had told me, that no matter how grotesque the crimes of the regime, the people who'd always been on top had survived and thrived. In nineteen fifty-one, the prime example, Alfried Krupp, had simply been pardoned three years into a twelve-year jail sentence and given back his industrial empire.

I even began to see Johannes' point, about how East Germany had at least been on the side of the anti-fascists from the start, even if the Stasi files on my four relatives suggested that, as far as gentile Germans were concerned, they'd ended up at a similar destination.

Dupont and I listened to the radio news - turnout for the referendum had been high, up to eighty percent by some estimates. The exit polls were pointing to a defeat for de Gaulle - Kramer's political cover gone for the time being. I was sure he'd made back-up plans, though. He had the inside knowledge of how the EEC really worked, and with von Barten out of the way, he would be able to claim a new freedom of action.

At midnight, the radio presenter's voice raised a notch, an announcement was expected from the President imminently. Ten minutes later, the de Gaulle era came to an end. To my ear, he was still the same obstinate, cantankerous Frenchman who Europe had been forced to get to know over the past thirty years, even to the last word: *"Je cesse d'exercer mes fonctions de président de la République. Cette décision prend effet aujourd'hui à midi."*

I heard a couple of shouts from the street. Down the promenade, the Hôtel du Somme was still lit up brightly.

I had the sudden urge to get away and meet people my own age, to hear what they thought. I excused myself, as politely as I could, took a key, and walked out.

I felt sick in my heart once more. Irrational as it seemed, I felt that von Barten's murder really had been for nothing now. Not that I approved of the plot which Kramer and Freybourg had originally cooked up, but with de Gaulle now definitively out of the picture, his alternative vision of a *Europe des patries* was surely going to die too.

The bar of the Hôtel du Somme was abuzz, people were talking excitedly, looking forward to the future. I watched them, perched on my stool, as if from afar. Suddenly, I now craved that forgiveness, a chance to rejoin the human race, not to remain condemned as a murderer like Cain, expelled from his clan and doomed to wander the earth.

I knew too, that before anyone else, I needed to somehow earn forgiveness from Sophie, but what if she never gave it? Some people moved away from the bar and at the end of the counter, where I'd seen her last time, sat Claudine. I moved along and sat beside her, bought her a drink. I supposed that although what she offered was a pale imitation of love, in one small respect it did precisely match the real thing. After you'd agreed and paid for that hour or for that night, you had her acceptance unconditionally, freely and without question. That wasn't any kind of absolution, but it would have to do for now.

Afterword

By 1965 de Gaulle's multiple attempts since 1958 to change the EEC's supranationalist character had been seriously checked and his patience at the Five had run out. Hallstein's plan for the Commission to take control of the Common Agricultural Policy – the controlled system of price-fixing and punitive tariffs on external imports - away from the Council of Ministers was the final straw. France brought the work of the EEC to a halt for six months until the so-called 'Luxembourg' compromise was devised. Majority voting at the Council of Ministers was instituted as planned, suiting the supranationalists, but each Member State had a veto on matters of 'very important national interest', protecting the position of France and those nations more aligned to an intergovernmental view of the Community's development.

De Gaulle's successor, Georges Pompidou, was on the surface more pragmatic than his predecessor, blessing the accession of the United Kingdom, Denmark and Ireland which took place in 1973 – but only after France had locked down the funding arrangements for the Common Agricultural Policy in 1970 with the Luxembourg Treaty. Despite de Gaulle's departure, the work of European integration did slow down to a virtual halt until the early 1980s, when the need to accommodate a growing number of accession countries finally undermined the Luxembourg Compromise, paving the road to Maastricht.

Two weeks after his resignation, de Gaulle went to Ireland on a highly unusual six-week visit - a homage to his Irish ancestor from one of the 'Wild Geese' families who had fled Ireland in the seventeenth century to serve the

French crown. It is to Ireland that Lenkeit's footsteps will take him next.

The position of an EEC *chef de mission*, used in the text, is a literary construct only.

Short Bibliography

Antony Beevor, 2015: *Ardennes 1944,* 2007: *Berlin: The Downfall: 1945*

Christopher Booker & Richard North, 2005 & 2016: *The Great Deception: The Secret History of the European Union*

Louis-Ferdinand Céline, 1957: *Castle to Castle*

Alan Clark, 1994: *Barbarossa: The Russian German Conflict, 1941-45*

Artemis Cooper & Antony Beevor, 1994: *Paris After the Liberation: 1944 – 1949*

Richard Cobb, 1983: *French and Germans, Germans and French: A Personal Interpretation of France Under Two Occupations, 1914-1918/1940-1944*

Aidan Crawley, 1969: *De Gaulle*

Julian Jackson, 2001: *France: The Dark Years, 1940-1944*

John Rodden, 2005: *Textbook Reds: Schoolbooks, Ideology, and Eastern German Identity*

Frederick Taylor, 2011: *Exorcising Hitler: The Occupation and Denazification of Germany*

Adam Tooze, 2007: *The Wages of Destruction: The Making and Breaking of the Nazi Economy*

.

28828956R00156

Printed in Great Britain
by Amazon